SHARON'S HOPE

NEVA COYLE

THOMAS NELSON PUBLISHERS
Nashville • Atlanta • London • Vancouver

Published in Nashville, Tennessee, by Thomas Nelson, Inc.,
Publishers, and distributed in Canada by Word Communica-
tions, Ltd., Richmond, British Columbia.

The Bible version used in this publication is THE NEW KING
JAMES VERSION. Copyright © 1979, 1980, 1982, 1990 Thomas
Nelson, Inc., Publishers.

Library of Congress Cataloging-in-Publication Data
Coyle, Neva, 1943–
   Sharon's hope / Neva Coyle.
      p. cm.
   ISBN 0-7852-7760-2
   I. Title.
PS3553.0957S48 1996
813'.54—dc20
                                      95–26717
                                          CIP

Printed in the United States of America.

2 3 4 5 6 — 01 00 99 98 97 96

Special Thanks
At the end of this first series, it is only appropriate that I express my gratitude to Lori Wick, Carol Johnson, and especially to Jan Dennis for seeing the novelist in me.

Special Dedication
In loving memory to my dad, who, if he were still living, would be thrilled to know that I have finally found a practical way to use what he used to call my overactive imagination. I must admit, though, that I'll never be the storyteller he was.

Also by Neva Coyle

Fiction
Cari's Secret
Jen's Pride and Joy
Megan's Promise

Non-Fiction
The All-New Free to Be Thin
The All-New Free to Be Thin Lifestyle Plan
Learning to Know God
Making Sense of Pain and Struggle
Meeting the Challenges of Change
A New Heart . . . A New Start

CHAPTER ONE

*W*alking quickly, Sharon Mason Potter crossed her tiny bedroom to shut the window against the angry voices coming from the main house.

"You don't understand a thing I'm saying, Mac!" Kenneth Matthews' shouts carried clearly across the yard and into Sharon's room.

"Don't talk down to me, young man!" Jack McKenzie spoke in a tone Sharon recognized and knew to avoid. Both she and her mother had learned years ago that in some things it was best to let Mac have his opinions and not to argue with him. "Poor Kenneth," she whispered into the night air. "Might as well give it up. Uncle Mac will never hear you."

"Mommy?" Six-year-old Richie came to stand beside her, encircling her small waist with his little arms. "I'm scared. Why are they fighting?"

"They're not fighting, honey." She slid the window down against the angry voices, then stooped to embrace her son. "They're having a discussion."

"Why are they yelling like that? Is Uncle Mac going to hit 'em?"

"Of course not, Sweetheart. They're having a disagreement, that's all."

"But Daddy hit us when he yelled, didn't he?"

Sharon's heart lurched. For the last four years she and her two small children hadn't even seen Richard Potter, let alone felt the force of his rage. Frannie never really knew her father. But for Richie it was a different story. Barely two when Richard Potter was sent away, he still had bad dreams about the abuse he and his mother had suffered.

Usually happy and content in her little house on the McKenzie egg ranch, her stomach now tightened with painful memories of violence and abuse she endured before she came to live here with Mac and Meg—memories she successfully shut out, most of the time.

Sharon was beginning to feel she needed to protect herself and her two small children from the tension building between Mac and his stepson, Kenneth. She pulled the short fiberglass draperies closed in a decisive effort to keep not only the noise from entering her small, safe home, but the strife as well.

"Come on, sweetie," she said to her son, "let's go back to your room. I'll read you a story."

"I don't want a story," Richie pouted.

"You don't want a story?" Sharon feigned shock. "What do you want then?"

"Sing me a song." He ran on ahead and leaped onto the twin bed arranged head to head with his sister's. "And," he added, quickly holding out his arms toward his mother, "I want you to hold me."

After her son was once again sleeping, Sharon returned to her own room. Glancing around, she found comfort in the orderliness. At least her little home and family were safe here. She smoothed an imaginary wrinkle from the ivory-colored quilted bedspread she had purchased at the Goodwill store in San Bernardino a few weeks back. Looking up, she noted with satisfaction that the print in the short draperies coordinated nicely with the colorful pillow tops Meg had shown her how to smock using gingham check. Living on public assistance didn't leave her any extra money, but Sharon found a special satisfaction in refinishing used furniture and thriftily decorating her house exactly the way she wanted it. Mac had been especially helpful repairing table legs or reinforcing chair backs. Her mother's cousin was more like a father to her, so she affectionately called him "Uncle Mac."

She could still feel argument going on in the main house, though she really couldn't hear it now. She knew what it was about—Kenneth's future in general, his views on the Vietnam War in particular. Neither subject was any of her business or affected her or her kids even slightly — except, of course, that their peaceful life was being momentarily upset. But Kenneth was only home for a thirty-day leave. As soon as he left, life would resettle into their untroubled routine.

As much as she knew Meg would hate to see Kenneth return to his military career, Sharon looked forward to his departure. She didn't blame Kenneth, but she knew his presence disturbed an otherwise happy home. Meg's four years of marriage to Mac had been, in Sharon's opinion, idyllic. No one could have been happier than the McKenzies. Both in their sixties and alone, Mac and Meg had courted like teenagers and eloped unexpectedly. They still did everything together, never wanting to be apart any longer than necessary.

When Mac and Meg bought the old run-down egg ranch in Yucaipa, they extended the invitation for Sharon and the kids to live in the little guest house out in the back. As much as she loved Redlands, Sharon welcomed the change to the higher elevation, the new surroundings, and the security for her little family. Sharon helped with gathering the eggs each evening. Meg pulled the morning shift. Mid mornings Sharon and Meg worked in the small egg processing room, where they washed, sized, and candled the fresh eggs before Mac took them to their growing list of regular commercial customers. Meg kept a few dozen of each day's gathering in a large refrigerator on her back porch for selling to friends and neighbors.

The routine and order of daily life at the ranch gave Sharon and her kids security and stability. Mac was crazy about Richie and Frannie, her charming five-year-old. Papa Mac, the kids called him adoringly. The kids loved Meg too, and she doted on them like a grandmother. But Meg took special care not to offend Frances Mason, Sharon's mother, and encouraged the children to refer to her as "Auntie Meg."

It had been close to perfect until Kenneth arrived a few days ago. Within hours he and Mac were at it. Tense at first, then heated debates, and finally this—full-blown shouting matches.

Sharon felt sorry for Meg, who was caught in the middle of the two men who meant the world to her. Perhaps it was difficult for Kenneth and Mac, but Sharon knew Meg's heart was breaking.

Walking from her bedroom to the small L-shaped living area, Sharon lifted the colorful cotton curtain that hid her dishes from view. She took a large jelly glass from its place on the shelf and filled it with ice water, saving the Kool-aid for the kids. Momentarily she pressed the cold glass against her face. It was hot for June. Evenings were always cooler, but with her bedroom window shut she lacked the ventilation she needed to cool the little house from the buildup of the afternoon heat.

She checked the sleeping children in the other tiny bedroom. Mac had built bunk beds for them, and last week she had pushed them in front of the window to catch the evening breeze. Not wanting her children to hear Mac's and Kenneth's angry voices, she stood quietly in the darkness of the room until she was satisfied that here on the opposite side of the tiny house they could not be disturbed. Finally she walked silently from the room and headed outside to sit on the patio. The angry tones from the house had subsided, and Sharon hoped the argument was over.

Sitting in a folding aluminum chair that she had recently rewebbed with Meg's help, Sharon relaxed. She had a hard time shaking the fact that five years ago today the Redlands High School class of 1960 had graduated. Had she not been expecting Richie, she would have graduated too. Saturday night, June 12, read the notice in the *Redlands Facts*, was the first reunion of the graduating class of nineteen hundred sixty. Five hundred or so classmates would meet to compare notes, share pictures of kids, or brag about college degrees and jobs. Tonight, as she did five years ago, Sharon stayed home, sitting in the darkness—alone.

"May I join you?" Kenneth asked from somewhere in the shadows.

"Oh, I'm sorry," Sharon said. "You scared me."

"Sorry?"

"I didn't see you."

"Do you prefer to be alone? I can leave," he offered gently.

"Oh, no," she said, almost too quickly. "I mean—" she tried to act calm—"sure, come on, sit down." She motioned toward a matching folding chair.

"Do you often sit out here in the dark like this?"

"Uh-huh," she said, taking a sip from her glass. "It's too hot in the house."

"Didn't you open up for the evening breeze?"

"For awhile." She didn't want to tell him she shut the window to keep out his and Mac's angry voices. "I'll open it again before I go to bed."

"Sure is amazing how it can be so hot in the afternoons and so cool at night. I can't get over it. Where I'm from, once it got hot it stayed hot. Air conditioning's a must back east."

"Would be nice here too," she said. "But the evening gives us the break we need."

"Low humidity, too."

"Yeah."

"Makes it easier to take."

"I guess," she said.

"What's that?" Kenneth asked nodding toward her glass.

"Water."

"Got some more?"

"Of course, I'm sorry." She stood quickly and went inside to get another glass from her curtain-covered cupboard.

Kenneth followed her but stayed in the doorway. "I've never seen the inside of your house before. Nice."

"Thanks." Sharon hoped he wouldn't come in any further and wished she didn't feel so uneasy with him. At the same time, she was glad she had showered and changed into a sundress while the kids watched *Beanie and Cecil* before supper.

"You do it yourself?"

"No, Mac and Meg helped."

"Thanks," he said, taking the cold glass from her. Within seconds he had drunk more than half the water. "I guess I was thirsty," he said. "The water here tastes so good." He held the glass out toward her. "Can I get a refill?"

"I'm sorry." She took the glass from his outstretched hand. "One thing we've got plenty of is water." Sharon didn't notice the slight frown cross Kenneth's face. She avoided looking at him directly and refused to let her eyes meet his.

"Want to go back outside?"

"Sure," she said simply.

Kenneth swirled the ice cubes in his glass as they sat in silence. "How long have you lived here?" he asked finally.

"Almost a year."

"Did I meet you last time I was home on leave?"

"No, I don't think so."

"I didn't. I would have remembered," he said.

Even in the darkness, Sharon knew he was smiling. She shifted uncomfortably, hoping he wouldn't notice.

"When were you here last?"

"I wasn't ever here—not on the ranch at least. I came out to see Mom and Mac shortly after they got married. Before I went back to Nam."

Sharon's head shot up and her eyes searched in the shadows for his, settling on where she thought his face was. "Went back? You were there before?"

"Yeah, once before."

"Why'd you go back? I mean, didn't you have a choice?"

"Do you know anything about the military?"

"Not much."

"Good." Kenneth drained his glass. "Then do you mind if we drop it?"

"I'm sorry," she said. "How long have you been in the service?"

"All my life," he said without emotion. "My dad was a career man. I've never known anything else."

"Are you a career man too?"

"I thought so." Kenneth's voice thickened. "Not sure anymore. Can we change the subject now?"

"I'm sorry," she said quickly. "I didn't mean—"

"You said that before."

"Said what?"

"Sorry," he said. She knew Kenneth was looking at her. She wished she was sitting away from the light coming out of the window and hidden in the shadows like he was. Suddenly, even in the semidarkness, she felt exposed. "You shouldn't apologize so much."

"Sorry," she said. Her response was instinctive.

"See?" Kenneth said. Sharon knew by the familiar squeak of his chair that he had changed positions. Glancing his way, she could see he was leaning forward and resting his elbows on his knees. She heard the soft sound of ice jingling in his glass.

"Want some more water?" she asked.

"No thanks." Kenneth stood, and Sharon both hoped he was leaving and was afraid he would all at the same time. "It's late," he said. "I only came out to get cooled off. Thanks for the water."

"That's okay," she said without moving. "It's not that late," she added barely above a whisper.

"Yeah, well . . ." He walked to the edge of the patio and leaned against one of the posts that led to the framework that supported the lattice covering. "It's nice here."

"I like it," she said.

"I can see why." Kenneth stepped into the darkness. "Goodnight," he called softly over his shoulder.

"'Night."

Sharon sat listening to his footsteps as he walked down the gravel driveway toward the main house. She heard him greet Major, Mac's friendly old German shepherd, and closed her eyes when she heard the screen door squeak open, then close behind him. She felt embarrassed, even slightly ashamed, that even though she hadn't moved, in her mind she had watched every step he took.

Closing the door of her little house firmly behind her, Sharon slid the lightweight lock into place. She didn't always lock the door. She felt perfectly safe in her little house with Mac and Meg nearby. But tonight was different. Tonight she didn't feel as safe.

Sharon leaned against her front door and touched the frame with her forehead. An unexpected tear fell down her cheek. She quickly brushed it away and took a deep breath in an effort to keep any others from forming.

Back inside her bedroom she opened the window only slightly, keeping the drapes closed. She knew the drapes would not allow enough breeze to cool down her room, but somehow she needed to keep something between her and Kenneth Matthews. The distance between the houses seemed insufficient, and while the drapes weren't much, they were something at least.

For a long time she lay on her twin bed, hoping sleep would come. Thunder rolled in the distance, and she knew that somewhere in the mountains heat lightning could start a wildfire. Such fires were quite natural for this part of the country, a normal part of life in the California foothills and the rugged mountains above. But tonight the thunder seemed to carry an ominous personal message with it, and Sharon was both fascinated by and frightened of the undefinable emotional stirring she felt inside.

CHAPTER TWO

Sunday, June thirteenth, 1965 promised to be a hot, sunny day. *Perfect day*, Sharon told herself, *to take the kids and get away for the day*. Even before the kids woke up, Sharon busied herself making peanut butter sandwiches, cutting carrots into slim sticks, and packing them neatly wrapped in waxed paper into a small, clean cardboard box. She filled a two-quart pickle jar with Kool-aid and tucked three small plastic cups into the corner of the box. Potato chips, apples, and cupcakes rounded out the menu. In large paper grocery sacks she stuffed extra clothes, bathing suits, and towels, hoping the wading pool at the Redlands Plunge would be open.

"After church," she told her children over breakfast, "we'll go to the park and eat and play in the water."

Richie was beside himself with excitement, and at the last minute he stuck in the baseball glove, bat, and ball Mac had given him for his birthday last month. Frannie rummaged through the toy box to find her "floaty" and came up with a Donald Duck sadly deflated beyond repair.

"Tell you what," Sharon promised, "before we go swimming next time, we'll get you a new floaty. Today, I think poor old Donald needs to stay home, okay?" Then she gathered her disappointed daughter in her arms. "We'll have fun without Donald. And besides, the wading pool is almost too shallow for him anyway."

By the time they were finally in the car Frannie had dismissed the disappointment of leaving her water toy behind and was, as usual, optimistically cheerful and happy. She didn't have the dark, moody side her brother had. But then, she hadn't experienced the same abusive beginning either. Even their different appearances seemed to underscore that fact. Richie's straight thick hair was medium dark brown, his eyes deep hazel. His skin tanned easily and by the end of summer he'd be what Meg called "brown as a berry." Frannie, on the other hand, was almost cherublike with her little round face, fair complexion, and soft, curly, baby-fine blonde hair. She burned easily, and by the end of June her little nose and cheeks would flame bright red, eventually peel, and then settle down to display a few tiny freckles. Sharon often put a light slip-on shirt over Frannie's bathing suit just to keep her shoulders from burning. She tried to get her to wear a hat, but as eager as Frannie was to put it on, more often than not it was tossed carelessly away within an hour.

"Hey!" Kenneth's voice boomed from the back porch as Sharon put her Volkswagen bug in reverse. "Where're you guys going?" Before she could even accelerate and back out of the driveway, Kenneth was beside her with his hands firmly planted in the open window of her car door.

"We're going to Sunday school!" Frannie said from her place in the back seat.

"And a picnic," Richie added.

"No kidding," Kenneth said, smiling broadly.

Sharon's stomach tightened. "We're running late."

"Wanna go?" Richie asked innocently from behind her.

"Sounds like fun," Kenneth said, still smiling. "But you'd better ask your mama about that."

"Can he, Mama? Can Kenny go with us?"

"Kenny?" Sharon asked turning to face her son as he leaned over her shoulder. "You call Mr. Matthews, 'Kenny'?"

"He said I could, Mama. Didn't you, Kenny?" Richie's expression begged Kenny to defend him.

"I did," Kenneth said. "All my friends call me Kenny."

"I see," Sharon said softly. She knew she had been out-maneuvered.

"Can Kenny go, Mama?"

"Well, I don't know . . ." Sharon searched for a plausible excuse to exclude Kenneth from the day's activities. It was because of him that she was taking the children away for the day. Otherwise, Mac and Meg might have joined them. But the tension in the main house was causing them to pull away. Sharon's thoughts were interrupted once more by her son's pleading.

"Please, Mama," Richie said, touching her face gently with his hand. "I want Kenny to go. He can play ball with me—can't you, Kenny?"

"You betcha!" Kenneth said.

Sharon wished Kenneth wasn't so willing.

"Mama," Frannie said softly.

"Hush, baby, Mama's thinking."

"Miss Hannah said we could bring a friend to Sunday school and get a fishy pinned to our line," Frannie said, ignoring Sharon's hushing. "Kenny's my friend, isn't he, Mama?"

"See?" The look of triumph on Kenneth's face made Sharon uncomfortable, but not unpleasantly so. "I can go to Sunday school and get Frannie a fishy, then play ball with Richie. Everybody wins!"

"Okay, Mama?" Richie begged.

"Please, Mama!" Frannie pleaded dramatically.

"Well, Mama?" Kenneth teased. "You're in charge here. You make the decision."

"Right." Sharon stared straight ahead, knowing she was defeated. Kenneth Matthews would be included in her little family outing—like it or not. "Then we'd better get going. We'll be late as it is."

"Wait!" Richie shouted from the back seat. "You got swimmin' trunks?"

"We're going swimming?" Kenneth asked with enthusiasm. Sharon decided he was enjoying himself far too much. "I'll be right back."

"Yippee!" Richie yelled, tossing himself back into a sitting position.

Frannie giggled and clapped her hands together. Sharon turned to face her children. "Now listen to me, you two, you calm down and behave yourselves, you hear?"

"Okay, Mama," Richie said with an effort to sober up. But once Sharon turned around, the two children looked at each other and noisy childish celebration overcame them both.

"What's all the ruckus about?" Kenneth said as he folded his tall, lanky body and stuffed it carefully in Sharon's little car. "It's nothing. They're just glad you're coming with us," Sharon said.

"We *all* are, aren't we, Mama?" Richie asked leaning up to touch Sharon's shoulder.

Sharon turned in her seat so that she could see to back down the long driveway, already feeling awkward having her face so close to Kenneth's.

"Yes," Kenneth said, "I think we're all very happy today." Sharon hoped he wouldn't see the slight smile she felt tugging at the corners of her mouth. She also hoped the flush she felt at the base of her long slender neck wasn't visible as it crept toward her face.

At church, she turned her eyes away from his and tried to focus on the service and the pastor's message. Her mind was difficult to control, however, and she found herself repeatedly worrying about having to introduce Kenneth to friends after church.

Glancing around the small congregation that had come to mean so much to her in the almost five years since Frannie was born, Sharon spotted Cari Bennett smiling in her direction. *Jeff and Cari!* she thought, trying to encourage herself. *I'll start with them.* She knew she could count on them not to jump to conclusions. Cari had always shown her true friendship. *Then Jen and Dan Miller,* she planned silently. Jen and her stepdaughter, Joy, were always coming to make a fuss over Frannie. Sharon caught a glimpse of her mother, sitting alone, as she did every Sunday near the back of the church. Frances was looking in her direction, and Sharon could read the look of disapproval on her face. Leave it to her mother to read more into a situation than was really there.

It was hard for Sharon to handle the changes in her mother's moods. Less than five years ago she had been loving and supportive—even forgiving. But in recent years that had all changed. Confusing and many times hurtful, Frances made Sharon feel grateful for being able to live apart from her.

Maybe it would make a difference once Frances knew that Kenneth was Meg's son. No, Sharon guessed, probably not. Once she found out that Kenneth was staying on the ranch, Frances would make up her mind to fear the worst. She'd be up at the ranch this week, no doubt, just to check things out and to have one of *those* talks—again.

In spite of the heat, a gentle breeze made the afternoon quite pleasant. Sharon managed to relax, and she even enjoyed having Kenneth along to play ball with Richie while she and Frannie made chains out of blades of grass and watched a ladybug that kept the delighted preschooler occupied for nearly an hour. Kenneth took Richie and

Frannie into the wading pool, and Sharon was content to watch from the shade of a nearby tree. Richie was excited about learning to throw what Kenneth called a Frisbee, and Frannie, cold and shivering when she left the water, wrapped up in a towel and snuggled close to her mother.

By late afternoon everyone was hungry again, and Kenneth offered to buy hamburgers at the Burger Bar drive-in before they headed up the highway toward home. Once the kids had eaten, they settled quietly in the back seat and both were sound asleep within five minutes of leaving the drive-in. Sharon was more than happy to have Kenneth drive home. Without the children's constant chatter, the silence became awkward and Sharon's now familiar self-consciousness returned.

Thankfully, Kenneth didn't press her into conversation. In fact, it seemed to Sharon that he was lost in thoughts of his own.

Back at Sharon's, Kenneth carried Frannie into the house and Richie managed to wake up enough to walk in unassisted. It didn't take long for the children to change into their lightweight summer pajamas, and by seven they were both ready to settle down with popcorn and watch *Disney* on the small TV in Sharon's cozy living room. Kenneth stood, as if waiting for an invitation to sit down, which Sharon hesitated to extend.

"Here, Kenny," Richie said, patting the couch beside him, "sit here and watch with me."

Kenneth found his place easily beside the little boy. Within a few minutes Frannie was sitting on his lap feeding him popcorn, one kernel at a time, from her bowl. Sharon fussed around a bit in the kitchen, putting away the picnic supplies and killing a couple of ants that had hitchhiked home in the paper bags. Eventually she settled in a bean bag chair in a corner of the room and waited—for what, she wasn't quite sure.

As soon as the program ended, Sharon hustled the children into their rooms and tucked them into their beds. Within minutes both were sleeping soundly. Sharon bent to kiss their foreheads and noticed Frannie's nose and cheeks turning bright pink.

Kenneth wasn't in the living room when she left the children's room, and for a moment Sharon thought he had gone. Then she heard the familiar sound of the folding lawn chair squeaking under his weight.

"Want some tea?" she asked as she held out a tall, cold glass filled with the light brown liquid. Kenneth had situated his chair in the grass just beyond the cement of Sharon's covered patio.

"Thanks." Kenneth's mood was once again growing serious. Sharon didn't know which she found more discomfitting, this shadowed sad side of him or the lively, playful side she had seen earlier in the day.

Instead of sitting in the other folding lawn chair, Sharon chose to sit at the heavy wooden picnic table Mac had made for her and the children. Most picnic tables were oblong, but Mac had made this square version to fit perfectly on her small patio. She and the kids ate breakfast out here often in the summertime before the morning sun hit this side of her house. It was too hot to sit out here on summer afternoons, but when the sun finally dropped behind the distant horizon, it wasn't unusual to need a sweater to stay out long enough to enjoy the bright stars of the evening sky.

"I've never seen such spectacular sunsets before," Kenneth said gazing up at the long pink and purple tinged clouds stretching lazily across the sky.

Sharon didn't move from her place at the table.

"How long have you lived in this area?" he asked.

"All my life. In Redlands, that is. Then when Mac and Meg bought this place and invited me to come and live here, I was glad to come."

"Redlands is beautiful. This is so—I mean, this is nice, too. Don't get me wrong. But in town, the streets all lined with tall palm trees, all the ivy, the charming lampposts—do you really like this better?"

Sharon shrugged. He was approaching a subject she did not intend to open with anyone, let alone Kenneth Matthews. "I like it here," she said simply. "I wonder if Mac and Meg are back yet."

"Changing the subject?" Kenneth asked.

"It's not like them to miss church."

"Yes, I guess you are." Kenneth leaned forward, resting his elbows on his knees, and studied the ice in the bottom of his glass.

"Your mother avoided us this morning, didn't she?"

"My mother isn't . . ." Sharon let her voice trail off. Her mother was another subject she didn't care to discuss with Kenneth. "Well, let's just say my mother is a bit different."

"Like Mac?"

"No." Sharon laughed. "Not like Mac at all. Mac is my mother's cousin."

"Yeah, I know." He paused. "And your father, was he in church too?"

"Probably not." Sharon was unaware of the slight wince that crossed her face. Long ago she had learned not to feel anything concerning her father. The hurt was still there, she just didn't feel it anymore. "My parents are divorced."

"Sorry," Kenneth said.

"Well, you know. That's how things go sometimes."

"No."

"No?" Sharon asked involuntarily, searching Kenneth's face for an explanation.

"No," he said gently. "I don't know. My parents had a good marriage, from what I know of it. My dad died while I was away in college. He was transferred out here just after my second birthday. My mom liked it out here so decided to come back after I left home for college."

"She worked for Cari and Bennett's grandmother. You met Cari and Jeff this morning."

"I remember." Kenneth swirled the melting ice cubes in his glass. "Are you divorced?"

Sharon's dislike of the word *divorce* began when her father walked out when she was only five and a half. Her hatred for *divorce* increased with her age. Most kids she knew lived with both parents. She felt left out of most of her life because her mother refused to go to any activities where families gathered and their children played together. That included church. Later, after her children were born, it was Sharon who took her mother to church. It was difficult to attend church as a single mother, but her children needed her to overcome that difficulty—something her mother either refused to do or couldn't do for her. "Sharon?" Kenneth repeated. "Are you divorced?"

"Yes." She took a deep breath and let it out slowly. "I'm divorced."

"What happened?"

"It's a long story," she said, hoping to discourage him from probing further.

"I've got time."

Sharon wasn't about to be prodded into talking about Richard Potter and the devastation he had brought into her life. She had come out of the marriage with two beautiful children; that was plain for anyone to see. What they didn't see were the deep inner wounds that remained long after the superficial cuts and bruises finally healed and disappeared. The scars on her back from his cigarette were the only remaining outer evidence of Richard's cruelty—but inside, that was a different story.

"We both have war stories, Kenneth. You don't want to talk about yours—I don't want to talk about mine."

"I'm sorry," he said. "I didn't mean to pry."

"It's okay—it's in the past. I've got my kids now. And I've got Mac and Meg and this place. And I've got my—" She dropped her eyes.

"Your what?"

"Nothing, never mind." It was not something she talked about to anyone. Mac and Meg knew about her gift at the potter's wheel, but no one else. Although she often sang solos at church, Sharon had managed to keep this talent to herself for over a year.

"Sharon, are you happy here?" Kenneth asked.

"If I'm not, then I'm very close," she said quietly.

"What would it take?"

"Take?" She wasn't sure she understood his question.

"To make you happy?"

"I try not to think about it."

"What do you think about instead?" he asked.

"How grateful I am." Sharon smiled. She realized suddenly that she was enjoying this conversation, even if she was uncomfortable being with Kenneth alone like this. "Listen, I'm sorry about giving you a hard time this morning. The kids had a great day. Thank you."

"And how was your day?"

"Nice." Sharon refused to look at him even from this safe distance.

"Nice? That's all? Nice? The kids had a great day and you had a *nice* one? I'm insulted," he teased.

"I'm sorry, I didn't mean—"

"Don't apologize. Man, there you go again." Kenneth stood and walked to stand opposite her with Mac's home-made picnic table between them. "I had a wonderful time.

Mom said I needed to get some perspective. Thanks for taking me along. Nothing like playing with kids to make you see things differently."

Kenneth put his empty glass on the table, stuck his hands into his pockets, and with a simple good night, turned and walked back to the main house. Sharon stared after him long after his image had faded into the shadows of the summer evening. Last night the three remaining weeks of his leave had stretched out eternally in front of her, but now she knew they would pass far too quickly. She'd have to be careful with her feelings. Like all the other men in her life, except for Uncle Mac, Kenneth Matthews would soon leave.

CHAPTER THREE

*D*uring the last couple of years, because of Mac and Meg's persistent encouragement, Sharon had returned to school. First, an adult education program helped her secure her high school equivalency certificate. Then at the community college nearby she discovered not only an interest in art, but a previously undiscovered artistic talent. Eventually she focused on pottery. Quickly she became proficient at throwing pots, and her skill soon revealed a talent just waiting to be developed into an art. By year's end she even entered a couple of her best creations in a student art show.

Mac and Meg surprised her on her birthday soon afterward by converting one of the ranch's smaller sheds into sort of a makeshift studio where Mac installed a used potter's wheel. Next, he came across a secondhand kiln, brought it home, and—under Sharon's close supervision—put it in good working order.

Sharon sat at the wheel for hours on end while Mac and Meg kept an eye on the kids. The comfort and peace she got from squeezing the wet clay between her fingers, shaping it into a ball, then fashioning it into a round, usable pot was a profoundly rewarding experience she rarely talked about. She certainly wasn't going to share it with Kenneth. Mac and Meg were the only ones who even knew about her work. Meg had a few pots sitting on her back porch filled with growing herbs and an angel-wing begonia, but no one knew the potter's identity. Over three dozen more finished pots sat on the shelves Mac rigged up with planks and cement blocks along the walls of her little hideaway workroom.

Are you happy? Sharon could still hear Kenneth's question ringing in her heart. Before she walked out to unload her kiln early a few mornings later, she thought honestly about the answer. Pausing at the side of her covered patio, she glanced down at the morning glories she was training up the heavy corded macrame webbing she had crafted a couple of months earlier. She poked the tiny delicate tendrils through the spaces and kept the trailing vine moving upward. Soon one whole side of the small patio area would be covered with the lush green leaves and every morning the bright periwinkle blossoms would greet her and the children during their summer breakfasts.

Happy? Sharon thought about the terror she felt in years past whenever she had displeased Richard and the gripping fear that came just before his fist or foot connected with some tender spot on her body. "At least I'm not scared out of my wits any more," she said to no one. *Happy?* She thought back further to the beginning of the relationship with Richard Potter. He had been so smooth, so attentive, and yet so demanding at the same time. Jealousy set him off when there was nothing to be jealous of. If she combed her hair a new way, he accused her of having another boyfriend. If she kept it the same, he yelled at her for not fixing herself up more. If she wore a sundress, he screamed at her for being a tease. If she wore a buttoned up blouse, he said she was dowdy and unattractive. When she resisted his advances, he said she was frigid and cold; when she gave in, he called her a slut. Then, when she became pregnant with Richie at the end of summer between her junior and senior years, he said it was her fault she didn't know how to be more careful. Afterward, when Uncle Mac saw to it that they married, he said he was trapped, even though she was the one who found herself locked in the bedroom for hours on end.

Am I happy? Sharon asked herself. Turning to walk the small distance to the shed, where she worked with her hands, got dirty, and came back having made something lovely from nothing, she let her eyes rake over the spaciousness of the egg ranch. Her mind embraced the memory of nights spent in her own bed in her own room with her children sleeping peacefully in the tiny room next to hers. How long had it taken before she stopped jumping every time she heard a car door slam? How long was it before she could answer the phone without dreading whose voice she might hear on the other end?

Suddenly Cari Bennett's face popped into her mind. Cari knew what Richard was like—knew firsthand. Jeff did too. As much abuse Sharon had taken from Richard, she also knew Cari had suffered because of him. Yet, Cari was happy. Anyone could see that. Sharon didn't think anyone could be happier than Jeff and Cari Bennett.

But then of course Jen and Dan Miller came close. Married less than a year, Jen and Dan were ecstatically happy, and it seemed to Sharon a happiness that would last.

Sharon knew she wasn't happy—at least not in the same way that Cari and Jen were. *But they deserved to be happy,* she thought. The most she could ever hope for was what she had here with Mac and Meg, Richie and Frannie. Sharon may not have been happy, but she was content. *All things considered,* she mused, *it's much better than I ever hoped it could be.*

Pondering her contentment and the peace she felt inside, Sharon began unloading several large pots from the cooled kiln. She ran her hand over the pots' textured exteriors and noticed the way the colors swirled and danced gracefully together. Formed under her careful, steady hand the delicate designs were frozen forever by the firing of the kiln.

It was then she noticed the worn belt attaching the electric motor rigged to power her wheel by an inventive Uncle Mac. Examining the belt closer, she decided it was unsafe and knew she'd have to report it to Mac for repair before she could sit at the wheel again.

Sharon headed toward the back porch of the main house. On the way she once again turned her mind to the question Kenneth posed a few nights ago. *Happy?* She decided the answer she had given him was the accurate one after all. *Almost.* It was enough. Enough for now, at least.

Kenneth watched her approach from the shed where she mysteriously disappeared several mornings this week. Sharon walked without hurry toward the porch, where he was enjoying a second cup of his mother's coffee and the small town's morning paper. He noticed how slender she was and how her long, straight blond hair blew softly away from her face in the summer's breeze. She was wearing a simple white sleeveless shirt, knotted at the waist, and faded jeans cut off mid-thigh. She wore no socks underneath the soft tan leather moccasins on her feet. He could tell she was lost in her own thoughts and unaware he was sitting on the porch. He let her walk silently up the few steps to the back door before he greeted her.

"Hi," he said over the rim of his cup. "You're up bright and early this morning."

"Kenneth," she said as one hand flew involuntarily to the base of her throat. "I didn't see you there."

"You weren't seeing anything if you ask me. You were pretty deep in thought out there."

"Is Mac around?" she asked. Unwilling to admit to him that her preoccupation was with the question he had asked a few nights before, she ignored his inquisitive approach.

"I think he's in the kitchen with Mom." Kenneth had liked the way she looked last Sunday when they were with the kids at church then at the park. Her simple straight cotton skirt and sundress-style top had complemented both her figure and her complexion beautifully. He even found it amusing that she would wear leather thong-type sandals to church without nylon stockings, then decided it was because she and the children were planning a picnic after the morning service. Now, seeing her dressed like this, he wondered if she ever covered her smooth legs with nylon stockings. . . . He forced himself to think about something else.

"Go on in," he said finally. "I think they're about done. Get yourself a cup of coffee."

"Thanks," she said, purposely not committing to stay long enough to drink a cup of coffee. Once the screen door to the kitchen closed softly behind her, Kenneth was disappointed that she stood where he couldn't see her. He didn't move from his place on the porch but heard every word exchanged between Mac and Sharon.

"That old belt seems almost ready to break, Uncle Mac. Sorry to bother you like this. No hurry, whenever you can get to it would be fine. Will it cost very much? I don't have much—"

"Listen, sweetheart." Mac's voice was more tender than Kenneth ever imagined it could be. "Don't you worry none about that. If'n it gets too expensive, we'll just barter one of them pots for it."

"Go on, you two. Let Mac have a look at it now," Kenneth heard his mother say. It was obvious how much they loved this young woman, and it was easy to see why. Kenneth sat very still behind his paper while Mac and Sharon left the house and walked together back to the shed where whatever Sharon was talking about needed repair. Kenneth drained the last of his coffee from his cup and slowly folded his newspaper. Setting the cup on the porch railing for retrieval later, he decided to tag along.

"Who knows," Kenneth said softly, stopping to pat old Major's head, "he might could use some help."

Major lazily wagged his tail and once again laid his head down in the cool dirt beside the porch steps.

"Need some help?" Kenneth asked, stepping inside the shed without knocking.

"Don't think so," Mac said abruptly. "I can handle it."

"Okay, just thought I'd ask."

"Thanks anyway," Mac said curtly from his vantage point. He was already on the rough, dust covered cement floor tugging at the troublesome belt with both hands. "Hand me that screwdriver there, will you, Sharon?"

"Going to loosen that pulley?" Kenneth inquired innocently.

"That's the whole idea," Mac said gruffly.

Without a word, Kenneth handed him a small wrench, guessing correctly at the lug size.

Mac simply grunted what Kenneth knew was acceptance of the wrench only—certainly not of his presence or help. He looked further into the shed's interior, and his eyes widened at the sight of the impressive display of Sharon's work. "You make these?" he asked. The expression on his face emphasized the wonder in his voice. Searching her face, he knew at once the answer to his question and saw too how awkward his discovery made her. "No kidding," he said softly as though she had answered him. "I'm impressed."

Sharon turned away from his admiring gaze and busied herself pretending to help Mac loosen the frayed belt. Kenneth saw the bright red flush beginning at the base of her long, graceful neck and creeping slowly toward her tiny earlobe. Her long hair fell across her face and when she didn't push it out of her way, he wondered if perhaps she was hiding behind it.

"This is tight here, girl," Mac said, straining to loosen the difficult nut.

Kenneth pushed both hands deep into the pockets of his Levi's and leaned slightly against a four-by-four-inch support pole inconveniently placed just off center in the middle of the roughly constructed shed. *Beautiful, talented, good mother.* His thoughts were interrupted by Mac's angrily barked order.

"Give me a hand here, Ken!"

Kenneth squatted, reaching to take Sharon's place holding a wrench steady while Mac strained to loosen it from the other side. At his quick movement, Sharon jumped. The thought crossed Kenneth's mind that it wasn't because she was knocked off balance, but because she flinched at his sudden closeness. Kenneth was grateful for the cramped space of the shed that forced them together.

"I'll hold 'er steady over here. See if you can free 'er up on that side." Mac's order brought Kenneth's attention away from Sharon to focus on the stubborn nut and bolt.

"Sharon," Mac barked, "wedge that bar in there and see if you can stop that wheel from turning!"

Instantly Sharon leaned over from behind Kenneth and tried to reach the place Mac indicated with a small crowbar.

"Jam it in there as far as you can," Mac said.

"Can't reach," Sharon said.

"Stretch!" Mac shouted.

"Sorry," she said gently as she leaned forward, placing her hand on Kenneth's shoulder for support and jamming the crowbar between the pulley wheel and the taut belt.

"No problem," Kenneth said as his mouth widened into a broad smile. He felt her long hair brush softly against his ear, and her grip tightened on his shoulder as she stretched precariously forward to obey Mac's orders.

"Now," Mac yelled, "hold 'er steady. Ready, Ken? Now!" Mac and Kenneth strained in opposite directions against the stubborn nut and bolt. Sharon struggled to stay upright without leaning too much of her weight against Kenneth.

"Almost!" The encouragement was strained between Mac's clenched teeth. Suddenly the rusty bolt gave way, and Sharon was unable to maintain her balance. Only Kenneth's quick reflex as he grabbed her around the waist kept her from tumbling head first over his shoulder.

"You okay?" Kenneth asked as she scrambled to her feet and away from his grasp.

"Fine," she said, stepping toward the doorway.

"That was a stubborn one!" Mac exclaimed, holding the brown-stained bolt and nut in his hand. "This whole motor could use a good cleaning," he said upon closer examination. "The moisture here is doing quite a number on your equipment, Missy." Mac stood and rubbed his back. "Got a backlog of deliveries this morning or I'd take it on right now. Can't get to it for a day or two."

"That's okay," Sharon said, but Kenneth was almost certain he heard disappointment in her tone.

"Mind if I have a look?" Kenneth offered.

"You know anything about small engines?" Mac asked warily.

"I've had some luck with them." Kenneth didn't add that he had saved not only his life, but probably the lives of several others in Vietnam repairing small electric generators for medical teams long into the night. His skill with small motors often kept him at the base camp when men around him were sent into the field—some never to return. He repaired jeeps, generators, small pumps, and even a dentist's drill once. His mechanical knack spread to small electronics, keeping him busy maintaining radios essential to communication packs carried on some soldier's back. When something broke down and there were no spare parts, it often fell to Kenneth to somehow keep the small but essential engines running. He managed to rummage parts from machines and devices thought beyond repair. He wondered how many times his seemingly uncanny ability to work on even the smallest of motors saved his life—a fact he was grateful for and felt guilty about at the same time.

"Not like those jet engines," Mac warned.

"I know." Kenneth fought to keep his temper in check. "But, hey, if I run into trouble I'll give you a shout. I don't have much to do around here anyway. I'd like something to do, really." He heard his own tone of voice almost begging to be trusted with something he knew would take him only an hour or two at the most. Underneath it all, he also knew without having to admit it that it was the perfect excuse he needed to be near Sharon and perhaps give him a chance to see her work.

Mac's face told Kenneth that his stepfather suspected his ulterior motive. He could tell that Mac wasn't completely in favor of the idea but couldn't think of a credible objection either.

"I'll have her back to work right after lunch." Kenneth hoped his offer would be irresistible.

"I only work out here mornings," Sharon said. Kenneth knew she was trying to find an excuse to keep him out of her pottery shed. "I'm in no hurry."

"Good," Kenneth said, "then I'll be able to take my time and do it right. You'll want to look at it once I get it apart anyway, right?" He directed the question to Mac.

"Right," Mac said. Kenneth noted the defeated tone in Mac's voice rather than the enthusiastic agreement he had hoped for. "Okay, then. You can pick up a new belt down at Smittie's over on the boulevard if I don't have one hanging in the tool shed. You take that motor completely off there and take it to the work bench. Then, young lady—" Mac turned to Sharon. "While he's got it out of here," Mac pointed to the mounting plank, "you see what you can do about getting that powder out of there. I'm surprised you haven't burned that engine up by now. Get the shop vac out of the garage and give this place a good going over." *And stay away from each other!* Mac didn't say it, but Kenneth heard his unspoken command loud and clear.

In spite of their differences, Kenneth knew he and Mac were both concerned with Sharon's best interests. Watching her walk toward the garage to retrieve the large shop vac, Kenneth found himself wondering what it would take to become one of those interests.

CHAPTER FOUR

*W*ith her potter's wheel dismantled, Sharon threw herself into giving her workroom a needed, though impromptu thorough cleaning. The motor from under her wheel removed, she scraped, swept, and vacuumed every last particle of accumulated dust and clay from even the remotest nooks and crannies.

While she cleaned, Kenneth labored over the little electric motor that powered her wheel. Taking it apart was nothing like the engine repair and maintenance he performed in the military. This was simple and fun. For a couple of hours he totally lost himself handling the familiar tools of his trade. Before the morning passed, Kenneth not only completely cleaned and reconditioned the small engine that brought Sharon's pots to life under her long graceful fingers, but had replaced Mac's simple three-speed switch with a variable-speed foot-control.

Later, just as Sharon and the children were finishing lunch, Kenneth appeared at her doorway.

"Whenever you're available," he said, "I'm ready to put the motor back on."

"Now?" she asked, suddenly aware of how pleasant his unannounced visit was.

"No better time than the present, is there?"

"Yes," she said, "there is. It's hot out there. We could wait until later."

"I don't mind the heat. This is nothing compared to . . ." he changed his comment mid-sentence. "I don't mind the heat."

"Suit yourself," she said shrugging her slender shoulders. "But the kids and I are going to play in the sprinkler. That is, of course, unless you need my help." She secretly hoped he would.

"Nah," he said with a smile that caused her pulse to quicken. "I think I can manage."

"Too bad," she said softly, then immediately wished she hadn't.

"Pardon me?" he said. Sharon felt her cheeks flame with embarrassment.

"Can't you play in the water with us?" Richie moved quickly to Kenneth's side and Frannie moved to the other.

"Yes, yes," the little girl begged. "Please, Mommie. Can Kenny stay and play?"

"I don't know about that," Kenneth said without taking his eyes from Sharon's. "I probably should get that motor back on."

"Yeah, probably," Sharon said, wishing he'd change his mind.

"Shouldn't take more than an hour or two at the most," he said.

"I don't need it until tomorrow morning," she offered.

"Could do it after supper, I guess."

"It'd be cooler then."

"It is pretty hot out there."

"We're going to play in the water, Kenny. Come on!" Richie was already pulling Kenneth out the door and toward the small patch of grass shaded from the afternoon sun by thick oleander bushes and a tall walnut tree.

Frannie ran to the faucet by the side of the house and Richie stood over the sprinkler head, tensely waiting for his sister to turn on the cold spray. Sharon settled comfortably on a lawn chaise pulled into the shade to watch her children play as she did on many summer afternoons. Kenneth lowered himself onto the cool grass nearby. He kept his eyes on the children, but Sharon could tell that he was as much aware of her as he was them—maybe even more.

It's good to be home, Kenneth said to himself as he watched Sharon's happy children run and jump in the fine, cold spray. Their squeals and laughter seemed to reach into his very soul, soothing away the dark memories of other children far away—children pressed into war by heartless and cruel men who had no regard for the value of life or the innocence of childhood. He closed his eyes in an attempt to shut out the memories. Opening them again, he found Richie creeping toward him, squirt gun in hand and a mischievous gleam in his eye.

"Hey!" Kenneth shouted in mock protest. "I'll get you for that!" he yelled playfully when the first stream of water hit his chest. Leaping to his feet, he quickly overtook the small boy from behind, sweeping him easily into his arms. He turned Richie upside down, and held the boy by his ankles, threatening to suspend him face down over the sprinkler. Laughing and screaming at the top of his lungs, Richie begged Kenneth to let him go, and Frannie tugged at Kenneth for her turn to hang upside down. Sharon watched with interest as Kenneth played as hard and laughed as easily as her children. Mac loved the kids, but safely, from a distance. Rarely, if ever, could she recall him roughhousing with Richie or tickling Frannie. Mac had provided the safety and security that both she and Richie so desperately needed. Thankfully, Frannie had never experienced the trauma that Sharon and Richie had; Mac had seen to that too.

Kenneth was different from both Mac and Richard. *Why couldn't I have met someone like him before I met Richard?* Sharon immediately pushed away the thought. *What's done is done,* she told herself, just as her mother had many times before. *No use rehashing past regrets. Living with the consequences of them is bad enough. Better get on with things as best you can.* Frances's words had stung Sharon more than once. *Don't kid yourself into thinking life will offer you any more than you have right here,* her mother's warning flooded Sharon's mind. *Mac and Meg don't have to be this good to you, you know. Don't do anything that will make them regret having you here.*

"Mommy," Frannie's voice brought her back to the present. "I'm freezing."

"Come here," Sharon said opening her arms. The little girl's cold body was refreshing on such a hot day, and her cool, damp head felt good tucked under Sharon's chin. Richie took himself off to play in the dirt with his Tonka truck.

"He'll be caked in mud before long," Kenneth said, nodding in Richie's direction as he lowered himself on the grass near Sharon and Frannie.

"He'll wash," Sharon said simply. She knew the boy would be in the sprinkler again before long. Sharon felt Frannie's body relax and knew her daughter was getting sleepy.

Kenneth stretched himself out full length and folded his hands behind his head. "Sharon?" he asked, then paused.

"Hmm?" she responded quietly.

"Tell me about the children's father."

"It's a long story," she said, wishing he hadn't brought it up.

"I've got all afternoon."

Sharon closed her eyes and turned her face into Frannie's hair. She searched for a way to tell Kenneth she didn't want to talk about Richard Potter with him—or with anyone for that matter.

"I'd like to hear it," he urged.

"I'd rather not." As soon as she said the words, she knew they weren't true. The realization surprised her, and if Frannie hadn't been on her lap she would have turned to Kenneth and retracted the statement. But she didn't discuss her ex-husband with anyone—especially in front of her children.

"Sorry," he said quietly. "Didn't mean to pry."

Sharon mentally groped for the right way to tell Kenneth that he wasn't prying—at least, she didn't feel he was. Words to say that while she didn't talk about it to anyone, she would like to talk about it with him—but later.

She lifted her eyes to meet Kenneth's and an involuntary smile tugged at the corners of her mouth. "Really," she said barely above a whisper, "you're not prying."

"Thank you," he said.

"For what?"

"Letting me off the hook like that."

Sharon smiled again. Kenneth Matthews was different from anyone she had ever met before. He had his mother's gentleness and sweet disposition. She couldn't imagine what it was about the war that caused the tension between him and Mac.

"What's the problem between you and Mac?" she ventured.

"Problem?"

"Voices travel on summer nights," she said.

"Oh, that." She knew he was looking at her and she avoided his gaze. "Then if you've heard us arguing," he said, "why do you ask?"

"I shut my window. I didn't want to hear you fighting with him."

"It's complicated."

"That much I gathered."

"I'm not sure I can talk about it," he said.

"Now *I'm* prying. Sorry."

"He's just so—" Kenneth said, ignoring her apology. "I don't know—so sure of himself."

"Stubborn. I know."

"He gets something stuck in that thick skull of his and he can't see it any way but his own."

"I know that too." Sharon had come up against Mac's stubbornness more than once.

"He won't even listen to anything that might make him rethink his position. It's like I threaten his whole purpose, or point of view or something."

"Yeah, that sounds like Uncle Mac."

"I'll say this for him, though," Kenneth softened his tone. "He loves my mother."

"And she loves him," Sharon added.

"Soft heart and a thick head. What a combination." Kenneth turned and raised himself up on one elbow and looked at Sharon holding her sleeping daughter. "He loves you too, you know. And he adores these kids of yours."

"I know. We're very lucky."

"So, will you tell me sometime?"

"Tell you what?" Sharon asked even though she knew what he meant.

"About the kids' father."

"Maybe, sometime. Sooner or later." Sharon's matter-of-fact tone belied her hope that it would be sooner rather than later.

Sharon watched as Kenneth stood then walked away toward the main house. She tried to shut out her mother's harsh warnings that all men were alike and only after one thing. Maybe her mother had never met anyone like Kenneth Matthews. The extremes of Frances's life hadn't left much room for men of consistent character. Mac was the only trustworthy man in Frances's frequently stated opinion. Even then, although he was "a wonderful cousin," Frances often said, "he'd be a boring husband." But it was obvious to Sharon, and to everyone else who cared to look, that Meg didn't agree.

After dinner, Sharon eagerly waited for her children to fall asleep so she could go out to her workroom where Kenneth had already been working for nearly an hour. Finally at nine, she slipped out to join him.

"There you are!" Kenneth's voice called from the doorway of her pottery shed. "I thought you were going to give me a hand," he said good-naturedly.

"Thought you didn't need any help," she countered.

"Well, maybe not help. But your company would have been nice. It is for your benefit, you know."

"Finished?" She was almost beside him now.

"Almost. Need a test run. Ready?"

"Sure."

Sharon straddled the bench and faced the empty flat surface of the wheel. "So," she said, reaching to a familiar spot but not finding the switch, "what have you done with the switch?"

"Down there," Kenneth pointed to a small wooden box by her foot. "I gave you a foot switch. Thought your hands might be messy or wet. Not the best idea to touch an electric switch with wet hands. Didn't anybody ever tell you that?"

"So you installed this? A foot control?"

"It works sort of like an accelerator in a car. Push."

Sharon pressed the pedal with her foot—gently at first, then harder. "It's really smooth," she said after varying the speed several times. "I'll have to learn a new technique. I guess I had adjusted to the . . ."

"Have you ever used this type before?" Kenneth picked up the conversation when she let her sentence drop.

"Sure, at school. But when Mac built this for me, he put in the hand control. It took a while but I learned how to use it."

"Didn't you tell him how much easier a foot pedal would be?"

Sharon shook her head.

"You didn't want to hurt his feelings, right?"

"Well, he's been so good to me and the kids. He didn't have to do this. I—well, I'm just so grateful to have it at all."

"Come on," Kenneth urged. "Make something."

"What?"

"Make something. Give it a real test. Don't you have a lump of clay around here somewhere?"

"Over there," Sharon pointed to a large plastic paint can in the corner. "I mixed it a few days ago. It may need some water."

Kenneth watched with admiration as she carefully added a bit of water and turned a lump of clay onto the wheel and began to knead it into a soft pliable blob. Gently she pressed her foot on Kenneth's homemade accelerator and the wheel began to spin—slowly at first, then faster at her command. Soon a small round pot took shape under her touch. Kenneth stood in awe of her ability to swirl just the right amount of water from a nearby bucket to give the pot the exact amount of moisture to remain moldable while holding its emerging shape.

"What shall we make?" she asked when the pot seemed perfectly formed to Kenneth already.

"We?" he asked incredulously.

"This one's for you," she said simply. "What kind of pot shall it be?"

"I don't know anything about pots. How do you decide?"

"What would you like to use it for?"

Remembering this night, he wanted to say, but decided against it. "I don't know. What are pots usually used for?"

"Holding something." Sharon smiled in his direction.

Kenneth realized she was amused at his sudden awkwardness. He was definitely in her territory now, and she was in complete control and at ease. He, however, was not. "Better hurry up, the destiny of this little pot is hanging in the balance here," she said.

"Hanging. That's good. Let's make a hanging pot."

"Do you know why you never ask a hanging pot for an opinion or decision?" Kenneth loved the sparkle in her eyes as she worked.

"No," he said with mock resignation. "I give up. Why do you never ask a hanging pot for an opinion or a decision?"

"Because they're always up in the air about something." Her answer was accompanied by the little shrug that Kenneth had noticed before.

"Oh, no. That one stung!"

"You mean with a bad smell?"

"Only with a stinger too." He was aware of how easily they laughed at the lame joke together.

"So a hanging pot, right?"

"Right."

"And, what, pray tell, will you hang in it?"

"Do I have to put something in it?"

"Do you plan to leave it there just hanging, empty and useless?"

"I never thought about it. What do you put in a hanging pot?"

"Whatever you want."

"Why do I have to make all these decisions?"

"It's your pot."

"You're making it!"

"But it's for you!" she protested. "You have to decide the destiny of this pot—I told you that already."

"Do I have to decide right now—at this very moment?" he exaggerated his discomfort. "Man, the pressure!"

"Take all the time you need," she teased. "Take a minute."

"A minute," Kenneth squatted down near her and examined the messy little pot closely. "Okay," he said. "I've decided. This little pot will be a hanging pot and hold a sweet smelling, oh, I don't know—some sort of plant that smells good."

"You're really creative," she said sarcastically. "I thought you'd be more original than that."

"You are really tough, you know that?" He pretended to be defensive. "I have never had to decide on the fate of a pot before. Give me a little room for inexperience, okay?"

"Sorry," she said softly. Kenneth thought he could detect a smile playing at the corners of her mouth. He forced his eyes away from her face to the pot between her hands.

"I know," Kenneth said emphasizing relief at reaching a decision. "It will be a jasmine pot!"

"Jasmine?" Sharon laughed.

"Jasmine. That's a plant isn't it?"

"I guess it is. Sounds more like incense to me."

"Okay, an incense pot. That's it—an incense pot. You know, like the hippies! Real cool man. Dig it?"

"I don't make incense pots."

"Okay, a jasmine plant pot then."

"Better than nothing, I guess. Sorry little pot. But this is his decision, not mine. I'm only making you—but I've given you to him. I hope you'll forgive me and not kill his jasmine plant." Kenneth stood and watched as Sharon put a small indentation spiraled from the bottom to the top with a gentle steadily held curve of her fingernail. Then she reached for a small wooden tool and slowing the wheel, carved an even wavy line criss-crossing the indentation making an intricate pattern. Suddenly as if struck by another idea, she stopped the wheel completely, and after rewetting her hands, folded the sides of the pot in on themselves and once again kneaded it into a nondescript blob.

"Hey what did you do to my pot?" Kenneth was surprised at his sudden, even intense disappointment. "You ruined it."

"I did not," she said so simply that Kenneth found his disappointment turning to anger. "Calm down." Once again she pressed the foot control and the wheel obeyed. "Watch."

Kenneth stood back this time and watched her from a distance. Within a few moments she once again produced a small, round, hollow creation and once again he saw her make steady, even impressions as the object whirled at her command. This time the pot was a slightly different shape, taller, not as round. The sides looked different, too. Sticking her fingers deep within, Sharon coaxed the moist substance toward the palm of her hand bringing the top into a small-mouthed opening. Eventually, she brought the wheel to slower rotation and finally to a complete stop. Reaching down into the covered paint container, she retrieved a small amount of clay and began to work it between her hands. Within moments she had fashioned four loops and with ever so gentle pressure placed them evenly spaced around the outside of the pot. Then with a sharp tool from her box she cut petal shaped curves above each little handle. Moistening her hands once again, she stuck her long fingers in the small opening at the top and gently pushed the petals outward to rest on the looplike appendages.

Kenneth watched without a word as her graceful, artistic touches gave the little pot personality and brought it almost to life.

"There," she said finally. "A jasmine pot."

"A jasmine pot," Kenneth said with admiration. "I always wanted to know what one of those looked like."

"Me too," she said.

"And now we know."

Once the pot was removed from the wheel and set on a shelf to air dry before firing, Kenneth watched Sharon clean up her work area and then rinse her hands a final time. Before leaving the shed, Sharon coated her hands with Vaseline and stood looking at the little pot while she rubbed the thick substance into her skin.

"Hi there, little jasmine pot," she whispered leaning toward the small delicate creation. "I think I like it," she said, turning to Kenneth.

"I know I do," he said. Hearing his own voice, he realized his tone revealed more than just his admiration for the pot. "I also like the artist," he added quickly before he could change his mind.

"Does that bother you?" he asked a moment later as he walked Sharon slowly toward her little house and her sleeping children.

"Does what bother me?"

"The fact that I like you."

"No," she said, but he heard the hesitation in her voice. Even in the darkness he knew she had dropped her eyes to the path at her feet.

"Then what?" he asked.

"I don't know," she said.

"Yes, you do. Would it be better if I hadn't told you?"

"Kenneth," she said. He liked the sound of his name coming from her.

"Are we breaking some unwritten laws if we like each other?" Kenneth wanted to see her face, to see for himself whether she would reveal how she felt at this moment.

"I don't know . . ." she started. "It's just that, well, my Uncle Mac—"

"What? Doesn't like me? Is married to my mother? What?" Kenneth wanted to reason away every possible objection to their becoming close. "We're not exactly relatives, Sharon."

"I know that."

"Then what? Because we just met? Because you've been married before?" Kenneth's tender emotions were beginning to be tinged with panic. "Maybe *you* don't like me."

"It's not that." Sharon's voice thickened.

"Then you do like me!" Kenneth felt his panic subside. "Good, I was afraid for a minute—"

"I'd better go in," she said.

"I guess," he said, unconvinced it was what either of them wanted. "Sharon?"

"Yes?"

"Can I take you out sometime before I leave? I mean on a real date?"

"I don't know," she said. "I . . ."

"You do date, don't you?" Kenneth was almost afraid of her answer.

"No, I don't date." Somehow her response relieved him.

"Will you make an exception in my case?"

"Maybe. Can I think about it?"

"Will this make things, well, difficult for you?"

"I don't know." Sharon turned to walk toward her front door. "I hope not."

Kenneth waited until he heard her door latch and the lock being slipped into place before he turned and headed toward the main house.

He took the steps up Mac and Meg's back porch slowly, processing more than thinking about the evening. Kenneth Matthews hadn't counted on meeting anyone like Sharon while he was home on leave. In fact, he hadn't counted on anything other than being with his mother and her husband, sorting out his confused feelings, and perhaps coming closer to making some very difficult decisions. Meeting someone like Sharon was definitely *not* in his plans.

"Kenneth." Mac's voice seemed to boom out of the darkness, almost assaulting his mind.

"Mac," Kenneth said quickly. "I didn't see you there."

"Have a seat." Mac's invitation sounded more like an order.

Kenneth lowered himself onto a lawn chair a few feet from where Mac sat in the summer night's darkness.

"Get that motor back on Sharon's wheel?"

"Sure did."

"She test it out?"

"Yeah."

"How's it working?"

"Fine."

"She's a nice girl, Kenneth."

"I know that."

"Make sure you remember it." Mac's voice was gruff.

"Don't worry, Mac. I won't forget." Kenneth tried to control the anger he felt whenever he tried to have a conversation with the rough man.

"She's been through a lot. I won't stand for any—"

"That's enough, Mac." Kenneth stood and walked quickly toward the back door. "In case you haven't heard, I did have a decent upbringing. Knowing my mother like you do, you should know that."

"Don't smart off, Ken."

"Don't push me, Mac."

"Here you two are!" Meg said cheerfully as she opened the screen door to the porch. Kenneth was grateful for her intrusion into their conversation. "How about some strawberries and ice cream, Kenneth. It's homemade."

"No thanks, Mom. I'm ready to call it a day and turn in. 'Night," he said and quickly kissed his mother on the cheek as he brushed by her into the house, leaving her on the porch with Mac.

CHAPTER FIVE

"I'm worried about him," Meg said to Mac when Kenneth was out of their hearing. "He seems so on edge."

"He's got a king-sized chip on his shoulder," Mac said. "That's something he's got to deal with on his own."

"Is he the only one?" she asked her husband.

"I don't know what you mean," Mac said defensively.

"You seem a little edgy yourself lately."

"Nothing to bother you with, Sweetheart," Mac said.

"Jack McKenzie," Meg said firmly, "how can it not bother me? My husband and my only son can hardly say a civil word to one another, and it's not supposed to bother me?"

"What do you want from me, Margaret? The kid comes in here all filled with anger and remorse over serving his country. My God, Meg, you'd think he was the only one here who had ever been to war. I was in a war too, you know."

"I know," Meg said. "But somehow this is different, can't you see that?"

"Why?" Mac said, raising his voice. "Why is serving your country and fighting for our freedoms any different now than when we fought in '42?"

"It's not 1942 any longer, Mac. It's 1965. You had the whole country behind you. Everybody and his brother enlisted back then. Those of us who stayed at home prayed, cried ourselves to sleep at night, and sacrificed right along with those who went. It's not the same now. Not everybody is behind this war like we were back then."

"You're wrong, Meg. War is war. France, Italy, Germany—they all know what war is. What did these kids expect when they went over there? A picnic? War is hell, it's always been hell and it will always be hell. For crying out loud—I was on the front, Meg. I know the horrors of war. Did I come home whimpering and back-stabbing my government? Of course not. I would have considered it treason to talk the way he does. And he hasn't even been on the front lines. He's been behind the scenes, working on motors and engines. He's had it too soft, maybe. Maybe he'd have a different opinion if he'd been right out there fighting with the others. He needs to go back there, Meg. He needs to go back and have a taste of what real war is like."

"This is my son, Mac. My *only* son. I've sent him to that war, not once, but twice. He's been to that godforsaken part of the world twice, Jack McKenzie." Meg's eyes flashed with anger even in the darkness. "You'd have me send my only son back to war just because you think he needs to learn a lesson?" Meg's voice broke with emotion. "What do you know about praying every night for a son fighting for a cause that's uncertain and unclear? For a president who changes his mind every time he opens his mouth? What do you know about looking forward to a letter from him and dreading the day when you might get notice of his death? How can you say that he or I don't know about war? Do you forget that my own husband, his father, died in the very war you survived? You have your medals, your decorations, your glorious memories. All we have is a flag, folded neatly in its box and stored in a trunk. Don't you dare tell Kenneth—or me, for that matter—that we don't know about war!"

"Meg—" Mac had never heard his wife speak in such angry tones. "I'm sorry. Honey, believe me, I'm sorry. I don't mean to hurt you. But a man has his convictions.

When your country calls you to battle, you go. No if's, no and's, no but's about it. You go. You do what you have to do. These kids today undermine the very effort they've been sent to—"

"No," Meg said angrily. "I won't discuss this with you. You talk about convictions as if you're the only one who has them. Anyone else's convictions can't be real or genuine if they differ from yours. Listen, to me, Mac," Meg ordered. "You can't live your whole life treating those with differing ideas or personal convictions as if they are traitors to our country and what it stands for. If you say your war was worth fighting, then—okay, you were there and I believe you. But if my son, who has been in Vietnam, says something else, then I for one think somebody ought to listen. You act as if he's betraying his country, and he feels as if his country has betrayed him. And like it or not, I'm caught in the middle. Can't you just let him have his views? Is he so threatening to you?"

"You don't understand," Mac said. "You simply can't understand."

Meg stood, squaring her body in an offensive position facing her husband. "Now, you not only question my son's integrity, but you insult my intelligence. As much as I love you, I won't take that. No, Mac, I won't take that from you."

Meg shut the door firmly behind her, and the sound of it ended their conversation with a decisive finality.

Mac stayed on the back porch, staring out into the summer night. Thrusting his hands deep within his pockets, he made up his mind to do something he thought he'd never do: he'd talk to Frances about Sharon and Kenneth. Maybe Sharon's mother could talk some sense into her. He couldn't do anything about Kenneth being Meg's son, but Sharon was an entirely different matter.

On Friday morning, Frances Mason made an unannounced visit to Sharon and the children.

"Can't a grandma come visit her grandbabies without an appointment?" she asked in response to Sharon's asking why she was there.

"Of course," Sharon said without conviction. Frances and Sharon hadn't been especially close and were even almost distant since Sharon's marriage to Richard Potter. She was opposed to the marriage, and gave in only because of pressure from Mac. Only when Sharon left Richard did Frances seem to warm up to her daughter. And, then, only briefly. Living together for a short time after Frannie's birth only enhanced their differences and set Frances on edge.

Sharon looked at her mother. Years ago, Frances began coloring her hair, "to hide the premature gray," and now her once luscious red-brown hair looked brassy and damaged. Teased and piled high, Frances sprayed it until it was as stiff as straw. Once nearly a sun-worshiper, Frances's skin had taken on a rough, weathered look. The cosmetics she used in an attempt to hang on to her suntanned, youthful appearance only made it worse. Her most recent additions were heavy black eyeliner and false eyelashes. Plucking her eyebrows and replacing them with pencilled ones made her eyes stand out in stark contrast to her pale mouth. A holdover from her strict upbringing prevented her from using anything but the palest of lipstick—which, fortunately, was in fashion these days.

Sharon noticed that her mother's usual mixture of fragrances was slightly different this morning. Normally reeking coconut oil suntan lotion, a sickening sweet hair spray, and a generous dab of Chanel Number Five, this morning she also smelled of cigarette smoke.

"Mama," Sharon said without trying to hide her shock, "have you started smoking?"

"It's not what you think," Frances offered with a smile. "It's not a habit with me. I'm just doing it to keep my weight down. You know the battle of the bulge gets harder when you get a few years on you. I can quit anytime. I just want to take off another ten pounds or so."

"You're too skinny now," Sharon said.

"Not for that two-piece I want to wear to the beach next week. We're all going from work and—"

"I don't believe it," Sharon said. She decided to drop it. "So you want to play with the kids. Well, come on then. They're probably out with Meg. They help her take in the eggs in the mornings. I'll show you."

"Can't we wait for them in here?" Frances said. "I really don't care to go traipsing around the barnyard in these shoes."

"Suit yourself," Sharon said. "I just thought that since you drove all the way up here to see them—"

"Got any iced tea or soda pop?" Frances interrupted. "It's getting hot already."

"Sure, help yourself," Sharon said, pointing to her small refrigerator. "There's Kool-aid in there."

"What about you?"

"I have to go unload my kiln. You can come along if you want."

"I think I'll wait here. That room is always so dusty."

"I just cleaned it," Sharon said. "You'll probably never see it this clean again. Sure you don't want to come?"

"I'll be here when you get back. Hurry it up, will you? I'd like to talk to you before the kids get back."

"Really? Something wrong?"

"No, of course not. Well . . . at least I don't think so."

"Okay, Mama, what is it?" Sharon said, taking a seat across the small formica kitchen table opposite her mother. "I can unload the kiln later."

"Suppose you tell me," Frances said.

"About what?"

"Kenneth."

"Kenneth?"

"Mac is worried that you two might be getting, well, you know, too close."

Sharon felt the anger rise within her chest and knew her face was probably flooding with uninvited color. "Kenneth and me?"

"Is he wrong?"

"Uncle Mac is concerned about me having a relationship with Kenneth and he sends *you* to talk to me about it?" Sharon's hands were beginning to tremble as she fought to control her anger.

"He loves you like his own," Frances said. "You know that, Sharon. He just doesn't want to see you make another mistake that's all. He's only looking out for you and the kids."

"Let me see if I understand this." Sharon stood and slowly walked toward the sink. Slowly she turned and faced her mother. "Mac—the very man who forced me to marry Richard when I got pregnant, then stood by while I got beaten time and time again. Mac who nearly got Cari Bennett killed because he got Richard a job at her grandmother's house. The same Mac who finally realized that my situation was almost as much his fault as mine—have I got this right so far, Mother?"

"Sharon, don't talk to me in that tone of voice."

"This, your beloved cousin Jack McKenzie—" Sharon's whole body was now trembling with anger—"who finally, after two children were forced on me by that man, decided to help send him to jail so I could raise my two kids without fearing for my life is now afraid that *I* might make a mistake?"

"Sharon, listen to me—"

"No, you listen to me, Mama. Kenneth is a very nice man. He comes from a wonderful family, and I love his mother almost as much as if—"

"As if she were your own mother. Go on say it. I didn't come here to have you throw that in my face, Sharon Frances."

"Why *are* you here, Mama?" Sharon lowered her voice and came to stand closer to her mother.

"I came because Mac thought I should try to talk some sense into you about this man. He's a soldier home on leave. He *is* leaving, you know. He's only here for a short visit. You can only get hurt if you let yourself get involved with a military man, Sharon. He's got no roots, honey. He's probably got a girl in—"

"Every port?" Sharon finished her mother's chosen cliché.

"Probably," Frances said. "Many of them do. Military men don't make the best husbands and fathers, Sharon. They're restless and always looking for excitement."

"And you're an expert on military men, are you?"

"I've known a few in my time, yes."

"Did you ever have a relationship with any of them, or were you just the 'excitement' you say they're looking for?"

"Sharon!" Frances jumped to her feet as her open hand struck Sharon's cheek. "I won't take that kind of disrespect from you!"

Sharon turned toward the sink and her long hair fell forward, hiding her stinging cheek. "Mama, I can't believe you did that," she said quietly. "If you've said everything you came to—"

"I'm not finished." Frances's voice carried a triumphant tone of superiority. "You have two things to consider, Sharon. Those two kids out there depend on you to keep your life straight. Once they're grown, you can do what you want with your life and live as you see fit. But until then . . ."

Like you, right, Mama? Sharon wished she could say the words. *A normal life, Sunday school, PTA, and then, once you thought I could take care of myself, you decided to see how much of life you'd missed taking care of me.*

It had started occasionally at first. A night out with the people from work, bowling once in a while or a movie. Then it was every Tuesday night for the bowling league and eventually a weekend at Lake Arrowhead or Las Vegas. By that time Sharon was in high school and able to take care of herself. Left on her own, Sharon had discovered by the ninth grade that she could be popular, with the boys at least. If her mother could play the game, Sharon had decided early, she could too. In the eleventh grade she met Richard, and then she dropped out to get married and have his baby.

". . . Right now you have the kids to think about." Frances had been speaking the entire time Sharon's mind had wandered. "And you have Mac and Meg. They've been really good to you, honey. Think of them. What would it do to Meg if her son and you . . . well, if anything inappropriate happened?"

"Inappropriate? You think my relationship with Kenneth just has to be inappropriate don't you, Mama? Did it ever occur to you or to Mac that my relationship with Kenneth might be perfectly appropriate?"

"And what happens when he finds out about Richard? You don't come with a spanking clean past, Sharon. Once any decent man finds out—"

"Stop it, Mama." Sharon hated it when her mother paraded like this. "That's all history. Things are different now, you know that. I've changed. I have a new life now."

"Oh, sure, and I admire you for it. Getting religion has been very good for you, Sharon. And the kids, too. But come on, for some women men are like alcohol to a drunk. One little slip and it's over. Listen to me, baby," Frances begged, "you've got a good thing going here with a free place to live, and Mac to watch out for you. Meg watches your kids whenever you need her. You want to risk all this for a man home on leave? Come on, you're smarter than that, aren't you?"

"You know, Mama, you talk as if my relationship with Richard spoiled my whole life. Like there's never any chance for a happy life after that. I made a mistake, yes, I got pregnant. I got married—another mistake. Now, I'm divorced. And Richard Potter is who knows where, doing who knows what. Last I heard he's living with some woman up in Redding. I'm free of him, Mama. He even committed adultery while he was still married to me. In God's eyes, I can go on with my life. Now if you and Mac would just see me as free as God does."

"You're not free, Sharon. Not as long as you have those two babies out there. Can't you see that? You might be free to remarry—I don't know nothing about the church's rules on that—but you're not free to carry on with a soldier who's home on leave. At least not right here under Mac's roof with your kids sleeping in the next room."

Sharon took a deep breath and wished her mother would leave. "If you're lonely—and I understand lonely, honey—then go out to the base or the bowling alley and meet yourself someone. But for heaven's sake, do it away from here. Somebody besides Mac's stepson. You're almost relatives! Sharon, use some sense."

"You know what, Mother?" Sharon said, inwardly surprised at the control she felt returning. "You finally said something that I can agree with. I will take your advice."

"You will?"

"Yes, I will."

"What did I say? What advice?"

"I'm going to use some sense. I'm not going to do anything that will bring shame or disgrace to Mac and

Meg's household. I'll not 'carry on' with Kenneth, a soldier home on leave, as you say. And I'll not do anything inappropriate with my kids right there in the next room. I promise you, and I promise Mac—I'll not have a fling with Kenneth."

"Good girl!" Frances leapt toward her daughter and hugged her tight, planting a kiss on the fading redness on Sharon's cheek where she had slapped her a few minutes before. "Now when are the kids coming in? I was hoping to see them, but my goodness! Look at the time. Guess I'll see them some other day really soon. Tell them I was here looking for them, okay? Better run now."

Sharon noticed that once her mother had made her point, she was all too eager to leave. Sharon regretted that she hadn't acquiesced earlier—then felt guilty for the thought.

CHAPTER SIX

*B*y Sunday night, alone on her patio, Sharon had decided that even though Kenneth was a very nice man, she would not risk Uncle Mac's displeasure. *I like my life right now as it is. I have my kids, my little house, and my work. I may not be happy, but I am, after all, content.*

Her thoughts then took a different direction. *Some women are addicted to men,* Frances had warned. "Am I one of those women?" she whispered into the starlit sky. How in the world could she tell the difference between an attraction and an obsession?

"Penny for your thoughts," Kenneth said softly, coming to stand beside her.

"Kenneth," Sharon said, startled, "I didn't hear you coming."

"No kidding," he said. "But then, you've been pretty lost in your own world all weekend. Is something wrong?"

"Wrong?" she asked.

"It's just that last week I thought we were becoming— well, friends. You've hardly spoken to me for days."

"I guess I've been thinking, that's all."

"Want to talk about it?"

"No."

"No, you don't want to talk about it? Or, no, you don't want to talk to me about it?"

"It's late, Kenneth. I was about to go in." Sharon turned toward her front door.

"I don't think so," Kenneth said.

"Excuse me?"

"You just poured this," he said, holding out a tall glass filled with ice water. "I figure if you were about to go in, you'd be finished with this or you'd take it with you."

"Oh, thanks," she said reaching for the glass.

"Wait a minute," he said, lifting the glass out of her reach. "I think you're avoiding me."

"I can't stop you from thinking."

"You could answer the question."

"What question?"

"Are you avoiding me?"

"I need to go in. Good night." She felt his hand cover hers as she reached for the door knob. Her heart pounded.

"Sharon, have I said something? Done something? Are you angry at me?"

"No, of course not. It's just—well, you're leaving in a week or so and I . . ."

"I'm only going to Camp Pendleton, Sharon. I've got only six months left, then I have to decide what I'm going to do next."

"I'm really tired, Kenneth," Sharon said, pulling away from his hand and reaching once again for the knob. *I can't do this,* she screamed to herself. *If I don't go in, he might think I'm leading him on. Mac and Meg might get the wrong impression if they see us talking.*

"I haven't decided whether or not I'll reenlist," Kenneth said flatly.

"But I thought . . ." Sharon dropped her sentence, determined not to pursue the conversation.

"I'm rethinking my military career," Kenneth said as if he didn't notice her lack of encouragement. "In fact, I'm rethinking my whole life."

Sharon stepped inside her little house. It was all she could do to keep from turning around and going to him. *I know what it's like to rethink my whole life,* she wanted to say. *Only when I gave my heart completely to Christ did I find peace and hope.* But she didn't say anything. She didn't even look at him.

"I'd like to talk to you about it sometime," he said.

She didn't turn around. *And I want to listen,* her heart cried out.

"I was hoping you'd . . . well, be interested."

"It's none of my business," she said. *But I want it to be.* She could barely hold back her tears of frustration and loneliness.

"I'm sorry I bothered you," he said. Sharon stood motionless, knowing that just a few feet behind her stood a man who wanted to share his inner struggles with her, who wanted her to listen to the pain in his heart and to have a part in one of the most important decisions of his life. "I was hoping . . ." She could barely hear him. "Sorry," he finished.

She closed her eyes as she heard him step from her patio into the gravel of the pathway leading to the main house. Taking a deep breath, she forced her feet forward and walked through her door. Only when she heard the squeak of the screen door on Meg's back porch did she allow herself to turn around, shut the door, and lean her forehead against its cool painted surface. Then as the tears fell unchecked down her cheeks, she slid the dead bolt securely into place.

In the days that followed, Kenneth kept to himself, played with the children, and helped Mac around the ranch as much as Mac would allow. Only a couple of times when Meg insisted they have an outdoor supper on the back lawn, barbecuing chicken or hamburgers, did Kenneth and Sharon attempt polite conversation. Even then, it was for Meg's sake.

"How's my pot?" Kenneth asked one evening between bites of corn on the cob and potato salad.

"What pot's that, dear?" Meg asked.

Kenneth nodded toward Sharon. "She made a pot for me after I fixed her wheel."

"That was nice of you, Sharon," Meg said.

"So?" Kenneth insisted. "Is it done yet?"

"Yes," Sharon said, refusing to meet his eyes with her own.

"Well, when do I get it?"

"It's right out there on the shelf. You know which one. Help yourself."

"I'm not stepping foot in your studio—"

"Studio?" Mac said good-naturedly. "It's a *studio* now is it?"

"Most artists call their work places studios, Mac," Meg said.

"Artist?" Mac said, smiling. "You take a lump of mud and whirl it in a circle until you make a hole in the middle and you call it art?"

Sharon dropped her eyes to her plate. Kenneth was sorry he had put her in such an awkward position. He was just trying to make friendly conversation. *Why did Mac seem determined to downplay Sharon's work and talent?* Kenneth wondered. He had seemed so proud before. Surely Mac knew Sharon's pottery was more than just a hobby. Why else would he have invested so much in it? Kenneth looked again at Sharon but couldn't read her face. *You are so good at hiding your true feelings,* he thought. *And you,* he wanted to say to Mac, *you need to watch your mouth!*

Nothing else was said about Sharon's work in general or the pot she had created just for Kenneth in particular. But it wasn't the end of the subject as far as Kenneth was concerned. He resolved to speak to her about it when he could manage to see her alone. It wouldn't be easy, but if he had to knock on her door after the children were asleep, he would. He had admitted to himself his growing attraction for her and his deepening feelings. With less than two weeks left before he had to return to duty, Kenneth knew he didn't have much time to find out if she felt the same.

A few days later, Sharon had tucked her children in after giving them both showers. The hot summer days were thankfully relieved by Yucaipa's wonderfully cooler nights. Wearing as little as possible all day long, the happy and exhausted children welcomed pajamas and blankets after bedtime showers. Once the children were sleeping, Sharon turned off her small TV and stepped outside onto the patio.

Lost in her own thoughts, Sharon didn't hear the familiar sound of the squeaking back screen door up at the main house. When Kenneth's footsteps on the gravel path jarred her into realizing that he was headed her way, it was too late to go into the house and avoid him.

"Sharon?" he called softly from a short distance away. Her heart stirred at the sound of him speaking her name.

"Over here," she said.

"Can I come and talk to you?"

"Yes." Sharon agreed before she could think better of it.

"It's really pretty out tonight," Kenneth said, stepping closer.

"I know."

"Are the stars always this bright here?"

"Only in the summer."

"It's cooled off considerably."

"It always does."

"I'm confused," Kenneth said finally. Sharon's heart began to race again. Not knowing what to say, she kept quiet. "I thought we agreed we could be friends. Am I mistaken about that?"

"No."

"Then why have you been avoiding me?" Kenneth asked more bluntly than Sharon expected.

"I haven't been avoiding you," she said, even though she knew she had.

"It appears that way to me."

"I've been busy," she offered.

"You've been busy, or you've been keeping yourself busy. Which is it?"

Sharon's throat tightened. How she wished she could just spill out her inner turmoil to Kenneth. To once and for all tell him about her past, about Richard, about her prewedding pregnancy and the conditions under which Frannie was conceived and born. If she could only trust him enough to tell him, she thought, it would at least all be out in the open. Then if he backed off, okay—but if he didn't—

"There you go again," Kenneth said gently.

"Go again what?"

"Lost in thought. I wish I could tell what was going on inside that beautiful head of yours." Sharon blushed at the compliment and silently thanked God for the darkness. Maybe Kenneth wouldn't notice. "It's Mac, isn't it?"

Sharon spun around to face him. "Mac?"

"He doesn't like me very much. Anyone can tell that just by looking," Kenneth said, then added, "or listening. He's told you to stay away from me, hasn't he?"

"No, Kenneth, he hasn't." *He sent my mother to tell me,* she wanted to add.

"He's made it pretty clear how he feels about me. And it's obvious how much he loves you and the kids. It's just that . . ." Sharon waited for him to finish his sentence, then noticed that Kenneth had drifted off, into his own deep thoughts.

"I guess I'd need that penny now," she said, trying to lighten the mood.

"I'm sorry, what did you say?"

"It's my turn to pay a penny for *your* thoughts," she said.

"Just thinking."

"Yeah," she said without pressing him. Sharon not only liked Kenneth, she liked being with him. Being near him, just knowing he was in the main house with Meg and Mac, was a pleasant thought. She had observed his attempts at making friends with Mac. She could tell that he had decided to hold his tongue on the issues that separated them. Kenneth was not a compromising man; Sharon knew that just from listening to him talk to his mother. But he was a peace-loving man, and he loved and respected his mother deeply. Out of that love and respect he swallowed his pride where Mac was concerned and kept his opinions to himself more than once. Even when Mac tried to provoke an argument, Kenneth kept his mouth shut. Sharon came to recognize that while Mac appeared to be the stronger man, Kenneth had a kind of strength that Mac would probably never have.

"I'm thinking of leaving the middle of the week," Kenneth said, breaking the long silence between them.

"That soon?"

"Well, I thought I might go and visit my sister back east before I have to report for duty. I can fly military standby."

"I see," Sharon said, trying to keep the disappointment from showing in her face and in her tone of voice. "When would you have to go?"

" After the fourth—Wednesday or Thursday, I guess."

"Does Meg know?"

"I told her," he said. Sharon thought she saw the glimmer of a tear in Kenneth's eye, but in the darkness it was hard to tell.

"What'd she say?"

"She said it was up to me. It's hard for her having me here. I hate to see her and Mac at odds with each other. It's even harder when I know I'm the reason for the tension between them."

"Have they argued?"

"Not so that I can hear," Kenneth said. "But I know when my mother is taking a stand against something. She can be pretty stubborn. All smiles, polite and cheerful. But she can freeze you out all at the same time when she thinks you're in the wrong."

"Is that what she's doing?"

"Not to me," Kenneth said. "But your poor Uncle Mac."

"He's stubborn too—maybe even more than she is."

"But he'll wear down first. You watch. He's angry with his stubbornness, she's not. I don't quite know how to put this. My mother's only stubborn when she's right and she knows it. She never gets angry when she knows she's right, and with that kind of righteousness on her side, she can last forever."

"Righteous indignation?" Sharon asked.

Kenneth laughed softly. "Iron hand in a velvet glove." The way he laughed made Sharon feel good and she laughed as well. "That's more like it," he said, "I like to hear you laugh."

Kenneth turned to look at her, and as he took a step closer she backed toward the front door of her little house. As much as she wanted him to close the distance between them, fear kept her from standing still and allowing him closer.

"You're really determined to keep me at arm's length, aren't you?" he asked, his voice barely above a whisper.

"I—" Sharon hesitated. "It's just that, well, you're leaving and everything. I don't want to get something started and then . . ."

"You're too late," Kenneth said. The truth of his statement slowly penetrated her mind, and her heart raced in agreement.

Suddenly anxious to escape from his disturbing presence, she turned to leave without comment. Sharon froze at her doorway under the weight of his warm hand on her shoulder. "Sharon, don't do this," he said. She didn't turn around. He was too close. Turning around would mean facing him, and she was convinced she couldn't hide the truth of her feelings for him if he pulled her into his arms. *Addicted to men or attracted to Kenneth?* The question hung in her mind and shadowed her heart with fear.

"I can understand if you just want to be friends. If you don't want this relationship to go any further, just say so. I'm a grown man, Sharon. I've been to war—by now I thought I could take most anything—but I can't take this silence from you. Just tell me what you want from me."

Sharon turned slightly and fought for control. She looked to the dark, star-sparkling sky above as if searching for strength. Taking a deep breath, she tried to calm herself, but when she tried to speak her voice wavered.

"I can't," her voice broke slightly. "I just can't."

"Can't tell me? Can't be my friend? Can't what?"

She swallowed hard, trying to manage any suitable answer. "My life is—well, complicated."

"Is that what I am, another complication?" he asked. She could hear the emotional strain in his voice.

"Kenneth, please," she begged.

"Okay, listen. I'll leave. You know how I feel about you. But with the situation in the big house with Mac and me, for my mother's sake—and yours too—I'll go. I really didn't come looking for this, Sharon. But there you were, you and the kids. I'm as surprised as you are. But one thing is for sure, I didn't come to cause anybody any trouble. I won't stay where I'm not welcome."

Oh, Kenneth, her heart whispered in answer, *if you only knew how much I wanted*—She felt the weight of his hand lift from her shoulder, and she glanced back uneasily to where he was standing less than an arm's length away. Something disturbing charged the night air around them. With effort, she was able to force herself to look in his eyes. Even in the darkness, his blue eyes seemed to look within her soul to the empty place that even the intense love for her children was unable to touch.

"Sharon," he whispered, "don't shut me out."

She turned away, weary with indecision, unmet needs, and uncertainty. If he didn't leave now, her fragile resolve would break and she'd fly into his arms. Standing perfectly still, she waited, unable to move. Her mind raced with a crazy mixture of hope and fear.

Kenneth reached and with the tips of his fingers gently smoothed her long, blonde hair away from her face. "Please," he pleaded again, "don't shut me out."

Suddenly she realized that she was more afraid of herself than of him. Once again she forced her eyes to meet his. In the darkness the moisture in his eyes caught the moonlight. Her pulse raced erratically with panic-filled excitement. Taking a deep breath, she let her guard down for a brief moment. "I can't . . ." she began, but Kenneth's movement, stepping even nearer, stopped her from finishing. With him so near, all of her loneliness and confusion welded together in an overwhelming yearning to be wrapped in his arms.

Kenneth seemed to understand her vulnerability and pulled her into his embrace, resting his chin near her temple. Sharon stiffened as his arms slid around her. She quickly chastised herself for letting him get this close. Placing both hands on his chest, she braced herself against him, but she was powerless to move away.

"Sharon," he whispered, "look at me."

For a long time she kept her eyes riveted on the top button of his shirt. Only when he repeated the command did she lift her eyes to his.

"I won't hurt you," he promised. "Can't you believe me?"

Involuntarily, tears of fear and relief filled her eyes. His face blurred. Closing her eyes in an effort to refocus her vision, the tears spilled down her face.

Her breath stopped as, one by one, Kenneth kissed the tears on her cheeks. A sob caught deep in her throat as she felt his lips touch hers, gently, like a whisper.

"You'd better go in," he said as he stepped away from her.

"I think so, too."

"Sharon—"

"Good night," she said quietly.

"Good night," he whispered.

"Kenneth," she said softly before he stepped on to the gravel path leading to the main house, "I'm afraid."

"I know you are," he said, his voice low and gentle. "I'll see what I can do about that, okay?"

"Okay," she said.

CHAPTER SEVEN

*T*hat they managed to get through the Fourth of July without a major explosion between Mac and Kenneth was more to Kenneth's credit than to Mac's. Mac seemed determined to bring up last week's bombing of Hanoi several times throughout the day. Sometimes Meg was able to run interference and change the subject. Finally Kenneth addressed the issue directly.

"It's no use, Mac," he said maintaining a good-natured mood. "Today we're both just veterans—Americans who love our country and want what's best for her and for our family. I'm not going to argue with you today."

Sharon was grateful and Meg beamed with pride for Kenneth's ability to walk away from Mac's incessant goading. For her part, Meg preferred to give the children most of her attention, keeping a distance between herself and Mac. Sharon wondered if Mac knew how much he was hurting his wife. With Kenneth's persuasion and Meg's encouragement, Sharon agreed to drive Kenneth to the airport the next morning. Although she hated to see him go, she was happy in a way to have the space and time she needed to think things through where he was concerned.

Kenneth, on the other hand, hesitated to leave and even changed his mind a few times. He knew he needed to go, but he wanted to stay. Mac's surly attitude made up his mind. It was hard enough to think clearly being this close to Sharon day and night, but Mac's constant sniping made it nearly impossible.

Kenneth and Sharon arrived at the small airport nearly an hour before Kenneth's plane was scheduled for take off. Sharon waited nervously as he checked in at the counter. Finally he turned and together they walked toward the coffee shop.

"I may not make this flight," Kenneth said once they were seated with tall glasses of iced tea on the table between them. "It's pretty full. I'm traveling military standby, but since I'm not reporting for duty, I may have to wait until the next flight."

"Oh," Sharon said simply. Looking for something to help her manage the awkwardness she felt being in public with Kenneth, she wrapped both hands around the tall glass and let its coolness refresh her. She stared at the honey-colored liquid and then began to stab her index finger at the lemon wedge floating among the pieces of crushed ice.

"Sharon," Kenneth began, "I think we both need time to think—and to pray. Don't you agree?"

"Sure." How could Sharon begin to explain that she wanted him to go and never come back, while at the same time she wanted to grab on to him and not let him go—ever. She kept her eyes on her tea.

"It'll be good to see my sister. It's been nearly two years since I've seen her. And the kids, they must be getting pretty big by now. She has two."

"I know. Meg told me."

"I'm hoping to convince her to come out here for Christmas. Mom would really love that. She and Mac went back there last year."

"I know."

"I'll be here then too."

Sharon's eyes flew up to meet Kenneth's. "Not till Christmas?"

"That depends. I'll be at Camp Pendleton for the next few months. I won't be that far away. I could come up from time to time. Who knows, maybe I'll be home for Christmas and then . . . well, maybe before."

"I see."

"Sharon," Kenneth said, reaching to take her hand across the table, "you've barely said five words to me since we left Yucaipa. Have I said something to offend you? Have I . . ." Sharon sensed he was searching for the right words and as much as she wanted to help him out by pouring out her heart right then and there, she couldn't. Her words were choked inside her chest by her intense emotions.

"Kenneth Matthews, Lieutenant Kenneth Matthews." His name came through the speaker in the ceiling. "Please come to the United Airlines ticket counter. Kenneth Matthews, Lieutenant Kenneth Matthews, please come to the United Airlines ticket counter."

Sharon waited in the coffee shop while Kenneth checked on his flight. Upon his return she could see the look of concern on his face.

"It could be a while," he explained. "Something about fog in San Francisco and also L.A. I guess they've rerouted connecting passengers through here this morning. I think I'd better call Mom. Come on, let's find a phone."

After talking to Meg, Kenneth checked again with the airline and learned that it would be late afternoon or early evening before they would know whether he could get a flight out that day. "Check back with us around five or so," the ticket agent said. "We have only two evening flights, but by then we'll know more definitely."

"Let's get out of here," Kenneth said, taking her arm and urging her toward the outside doorway.

"Do you want to go home?" Sharon asked, dreading his answer.

"No," he said. "I don't. Is that all right with you?"

"I have my orders to stay with you until—"

"I love my mother," Kenneth said with a smile that spread across his entire face.

"I know," he said, obviously enjoying the change in plans. "Let's drive up to the mountains until our time is half gone, then turn around and come back. We'll stop and eat somewhere along the way. Sound good to you?"

It sounded wonderful to Sharon. An unexpected day with Kenneth—no kids, no family, no cutting remarks from Mac to spoil it. "Fine," she said, careful not to reveal her delight at his suggestion.

Kenneth expertly navigated the car around the broad curves and hairpin turns of the mountain road.

"You're really quiet," he said.

"Am I?"

Kenneth pulled the car into a large open spot edged with a rock wall. *Vista Point,* the sign read.

"Come on." Kenneth took Sharon's hand and gently pulled her toward him. "Let's take a look."

She let him pull her toward the wall and the view of the mountains and valleys below. "Not much to see," she said, nodding toward the valleys clogged with thick gray smog.

"There's plenty to see," he said, smiling down at her.

Sharon felt her heart beat faster under his admiring gaze. "At least it's cooler up here."

"I like the mountains," Kenneth said.

"I do too."

"Sharon, come here," he said opening his arms. "Please, come here." His voice, low and thick with emotion, made Sharon catch her breath. But she didn't move. "You are so beautiful." She shuddered when she felt the slight tickle of his finger as he stroked her long hair and tucked it gently behind her ear. "What am I doing wrong, Sharon?"

"Wrong? You're not doing anything wrong."

"Then what is it?"

"I'm just not sure—" Once again her voice was choked back by her feelings.

"Do I frighten you?"

"No," she said quickly—too quickly. "Well," she said wanting to be honest, "maybe you do."

"Why are you afraid of me?"

"I don't know." Sharon's strong feelings for Kenneth and her intense need to confide in someone brought her to a surprising decision. She fought back tears and panic and turned to face him without closing the distance between them. "Kenneth, I have to tell you something, and I don't know how you'll feel."

"You can tell me. Sharon, you can tell me anything. Don't you know that?"

"I don't know what I know," she said. Something inside her warned that she'd better keep her mouth shut, but a competing emotion screamed to be released and heard. "All I know is that I'm divorced." The word still had an intense distaste in her mouth.

"I'm well aware of that."

"And," she said as if she hadn't heard his response, "I have two kids."

"I know that too."

"I have to have a tight grip on reality, Kenneth." Even using his name in casual conversation sometimes caused her heart to flutter; now in this intimate conversation it brought him dangerously near—too near. "I've made some pretty bad mistakes in the past."

"Who hasn't?" he asked. He reached forward to pull her closer.

"Don't," she said, taking a step away from him. "This is difficult enough. Please let me finish."

"Sorry," he said.

"I . . ." Closing her eyes, she summoned as much inner strength as she could. "I was pregnant with Richie when I married his father." She forced the words out then turned away, afraid to see Kenneth's expression. "And—" She continued, even though tears now blurred her vision. "And—it wasn't a good marriage." She wasn't able to reveal the full truth.

"Obviously," Kenneth whispered. "Then you had Frannie," he added quickly.

"As you can probably guess, I really didn't plan on having either of them. It's just . . ." Her embarrassment prevented her from explaining any more. How could she tell Kenneth about the beatings and the cruel way Richard Potter had forced himself on her? How could she expect someone as gentle as Kenneth to believe, much less understand, what she had been through?

"Sharon," he whispered, closing the distance between them before she could resist him again. "Please, honey," he said, "I'm not going to hurt you. I promise."

Suddenly feeling warm and secure as he encircled her with his arms, Sharon buried her face in his shoulder. Silent sobs shook her, and she felt his arms tighten around her. Her mother's oft spoken words haunted her: *You have two children to raise before you can even begin to think of your own needs and desires.* She stiffened slightly and Kenneth didn't restrain her when she pulled away. "I'm sorry," she said softly, regaining her composure.

"For what?" Kenneth's voice edged with anger. "For having a bad marriage? For making a mistake? For having two great kids? What do you have to be sorry for?"

"I shouldn't dump all this on you," she said. "Please don't be angry with me."

"Angry with you?" But it was too late. Sharon heard the sharpness in his voice and edged away from him. "Sharon, I'm angry, but not at you. I get this close," he said, holding up his hand with his index finger and thumb nearly touching each other. "I get this close and you shut me out."

Sharon wrapped her arms around her rib cage and stepped away. "See? There you go again. Why do you do that? Am I the one who hurt you?"

"No," she said.

"Have I ever done anything to make you think I ever would?"

"No." She wished she could make him understand. "It's not you." She searched for the right words. "It's not you at all. It's me. I don't trust my own judgment. My own feelings . . ."

"Feelings?" he said. She heard his tone soften and turned to see a smile lifting at the corners of his mouth. "You have feelings for me?"

"Kenneth—"

"Well?"

"I can't say."

"Can't? Or won't?"

"It's not that simple."

"I think it is," he said. "You like me, don't you? Maybe even more than like me," Kenneth teased.

"Don't push me," she commanded, holding up her hands and backing away as he stepped closer.

"Okay, okay," he said in mock surrender. "I won't push. But let me tell you, lady. I have feelings—strong feelings. And the more I'm around you the stronger they get. So how do you like that? The career military man, the nearly confirmed bachelor—taken quite off guard by a beautiful young woman and two little kids. I don't know what I expected when I came to visit my mother, but it certainly wasn't this." He gestured back and forth between them. "I'm not used to being resisted, you know."

"And I'm not used to feeling this way," she blurted out.

"What way?" Kenneth's expression told her he had experienced a small victory at her admission. "Come on," he said, catching her by both arms and turning her to face him. "Finish what you started to say. Feeling what way?"

"I'm not used to feeling," she said simply. "Feeling anything at all."

For a long, silent moment, they stared into each other's eyes. Sharon surprised herself by letting Kenneth look deeply within her soul and thought for a moment he might even be able to see into her very heart. Suddenly, the intimacy they were sharing gripped her with fear and she closed her eyes.

"Sharon," Kenneth whispered, pulling her tightly into his arms, "please don't—don't shut me out."

"I'm afraid," she admitted. "I'm so afraid."

"I know, baby, I know." Kenneth didn't try to kiss her, even though she felt he wanted, even needed to do just that. He just held her, and for a moment she let herself believe that he could protect her from ever being hurt again.

Once again he impulsively covered her mouth with his kiss. "Sharon," he whispered hoarsely as he lifted his face to barely a few inches above hers, "you're not the only one who's scared."

$\mathcal{A}$t the small country airport, Sharon stood alone
at the chain-link fence separating her from Kenneth. She
watched as he climbed the stairs and approached the
doorway to the plane. Her heart stood still for the moment
he turned, waved, then quickly ducked his head and entered the aircraft. Too quickly he was gone from her view,
yet she stood with her eyes transfixed on the airplane's
open doorway. The hope that he might miraculously reap-
pear refused to listen to reason. Her fingers curled tightly
through the open mesh of the fence. She stared straight
ahead as his plane rolled back onto the runway and slowly
taxied to its takeoff position some distance away. Still clinging to the fence, she squeezed her eyes tightly shut as the
huge aircraft roared overhead, carrying Kenneth away.

"Hey, lady," a young coverall clad man said, "you okay?"

"What?" Sharon wasn't aware of the activity around her
or how long she had stood there at the fence. "Oh, yes," she
managed to mutter. "I'm fine."

She removed her numb fingers from the wire fencing
and forced her legs to carry her back inside and through
the small airport to the parking lot. With effort she recalled
where Meg's Plymouth was parked and commanded her
feet to walk in that direction. Finally, in the privacy of the
car where she and Kenneth had spent so much of the day
together, she laid her head against the wheel that he had
touched just an hour before. Nothing, not even her abusive

marriage, had ever caused her this much pain. Nor had she ever felt such fear—fear that Kenneth wouldn't return, or perhaps fear that he would. She fought to subdue an agony that was too deep for tears. Lifting her head from the steering wheel, she looked at her trembling hands. "I have to get hold of myself," she said aloud. "I have to somehow make it home in one piece."

It took days before Sharon found the courage to examine the pain she felt when Kenneth left. Mac was so worried about her that once again he pressed Frances into coming to "take care of her daughter."

"What's gotten into you?" Frances scolded Sharon a few mornings after Kenneth's departure. "Have you lost your mind entirely? Over what? Some soldier?"

"Mama, don't," Sharon begged. "You don't understand."

"You bet I don't. You have a perfectly good setup here. You'd better think this through before you make another royal mess for the rest of us to clean up after." Frances insisted on pressing the issue of Sharon's past. "If you want a boyfriend, for heaven's sake, try to find one Mac likes, will you? After all he's done for you—"

"That's enough, Mother." Sharon was shocked at the angry tone of her own voice. "Just because Mac has provided me a place to live—and I'm no freeloader, I might add. I do help out, you know. Mac hasn't the right to tell me who I can or cannot see. Good grief, Mama, this is Meg's son we're talking about, not some soldier I picked up at the bus station."

"Just because he's Meg's son doesn't mean there's a whole lot of difference, Sharon. Men are cut from pretty much the same cloth. You should know that by now."

"Mama, please, we're getting nowhere fighting like this. What's past is past. I've given my heart to the Lord, Mama. I've put my past mistakes into His hands. He's forgiven me.

Why can't you? I have two wonderful kids, can't you see that? I made mistakes, yes. But Richie and Frannie aren't mistakes any more than you and I are." Sharon turned just in time to see her mother wince. "Am I a mistake, Mama? Is that what I am to you?"

"No, of course not. I loved you. It's just that from the day I told your father I was pregnant, he started chasing. If it hadn't been for—"

"For me," Sharon said, finishing her mother's sentence and giving words to her lifelong suspicion. "If it wasn't for me, you'd still have Daddy. Isn't that what you were going to say? Isn't that what you believe? My God, isn't it what I believe?"

"Look, Sharon," Frances said, leaning over the table with both hands planted firmly for support. "Face the facts, will you? If it wasn't for Richie—as darling a child as he is, sleeping like an angel in there right now—you could've had a nice husband by now."

"You're wrong, Mama," Sharon said flatly. "If it wasn't for Mac's interference—"

"Don't you dare blame my cousin."

"If it wasn't for Mac's interference and insistence that Richard 'do the right thing by me,' I would have been able to get on with my life by now. After all, Cari Bennett—" Sharon stopped. She wouldn't tell Frances the whole story of Richard's attacks on Cari. His two years in prison and five years' probation had given Sharon not only relief but, with Jeff Bennett's help, a divorce and freedom from Richard's threats and constant abuse. With Jeff's love and support, Cari had even been able to forgive Richard. And, seeing her with the children in her Sunday school class and the love she gave Richie in spite of the fact he was Richard's son. Even having to give up a son that she'd never see or know, Cari was able to put Richard out of her life. Because of this remarkable young woman, Sharon was drawn and eventually convinced to give her heart completely to Christ.

"That's entirely different," Frances argued. "Cari didn't have a baby to contend with."

Yes, she did Mama, Sharon thought. But she kept the thought to herself. "The point is, Mama, there *is* life after mistakes."

"Yes, I agree," Frances said, her tone turning smug. "But only after those children in there don't need you."

"Isn't that strange?" Sharon challenged her mother even further. "Two people can get married, have babies, and raise them together, but a woman with kids can't get married and raise them with a husband. This doesn't make sense to me, Mama." Sharon poured herself another glass of iced tea and made her way outside into the safe darkness of the patio. She looked at the bright stars of the summer night, the same stars she and Kenneth had admired together. *Are they always so bright?* she remembered him asking. Turning when she heard Frances come out of her house, Sharon phrased her next question carefully.

"Tell me, Mama, if I was interested in anyone other than Kenneth Matthews, would Mac be this upset?"

"What do you mean?"

"Do you know they quarrel?"

I think he came here just to cause trouble."

"Mama!"

"Isn't that what's happened?"

"No, it's not."

"Mac says he and Meg are—well, how shall we put it?"

"He can't push her around, Mama. That's all. Mac's got to be king of the hill and Meg's nobody's patsy. For once Uncle Mac can't tell someone how to feel, act, or think. It's a new thing for him to deal with. If anyone can stand up to Uncle Mac, Meg can."

"If she doesn't lose him just to make that point."

"Is that what marriage means to Uncle Mac—to you? Some game in which the man has to win all the time? Is it only for the husband to have his say? Are his opinions supposed to be engraved on plaques and hung on all the walls around the house?"

"A woman has to put up with—"

"No, Mama. I won't listen to this anymore."

"I was only going to say that a man has a right to his opinion. If a woman wants to keep peace in her house, she'd best do so by keeping her opinions to herself when they differ with his. I don't mean she can't disagree, but is it worth it to lose a good man like Mac just for the sake of an opinion?"

Sharon shook her head. Was Kenneth so fragile that a differing opinion would threaten his manhood? Somehow she doubted it. The sudden, uninvited thought of him reminded her that the pain of his leaving was still there.

"You don't have to go on with this, Sharon. He's gone now. Forget him. After all, how serious could it have become in such a short time? You're both adults. He's probably already looking for someone else to swoon and—"

"I think you've said enough for one night, don't you?" Sharon stepped away from her mother. "You're right, it's getting late and I think you'd better go." Sharon kept her voice even and calm. She didn't care to argue with her mother again—at least, not tonight.

"But what am I going to tell Mac?" Frances said, following Sharon inside the house.

"Tell Mac to mind his own business," Sharon said.

"You *are* his business," Frances countered.

"Then tell him to talk to me himself. Don't do his dirty work for him, Mama. If Mac has something he wants to say to me, he's going to have to tell me himself."

"He doesn't want to upset you, Sharon."

"Now, Mama, that's quite a piece of news. Tell him it's too late. He already has."

CHAPTER NINE

*F*or days Sharon moved woodenly through her daily routine. She unloaded her kiln in the mornings, threw a pot or two before noon, then made lunch for Richie and Frannie. She sat in attendance most afternoons while the children played in a new inflatable wading pool Mac had purchased, Sharon guessed, as a peace offering.

On Wednesday night, Kenneth called unexpectedly.

"I miss you," he said. The wires carried his strained yet gentle voice to Sharon's ear.

"How's your sister?" Sharon tried to keep her voice calm and attempted to cover her own loneliness with false interest.

"How are you?"

"We're doing fine," Sharon said, thinking it best not to let him know how much she missed him and difficult her days were without him.

"How are *you*?" Kenneth's voice, calm but insistent, sent her pulse racing. "I want to know how *you* are."

"I'm fine," she lied.

"Sharon, are you all right? I mean, has Mac given you any trouble—about me, I mean?"

"No, not really."

"He doesn't like me."

"Kenneth, I don't think he . . ." She searched for the right words. "He just doesn't want—"

"He doesn't want me to see you anymore. He likes having you and the kids all to himself. I'm a threat to him, Sharon. I know that. But he's got no right to—"

"Please, Ken, don't make it any worse than it is, all right?"

"Then he has been giving—"

"No," Sharon interrupted, "Mac's only been kind to me. You know it's because of him and Meg that I even have a place to live and my work. I owe them a lot, Ken."

"Your gratitude isn't enough? Do you owe him your whole life too?"

"Not just him," Sharon said defensively. "Don't forget your mother is involved here too. We've become almost like family. She's great with the kids. Better than my own mother, that's for sure."

"Strange, isn't it?" Kenneth said. "You love my mother, I love my mother, and Mac loves her too. But he doesn't want me near you."

"It's complicated," she said.

"No kidding." His voice was soft and sad.

"How are you?" she tried to change the subject. "How is it to be in familiar territory again?"

"Okay, I guess. Margie threw a party the other night. I saw some of my old college buddies. Some of them have really gone off the deep end about this war. A couple of them, lawyers now, have grown long hair—can you believe it? I thought they'd be in grey flannels and navy blazers by now. But they've become almost counter-culture in their political views as well as their appearance. Mac would have a heart attack if he heard the way they talk. They even make me uncomfortable. I thought I was pretty far out as far as the war is concerned, but these guys make me look like a hawk. I guess I'm not as far out in left field as I—or Mac— thought."

"Is that good?" Sharon asked. She found it easy to listen to him.

"What do you mean?"

"Is it good that you found out that you're not as radical as you thought you were?"

"I'm not sure. I'm beginning to think that if I'm not totally on one side or the other—well, it's as if there's no middle ground in this. I don't agree with Mac, that's for sure. But I certainly don't agree with these guys either. Funny thing, the ones I've met with the strongest feelings haven't even been there. And even though I've been there, I'm not sure what the best policy is. No wonder President Johnson can't make up his mind. There are no winners, Sharon. Not now, probably not ever. I simply don't know what the solution is."

"Good thing you don't have to make the decisions, huh?"

"You're right about that."

Silence. Sharon wished he would say something else, but fearing that whatever he said might be too personal or get too close, she decided to end the conversation.

"I'd better go," she said. "It was nice talking to you."

"Sharon, I really do miss you."

"I know," she said, barely able to keep from telling him her own feelings.

"I report for duty on Monday—that's the twelfth."

"So, you still have the weekend at your sister's." Her comment had no other purpose than to fill space in the conversation.

"Sharon," he asked in a lowered, husky voice, "do you miss me at all?"

Awkwardly, she cleared her throat. When she tried to speak, her voice wavered, then to her dismay, broke slightly. "Y—yes."

Even though she was alone, she caught herself glancing uneasily over her shoulder, hoping no one was listening. She suddenly felt as if she was being watched.

"Sharon?" Kenneth's voice was gently demanding. "You still there?"

She jumped at a sound outside on her patio. "Yeah," she muttered. "I'm here."

"I miss you," he repeated. Sharon only half listened, struggling with her conscience. She swallowed hard, trying to manage a confident and believable decline of his invitation.

"Kenneth, I really should go. I think I heard something. I need to check on the kids."

"Sharon?"

"I'm glad . . . I mean, thanks for calling." Without waiting for his response she hung up the phone. Biting her lip, she stared at the phone. *Oh, Kenneth,* she said to herself, *do I miss you.* She closed her eyes tightly and felt the warmth of her tears falling down her face.

Another noise from the patio steered her attention away from the phone. Standing perfectly still, she listened. Something cold and still touched her spine, and she stiffened with discomfort. Without really thinking, she moved quickly into the bedroom and stood motionless beside her sleeping children. She waited.

Finally she gathered her wits about her and shook her head. "Must have been the wind," she whispered to her sleeping son. "Or, a cat. Nothing to be afraid of." She walked through the small L-shaped living room and kitchen area and noticed that the back door was still open in order to catch the night breeze. Glancing at the latch, she knew she would have to secure it before she went into her own room.

Trying to act calm, she approached the doorway. Ordinarily she would have walked without reserve to the dark patio, looked at the bright, star-spangled night sky to process Kenneth's call and try to understand the meaning in the fact that he missed her so much and that her own loneliness was becoming almost unbearable. But tonight she became increasingly nervous as she got closer to the door, and when she was finally within arm's reach, she simply closed the inside door and slid the simple lock into place.

Her heart thumped madly as she reached to pull down the shades on her living room windows. She tried to take a deep breath and relax as she once again approached the phone and dialed the number.

"Uncle Mac?" she said, her mind racing to find a plausible explanation for her fear. "Would you mind coming over? It's probably nothing, but I think I heard a noise outside. I shut the door. Yes, it's locked," she answered in response to her uncle's question. "But—well, it's probably just my imagination, but I think I smelled smoke. Cigarette smoke."

She felt a terrible tenseness in her body as she waited for the sound of Mac's familiar footsteps on her patio and his knock on her door. After a few minutes she heard him softly call her name.

"Sharon?" he said. "It's me. Open the door."

"Uncle Mac," she cried and flung herself into his strong, protective embrace. "I got so scared."

"I didn't see anything out there. You sure you heard a noise?"

"Maybe it was just my overactive imagination. It's just that I thought it might be . . ."

"I don't see anything. Come on, let's have another look. You'll feel better once you see for yourself. Come on, now. Don't be afraid. Where's that porch light switch?"

"It's on a pull string outside, remember?" she said as she joined her uncle on the patio. Together they circled her small house, and Sharon noticed a flowerpot overturned when they came around to the front.

"See?" she said, pointing to the pot. "I did hear something. Probably that old tomcat that comes snooping around at night."

"Or a fox," Mac said. "Maybe I'd better check down in the chicken coops. Can't have my hens upset. Why don't you lock your door, just to be on the safe side. It'll make you feel better. I'll have another look around before I go back up to the house. Leave the porch light on tonight. It'll help me see better."

Mac waited until she was inside and slid the lock into place. She listened as he called for Major and walked away toward the chicken coops. Sharon noticed how lightweight the lock was and wished she had replaced it when Meg suggested it. Sliding a kitchen chair under the knob gave her not much but a little more comfort.

A warning whispered in her head, arousing old fears and uncertainties. Mac hadn't mentioned the smell of cigarette smoke, so perhaps that too was nothing more than her overactive imagination. Without turning on the light in her bedroom, Sharon quickly dressed for bed. She slipped into bed and even though the warmth of the small house was stifling, she pulled the blanket up close to her chin. She shut her eyes and tried to see Kenneth's face and hear his voice. *I miss you,* he had said less than half an hour earlier. She tossed uneasily on her bed, trying to shut out the restive feeling within her chest. Feeling smothered, she fought to overcome her fear and slid the window open slightly. Suddenly her hand froze on the window frame and her heart jumped in her chest. *I'm not imagining things!*

Dropping to her knees she crawled through the house toward the phone. "Uncle Mac!" she whispered hoarsely when he answered the phone. "I know I'm not dreaming this time. Please come! Someone is outside. I can smell cigarette smoke again."

"Okay, honey," Mac said when she finally let him in. "It's okay. Let's get the kids. You come and sleep up at the house tonight. Tomorrow we'll make sure we put in some stronger locks, okay?"

"I'm sorry, Uncle Mac," Sharon said, choking back tears mixed with grief and fear. "I'm sorry to be such a nuisance."

"You're no nuisance," Mac said gruffly. "Don't ever think you're a nuisance."

Sharon didn't even bother to dress but simply slipped a cotton seersucker duster over her thin pajamas. They wrapped both children in their blankets, and Mac lifted Richie easily while Sharon carried Frannie.

Sharon walked in front of Mac, afraid to be even a few feet away from him. Stopping abruptly, she turned. "There, smell," she whispered. "Smoke. Don't you smell it?"

"Go on to the house, honey." Mac gently pushed her forward on the path.

"What's the trouble?" Meg said, taking Frannie from Sharon the moment they were inside the big house.

"A prowler," Mac said. "I think we may have a prowler."

"Call the police," Meg said.

"Nah, I think I'll—" Mac started.

"You'll do nothing of the kind," she said. The flash of decision in her eyes made her husband stop. Sharon saw the look exchanged between them. "You'll not go out there alone, McKenzie." Meg's tone was unmistakable. "I want a husband, not a hero. Call the police or I will."

"So," the kind sheriff's deputy said when he came in after walking the entire length of the ranch with Mac. "Can you tell me what you heard?"

"It was a sound. You know, like somebody sneaking around outside."

"You see anyone?"

"No," she said. "That's why I thought it was probably just my imagination. I was on the phone. At first I thought it might have been one of the kids—they were sleeping. But then I realized it came from the patio."

"A pot was overturned?" the officer asked. "Your uncle said something about a pot?"

"A small plant. I didn't notice it earlier. It may have happened today sometime, I don't know for sure. I just didn't notice it before I went in."

"Anything else?"

"Smoke."

"Smoke?"

"Cigarette smoke."

"You smell anything?" the deputy asked Mac.

"No," he said slowly. "But then I spend all day around chickens. Breathin' what I breathe all day, my smeller's sort of given up."

"But what about when we were walking up the path?" Sharon asked.

"Oh, yeah," Mac said. "I thought I might have picked it up that time."

"What about your old dog there?" the man pointed toward the back porch where Major was already sleeping soundly again.

"He's not much of a watchdog anymore, I'm afraid," Mac said. "Goin' on fifteen years old. You'd have to be right on top of him before he'd know you were even close."

"Anything of value on the premises?" the deputy asked.

"Not much," Mac said. "Our valuables are right in there, sound asleep." Mac glanced toward the living room where the two children were curled up on the sofa.

"I'll put a watch on the house tonight. And tomorrow we'll come back and have a look-see in the daylight. Someone will be by every couple hours or so. Don't be alarmed if you see a spotlight now and then. Try to get some rest."

Mac walked out the back door with the deputy, and Sharon put her head on her arms, grateful for Meg's kitchen table to lean on.

"How would you and the kids like to sleep upstairs?" Meg asked. California ranch style homes seldom had a second floor, but years before Mac and Meg bought their ranch, someone had closed in a spacious attic and Meg recently finished it to make a small, pleasant guest room. "It's a bit hot, but we can open the windows at each end. It'll cool down directly."

Meg quickly unfolded a feather bed topper and tucked the children in on the floor. The twin bed suited Sharon just fine, and she welcomed the caress of the cool, rough sheets against her legs. She felt somewhat safer knowing Uncle Mac was in the room directly below. Sharon turned her face to the wall. Unable to hold in her emotions any longer, she put a pillow over her head and released her muffled sobs until she lay spent and exhausted. *Not again!* she cried silently. *Please, God, not again!*

CHAPTER TEN

*T*wo days later, Sharon ventured out of the house and down to her workroom. Hoping to find comfort in her pottery, she ignored the stifling mid-morning heat and began working a lump of damp clay into a pliable mass between her hands.

"I thought I might find you here." Kenneth's unexpected appearance at the doorway caught Sharon off guard.

"Oh, my gosh!" she gasped. "You scared me. What are you doing here?" she said, jumping to her feet.

Kenneth stepped inside and closed the distance between them. Pulling her into his arms, he ignored both her resistance and her dirty hands and pressed his lips against her temple. "I didn't like what I heard in your voice on the phone. I couldn't sleep all that night. Finally my sister shoved me out the door and told me to go see for myself. Are you all right?"

"You came all this way . . . I mean, you came back here because you . . ." Sharon couldn't believe he was actually here. "How did you get here?"

"I rented a car at the airport and here I am," he said with his face near hers. "What's going on, Sharon? You act like you've seen a ghost."

"I didn't expect to see you, that's all."

"Not now. I'm talking about the other night. I could hear in your voice what I can see in your eyes now. Is something wrong?"

"It was nothing. Really. Probably just a prowler or a nosy neighbor. I overreacted, I'm sure. I didn't mean to scare you, Kenneth. You were too far away to—"

"A prowler. You mean like a chicken thief?"

"I suppose it might have been."

"Come on, Sharon, I tried to call back and you didn't answer your phone. I called the house and Mom said you were already upstairs sleeping. I tried the next morning and Mac said it was nothing. But I could hear it in his voice too. Somebody's not being totally honest with me."

Sharon hid her face in the crook of Kenneth's neck and took a deep breath, savoring the unexpected pleasure of his nearness. "I'm really glad to see you," she admitted.

"Sharon," he said softly, "I couldn't help myself. I had to come back. I wanted to see for myself that you were all right. I had to see you again."

Sharon lifted her head and let her eyes meet his. Somewhere deep within she knew that what she saw there was love. Even without him saying it, Sharon Potter let the hope she carried bottled tightly within her heart rise a little closer to the surface. She welcomed then returned his gentle, tender kiss.

"*What?*" Mac's voice boomed from the doorway where Kenneth had suddenly appeared only minutes before. Sharon jumped, pulling away from Kenneth. "What in the world are *you* doing here?" he shouted angrily at Kenneth.

"Uncle Mac," Sharon pleaded, "please, don't."

"As if you don't have enough trouble already," Mac yelled. "Then this," he motioned suddenly toward Kenneth and Sharon flinched automatically.

"It's all right, honey." Kenneth reached toward her without taking his eyes from Mac's. "Don't be scared. Come here." Sharon stepped toward him.

"I thought you were back east." Mac's voice tightened with anger. Sharon shuddered.

"I came back."

"I can see that!" Mac yelled. "Did you think to check with anyone else before you made that decision all on your own?"

"No," Kenneth said. "I didn't think it necessary."

"I see." Mac said. "You just think you can waltz in here any time you please and—"

"Uncle Mac," Sharon cried, "stop it. Don't, please don't."

Mac spun to face her. "You've got enough to deal with right now, Sharon. This is a complication you can't afford, believe me. Another guy on the side is the last thing you need."

"Another guy?" Kenneth turned to Sharon questioningly.

"Uncle Mac!" she said. "Kenneth is not *another* guy."

"Richard Potter might not agree!" Mac shouted.

"Richard?" Sharon could hardly believe her uncle's words. "What's Richard got to do with this?"

"Jeff Bennett just called trying to find you. That's why I came out here. He's on his way over now. You better come to the house." Mac turned to leave, then paused and turned to Kenneth. "Your mother know you were coming?"

"No," Kenneth said flatly. "And don't you dare take any of my actions out on her."

"Pardon me?" Mac spun around to face Kenneth squarely.

"I mean it, Mac." Kenneth's voice was firm and loud. "You take any of this out on her and I swear—"

"Stop it!" Sharon shouted. "Just stop it, both of you!" She pushed her way past her uncle and ran toward the main house.

"Sharon!" Meg's wide arms were waiting for her as she bolted through the back door. "Come here," she soothed. "Now, now. It's going to be all right. Everything's going to be fine. We're together in this. You and me and Mac, we're family. We'll handle this together."

Sharon collapsed in the arms of the woman that had become much more than just her Uncle Mac's wife. It was because of Meg that Sharon had learned to trust again, to hope again. Gently, patiently, Meg had led Sharon to deepen her relationship with Jesus Christ. She had taught her to pray and how to study the Bible. She had answered her questions and calmed her fears. She had listened to Sharon when she needed to talk and didn't press her when she needed time to think.

"Was that Mac's voice I heard out there? Was he yelling at you?" Meg asked when Sharon finally calmed down.

"It's Kenneth," Sharon said between tears. "He came back just a little bit ago. Mac came in when . . ." She stopped. How could she tell Kenneth's mother that Mac had caught them kissing?

"Kenneth came back?" Meg said. A smile tugged at her mouth but Sharon didn't notice.

"He's outside with Mac."

"Let them stay out, then. All we need is the two of them fussing at each other right now. Listen, my dear, Cari and Jeff are on their way over. Richard has broken his parole. Too bad, he was so close to finishing."

"Where is he?"

"Seems nobody knows for sure. But probably headed this way—if he hasn't been here already."

"Oh, Aunt Meg." Sharon's eyes filled with tears again. "Do you think he was here the other night?"

"Sweetheart," Meg soothed Sharon's long hair away from her tear-streaked face, "we don't know for sure. We just can't take any chances. You know that, don't you?"

"But how could he know where I am?" Sharon had taken special care to make sure that her phone was unlisted and that only a few people had the number. She had moved to the ranch after Richard was sent to prison for his attempted kidnaping and assault of Cari. Her divorce was granted just after that. Surely the papers he signed had her old Redlands address, not the Yucaipa one.

A few minutes later, Cari rushed in the house ahead of her husband Jeff. Mac and Kenneth followed close behind.

"Cari!" Sharon cried as she flew into the outstretched arms of the other young woman who had suffered so much at Richard's hands.

Wordlessly they clung to each other. No one could understand the pain they had experienced and how much they needed to be together at this moment.

"Where are the kids?" Cari asked finally.

"In the other room. I've been letting them watch TV as much as they want for a couple of days. Ever since—"

"Ever since what?" Jeff asked, coming to stand closer to his wife.

"We thought we heard a prowler the other night," Mac offered.

"I've been so scared it was him." Sharon moved tighter against Cari.

"Do you know for sure it was?" Cari said quietly.

"No, of course not," Mac answered for Sharon.

The two young women stared at each other with an understanding between them no one else shared.

"Sharon?" Cari asked gently.

"I've just had this feeling." Sharon's voice dropped to barely above a whisper. "I'm scared, Cari," she admitted.

"I know," Cari said softly. "Me too."

Over tall glasses of iced tea, Jeff quickly filled Mac and Kenneth in on the details of Richard Potter's failure to report to his probation officer. "One time," Jeff explained, "they might overlook, but he's not reported in for nearly a month. He's not shown up for work and his landlady said he moved out of his room and didn't know where he was going. He didn't have a car when he left, but that doesn't mean anything."

"So—" Mac cleared his throat and leaned back in his chair. "What does this all mean? Surely you don't think he'll show up here."

Sharon shot her uncle a surprised glance.

"Mac," Jeff said calmly, "are you sure he hasn't already?"

"He'd be a fool to . . ." Mac let his comment trail off.

"Richard is clever, Mac," Jeff said. "But he's not very bright. And he's driven by emotion. Who knows what thoughts of revenge he might be harboring."

"Do you know anything else?" Kenneth asked. "I mean, is there anything else we should know about?"

Jeff exchanged glances with Cari, then looked at the faces of those surrounding the table. Finally he looked squarely at Sharon. "You might as well know, Sharon," he said seriously. "Richard Potter has bragged that no one would be able to keep him away from his kids."

"What?" she nearly choked as she spoke. "*His* kids?" Sharon slowly stood and her fear turned to outright rage. "*His* kids? He beat Richie and left bruises on him before he was even a year old. He punched me in the stomach when he found out I was pregnant with Frannie and said I'd be lucky if the brat ever came out alive. And he says these are *his* kids?"

Kenneth moved quickly to stand beside her. Sharon trembled with anger more intense than she had ever felt before.

"If he thinks for one minute that I'm just going to stand here and let him creep up on us or harm one of my children, he's in for an enormous shock," she cried. "Being angry with me is one thing. But he's got no right to even see them. All he's ever done is hurt us. He never cared about anything but himself." Sharon's voice faltered. "This isn't about the kids, doesn't anybody see that? This is about him—what he wants, he takes. Dear God, what am I supposed to do, just wait here, doing nothing until he hurts one of us again?"

Cari came and stood alongside Sharon and slipped her arm around her waist. "No one expects you to wait for him to pounce on you. Really, we feel the same way. We're here to try to find a way to keep him from hurting anybody. You, the kids, even me."

"Oh, Cari," Sharon said, sobbing. "Do you think he'd try to hurt you?"

"After two times before, I'm just as scared as you are."

Kenneth said nothing, and Sharon saw him finger the long-handled spoon he had used to stir his tea earlier.

"How long will you be here?" Jeff asked Kenneth.

"I have to report for duty in about forty-eight hours."

"And where is that?"

"Camp Pendleton."

"So you'll be here another day then?"

"At least." Kenneth looked at his mother. "I could file for an extension, but it would be denied unless it was a family emergency."

"We can handle this ourselves," Mac interjected.

"Right," Kenneth said sarcastically.

"Kenneth," Meg's voice carried an unmistakable warning then shot Mac a glance that communicated the same message.

"I'm here." Jeff took control of the conversation again. Sharon was glad he and Cari were here. The last thing she needed right now was for Kenneth and Mac to be at each other's throats. "I'm here because I thought we ought to put our heads together and make some decisions. I agree with Sharon that the last thing any of us want to do is to wait passively for Richard to spring out of nowhere and catch us off guard. That's why I arranged for the probation officer to call me if there were any changes or if he were released."

"He violated probation?" Kenneth asked.

"Only a few months short of completing it," Jeff answered. "Broke up with a girlfriend, it seems. Caught her with another man."

Sharon shuddered to think what would have happened if Richard had been the one to see Kenneth kissing her instead of Uncle Mac. "He can be insanely jealous," she said to no one in particular. "I know from experience."

"Well, until I have to report for duty," Kenneth said, "I'll stay in Sharon's house. She'd be better off here with Mac and Mom."

"And the kids?" Jeff asked. "Jennifer and Dan have a place in Big Bear. They've offered it to us for a while. Cari and I were thinking this might be a good time for her and the kids to get away. Sharon, would you like to go there too?"

"I'd love it, Jeff. But then what? I mean, how long do we hide from him?"

"How about getting someone in?" Kenneth said. "You know, like a body guard or—"

"I hardly think that's needed," Mac interrupted.

"I think it's an idea worth considering, Mac." Jeff once again diverted Mac's attention away from Kenneth and toward the merit of his idea. "Why not at least consider a night watchman for a while?"

"We've got old Major there," Mac said, nodding toward the back porch. "He's been the only guard I've ever needed."

"He's pretty close to retirement, isn't he?" Jeff asked good-naturedly. "I was halfway across the porch before he even raised his head or wagged his tail."

"Gettin' near deaf," Mac admitted. "Don't see none too good lately either."

"I think a night watchman wouldn't be a bad idea, Mac. Maybe he wouldn't be needed at all, but I think you'd all sleep a bit sounder if you knew somebody was on duty." Jeff had a way of handling Mac that Kenneth needed yet to learn.

"I know I would," Meg said.

"Sharon?" Cari said tentatively. "How about it? Will you and the kids come with me to the mountains?"

Sharon hesitated.

"At least let me take the kids, okay?" Cari pleaded. "Dan is going along and said if he has to he can commute. Jennifer and Joy would love to have Richie and Frannie. At least they'd be safe until this all blows over."

"Cari's right, dear," Meg said, coming alongside Sharon. "Let's at least get them out of his reach. If you're here and Richard comes poking around, he'll probably not even suspect the children aren't here."

Cari accompanied Sharon to her small house to help pack what Richie and Frannie would need for their trip. Kenneth followed closely behind and waited in the shade of Sharon's patio.

Once inside and sure they would not be overheard Cari put her hand on Sharon's arm.

"Sharon, I have to tell you something," she started.

"Something else?"

"Sharon, I don't know how to begin," Cari said. Sharon watched the attractive young woman search for the right words. "Do you remember the conversation we had in the hospital when Frannie was born?"

"I remember," Sharon said while motioning Cari to sit on Richie's bed.

"Sharon—this is so hard to say—" Cari's eyes filled with tears. "Sharon, does Richard know I went to Minnesota to have his baby?"

"Not that I know of. He went to prison right after I found out."

"I gave his baby up for adoption," Cari said. Her tears fell unchecked. "What do you think he'd do if he found that out?"

"Are you afraid he might use it as an excuse to—"

"Harass me?" Cari stared deeply into Sharon's eyes then continued.

"Oh, Cari," Sharon said, sliding her arm protectively around her friend. "I had no idea at the beginning. Then that whole thing with Richard. And oh, my gosh, there I show up on your grandmother's doorstep holding Richie and pregnant again. Cari, I didn't know then. I'm so sorry." Sharon's voice broke with emotion she didn't even try to conceal from Cari. Stifling a sob, Sharon continued. "Cari, did I break your heart when I named Frannie after you?"

"Little did you know, my dear friend, that little Frances Caroline was a miracle for me. She was a sign, in a way. A sign from God that I could go on with my life. I can't explain it, but really, Sharon, a namesake meant the world to me. I felt like her godmother. For the first time, I felt that God would trust me with a child again."

"And He has!" Sharon said, smiling. "Just look at the two darling children you have."

"I've been afraid that if Richard ever found out that the baby I gave up was his, he might try to take it out on one of my babies." Sharon felt as much as heard the fear in Cari's admission.

"He's awful," Sharon said. "How did a nice girl like you ever get mixed up with him in the first place?"

"Me?" Cari responded. "What about you? You're a wonderful person, Sharon. A good mother and so talented. My gosh, what does a man like Richard have that either of us would fall for?"

"We were young," Sharon said. "Too young to know we were being handed a line."

"But then Jeff came along," Cari confided. "Jeff changed all that for me."

"Was it hard to trust him?" Sharon asked.

"Jeff? No, not really. He was wonderful, patient, kind. The total opposite of Richard. The problem I had was feeling I could *deserve* someone as wonderful as him. He helped me see that I did the right thing for my baby. He also helped me see that it would always hurt and that I would probably always miss my son. But you know, as surprising as it may seem, while the pain hasn't completely gone away, it is better. I still wonder, of course, I always will. But even now, Jeff helps me with that. Both times, when I had my other kids, I had a moment of terrible grief. Jeff, so understanding and strong, knew what the problem was. He urged me to write letters to my son—the son I'll never know. I write to him from time to time. Jeff reads the letters and keeps them in our safe-deposit box at the bank. He says you never know. The laws could change someday and my son may want to find me. If he does, I'll have the letters to show him that I've thought about him and prayed for him and his parents all his life."

"Cari," Sharon said, barely above a whisper, "if you ever doubt you did the right thing, just think of what Richie has suffered at the hands of his father. I'd do anything to keep that from happening again. Anything!" Sharon didn't even try to hide her anger.

"Then we'd better get these things packed." Cari motioned toward the children's clothes. "Dan and Jen want to leave for the mountains this afternoon. My kids are already over there, ready to go."

CHAPTER ELEVEN

*A*fter the children were gone, Kenneth suggested they make it an early evening. Sharon was disappointed but she understood.

Kenneth took her hand and led her to the back porch, where he pulled her close and kissed her cheek slowly then gave her a quick, light peck on the lips. "I'm glad I came back," he said. "My sister was right, I needed to be here with you."

"I'm glad you did too," Sharon said. "I can't wait to meet Margie. I want to thank her in person."

"Get some rest, will you? You look bushed." Kenneth brushed her face with his fingertips smoothing her hair behind her ear.

The next morning, Sharon descended the stairway and noticed how quiet the house was. *Maybe I'm the first one up,* she thought. *Wonder what time it is.*

"Good morning, dear," Meg said, warmly looking up from a dishpan full of green beans just as Sharon pushed the swinging kitchen door open. "Did you get a good sleep?"

"Good morning to you," Sharon said as she walked to the stove for a cup of coffee. "I thought I might have managed to be the first one up. What time is it anyway?"

"Oh, my dear," Meg laughed. "It's nearly ten. You slept over twelve hours."

"My gosh," Sharon spun around to check Meg's word on the kitchen clock. "Why didn't you wake me?"

"We thought you needed the sleep."

"We?"

"Kenneth and Mac went off to see about getting the motor on the chicken feed mixer checked out."

"Together?" Sharon could hardly believe it since they could barely get along in the same room, let alone in a car together.

"I laid down the rules before they left. Believe me, Sharon, once they get past this they'll be great friends. I know them both so well. If they'd just stop being so stubborn about their views on the war."

"What kind of rules did you give them?"

"They can talk about the weather, the farm—anything they choose. But not about the war, politics, or the President. Most of all the President."

"When will they be back?"

"They left about an hour ago. I suppose by lunchtime, anyway. Who knows, when men get in a machine shop there's not much telling when they'll come out. Especially Kenneth. He loves small machines. He was a real handyman by the time he reached his early teens. Kept our lawn mower running, my sewing machine in tip-top shape. Once he even changed the belt on my old washing machine. He was only sixteen when he did that. Just like his father. Always tinkering with machines and small engines.

Sharon paused with her forkful of waffle and berries suspended midway between her plate and her open mouth. Slowly she let the fork down until it rested on her plate. She dropped her eyes and without really seeing, studied the pattern on Meg's everyday dishes.

"I know what you're going through," Meg said. "Sharon, I raised my children all by myself. Thinking back . . ." The older woman stopped snapping her green beans and looked directly at the younger woman sitting across the table from her.

"My mother did the same with me," Sharon said softly. "It can be done, can't it, Meg?"

"Yes, it can. But I'm not sure whether I did the right thing or not. I had opportunities, and of course, had I taken any of them I wouldn't have been married to Mac now, so I really don't have any regrets about that. But I wonder. If I had to do it all over again, knowing what I know now— maybe I would make different decisions."

"Why didn't you?" Sharon felt embarrassed asking Meg such personal questions.

"I don't know," Meg said. "Perhaps it was because the young man who came calling hadn't served in the war. It seemed somehow like betrayal to find love and happiness and turn my husband's children over to a man that didn't even have to go. He was a preacher, no less. It was one of the most difficult decisions I ever had to make."

Sharon noticed the wistful sound in Meg's voice. "Auntie Meg," she said affectionately, "perhaps it was the right thing to do. Kenneth is a wonderful person. And you're very close. Maybe you wouldn't be so close if there had been different circumstances."

"Maybe so," Meg said. "But it was hard, Sharon. Your little ones are small yet. When they hit their teens—well, believe me it will be a different story then. When they reach the age where they can outsmart you, it will be a real challenge. And you've got the two of them so close in age. At least Margie and Kenneth were a few years apart. I had a rest between their growth stages. And of course, girls mature faster than boys. That meant in my family, Margie was finished and on to something new long before Kenneth."

"And Frannie and Richie will seem more like the same age, right?"

"They almost seem like twins now," Meg said.

"Except," Sharon said quietly, "Richie seems to remember his father. Frannie hasn't any recollection whatsoever."

"Do you think he actually remembers?"

"I can't tell for sure. It's little things. Like when he hears Mac and Kenneth arguing. He's sure they will start hitting each other. Richard was like that. Yelling first, then hitting. Richie was so little, I thought he wouldn't remember. He was only a little over a year old when Frannie was born. Richard went away right after that."

"For kidnaping Cari, I remember. I was there."

"I forgot you were taking care of Cari's grandmother back then. They didn't charge him with kidnaping because he didn't take her very far. Didn't even get her in the truck before Uncle Mac and Jeff . . ." Sharon paused. "It had to be awful for her."

"But he did go to jail."

"For a while. The official charge was assault and battery with intent to do bodily harm."

"But I thought . . . Mac said . . ." Meg groped for the right words. "Mac said he tried to, you know . . ."

"Rape," Sharon said bluntly. "I know. But they said that it would be hard to prove that she didn't provoke him. You know, lead him on."

"Caroline?" Meg was shocked.

"I know," Sharon said. "I wanted them to throw the book at him. But Jeff told me that cases like these often end up being her word against his."

"Except for one thing," Meg said. Sharon looked up into Meg's face. "Caroline had bruises."

"So did I," Sharon said just as she heard Mac's truck pull in the driveway.

"Sharon," Meg said tenderly, "let me just say this before the men come in: Don't make the mistake of thinking you have to be alone, okay? You don't have the same set of circumstances to deal with that either your mother or I did. We made our decisions according to what seemed best for us at the time. Do you understand what I'm saying to you, dear?"

"Oh, Meg, I don't know. I made the decision to marry Richard and what a mistake that was."

"Did you make that decision, Sharon? Or was that someone else's decision?" Meg asked just as the men opened the back door preventing Sharon from answering.

"Well, lazy bones," Kenneth said good-naturedly, "I see you finally decided to join the living, breathing, and I might add, productive part of society."

"I had to get up," Sharon said. "It was getting too hot upstairs to stay in bed any longer. Otherwise, I'd still be up there."

Meg smiled at Mac; Sharon knew without asking that he must have agreed to make more of an effort to get along with Kenneth.

"So," Sharon continued, "you've been at the machine shop?"

"Kenneth did most of the work," Mac said. Sharon thought she detected a slight tinge of pride in his comment. "Old Bob didn't know quite what to make of this young upstart of yours, Meg. Up until now, nobody in the whole town came close to matching Bob's way with motors and such. But Kenny here, I think he might have taught Bob a new thing or two."

Kenneth didn't say anything, but munched contentedly on Meg's fresh, raw snap beans.

The rest of the day passed smoothly, and even in the intense late July heat, Kenneth reinstalled the motor on the chicken feed mixer with Mac looking on.

At dinner, served in the dining room away from the warmer kitchen, Sharon glanced across the table at Kenneth, knowing that he would be leaving the next day. She poked silently at her potato salad and barely touched the chicken thigh Kenneth had barbecued over hickory chips and briquets.

"No wonder this chicken tastes so good," Kenneth quipped. "Mac feeds them a steady diet of his gourmet mixture."

"This isn't one of our chickens," Meg laughed. "Our old hens aren't good for much else but stewing once they stop laying. We buy our fryers and broilers from the chicken farm up the hill."

"No kidding?" Sharon listened without comment to the good-natured bantering around the table. Uncle Mac was really on his best behavior. Glancing at Aunt Meg, she noticed the looks of approval that kept him in line. *Margaret McKenzie, you're really something,* Sharon thought. Involuntarily, a smile spread across her face.

"What's that for?" Kenneth said between bites of his mother's home-cooked meal.

"Pardon me?"

"That smile," he said, motioning toward her with a half eaten chicken leg. "It's the first one I've seen since we sat down to dinner."

"It's nothing, really," Sharon said, sensing a blush beginning at the base of her neck.

"Come on now, share it with the rest. Not polite to have secrets at the table," Kenneth teased. "Isn't that right, Mom?"

"You leave me out of this," Aunt Meg said.

"But you always told us—"

"I said it wasn't polite to *tell* secrets at the table. I've never said anything about *having* secrets."

"Same thing," Kenneth said. Turning to Sharon, "Come on now, let's have it."

"I was just thinking," Sharon said timidly, "that Auntie Meg may have actually tamed Uncle Mac at last."

"Oh, really?" Mac said in protest. "Tame, is it now? Is that what you think the woman has done to me? Bullied me, that's what she's done. Keeps me in line for fear of my very life itself." Sharon loved the sound of Uncle Mac's totally contrived Irish accent.

"And, don't you go forgettin' it," Meg retorted. "It's the upper hand I've got, and it's the upper hand I intend to keep. Now get yourself away from this table and give me a hand in the kitchen. That is if you know what's good for you."

"And I do," Mac said, winking at Sharon while scooting his chair back from the table. "Margaret, darlin' wife o' mine, what's good for me is you." Mac followed Meg through the swinging door separating the dining room and kitchen.

"Jack McKenzie," Kenneth and Sharon heard clearly from the kitchen, "you keep your hands to your self! I'm warning you!"

Mac's laughter rang throughout the entire house. A scuffle of feet then silence told Sharon that Margaret had probably surrendered to the affectionate advances of her husband.

All the while Kenneth didn't take his eyes from Sharon's face. She refused to look at him. Her thoughts once again returned to the fact that tomorrow he was leaving to report back for duty. She was unaware that a frown crossed her face.

"I see that," Kenneth said.

"See what?"

"That worried look."

"I'm not worried."

"You're not?" he asked, reaching for his iced tea. "Then what?" He took a long drink from his glass while he waited for her response.

"It's just that tomorrow . . ." She couldn't finish without crying, so she let the comment drop.

"Hey!" Kenneth complained when his mother set a bowl in front of him. "How come my ice cream's melted already?"

"Don't blame me," Meg said defensively. "Blame him!" She nodded toward her husband.

"It's not my fault the woman is irresistible!" Mac said, his rugged, suntanned features softened by his wide open-mouthed smile.

"Mom!" Kenneth scolded.

Sharon turned to see Kenneth's mother shyly lower her eyelids as a crimson flush spread over her face.

"Go on, you two, eat your dessert," Meg ordered. Sharon knew the older woman loved every minute of peace between her husband and son. In spite of her protests, Sharon understood that Margaret McKenzie reveled in every moment of attention from the two men she loved so desperately.

CHAPTER TWELVE

*L*ate Saturday night, Kenneth walked in the darkness of Sharon's small house. Her surroundings seemed to assault his senses making it impossible to think straight and preventing him from sleeping. Just after midnight, he walked out the door and sat on the patio. Staring into the starry night, he let his mind and heart drift heavenward.

"Dear God," he whispered into the night, "it's been a while since I talked to you. In fact—" He looked down at the dark cement under his feet. Leaning forward, he rested his elbows on his knees and let his mind return to the last time he consciously remembered praying. "It's been months, hasn't it? Since that night. I was really scared. I thought I was going to die. Thank you for being there and helping me out of that mess." Kenneth could still recall the horror of being attacked in the night. "You'd expect something like that on the front line, but who would have ever guessed those little boys who played near us by day were soldiers by night?"

Kenneth took a deep breath and brought his thoughts to the current situation and to Sharon, Richie and Frannie.

"You know, Lord," he continued, "I gave you my heart a long time ago. Mom says I need to give you my life too. I guess I didn't know I hadn't done that already. But come to think of it," Kenneth said, barely audible, "I guess I have acted like—well, independently. Making my own decisions, hoping they were approved up there." He motioned toward the stars with his hand. "But I can see that I'm up against it here, dear Lord. I mean, I thought I had it all figured out. Military career—twenty years at least. Then I'd still be young enough to get my own shop and have a retirement pension to back me up while I got started. Seemed like an okay plan to me. But now . . ." Kenneth hesitated. "Now it's all different. I've met this really nice girl, and she's got two great kids. I don't know how you see it, but my plan doesn't seem all that great to me anymore. I don't know what to do. I want to—I mean, I know this is a little sudden, maybe—but I think I'd like to marry this girl. I'd like to raise those kids of hers as my own. Would that be all right with you?"

Kenneth paused as if waiting for an answer, but he didn't really expect one. "You know," he said after a short silence, "of course, she's divorced. But really, can you blame her? I mean, that guy she married—was that in your plan for her? Is she always going to be stuck without a way out of that mistake?"

Silence filled the night, and a shooting star propelled its way across the black sky.

"You know, God, I'd be good to her, I can promise you that. And the kids too. I wouldn't want to do anything that would hurt her relationship with you, though. If you're as definite about this remarriage, as some seem to say you are, well, I'll back off. It just seems so unfair. She's all alone—except for you, of course, but you know what I mean. She's so pretty and everything. Some guy is bound to come along, and maybe the next one won't even ask you, he'll just barge in. Well, I'm probably more afraid of that than you are."

Kenneth walked slowly toward the little building that held Sharon's workroom. "She's so talented, God." He opened the door and snapped on the light. "Look at all this stuff," he said, talking to God the same way someone else might talk to himself. "She's really good."

Kenneth walked around the small workshop and ran his hands affectionately over the finished pots where Sharon's hands had worked. What was once formless and drab was now graceful. From ugliness she had created beauty.

"I'd like to give you my life, God," Kenneth said once again, walking out into the darkness. "But I'd like Sharon included in it too. Would it be impossible to merge the two ideas?"

Kenneth opened the front door of Sharon's small house without turning on a light. The open windows let in enough soft moonlight that even in the shadows he could sense her artistic touches. Even in this little guest house with her meager resources, Sharon had managed to create a home. *What could she do,* Kenneth wondered, *if she had a real home and a modest income?*

The mood the next day was subdued, and both Sharon and Meg were quiet. Kenneth knew Sharon missed her children, but he also understood her relief in knowing they were outside Richard's reach. Without discussion, the family had somehow agreed to stay home from church and be together while Kenneth prepared to report for duty later that evening.

"You'll be back to work tomorrow morning then?" Mac asked from behind the sports section of the *San Bernardino Sun.*

"Yeah, I guess." Kenneth's tone was more a sigh than a comment. "Depending on where I'm assigned, I should be up to my elbows in grease by noon."

"Your mother tells me your enlistment is up in December," Mac said.

"Yeah, officially. But I could be out sooner if I decided not to re-up." Out of the corner of his eye, Ken saw Sharon's head lift from the newspaper. "I get some time off for extra time in Nam."

"Extra time? I didn't know about that." Mac's interest was obviously piqued.

"It's nothing really. Just a bargaining chip the military uses to get men to stay over there longer, since I wasn't in any real danger." Kenneth omitted the nighttime attack from his conversation. "I thought only about the extra pay. I wanted to buy a car when I got home."

Kenneth glanced toward Sharon. She was staring at him. He didn't want to tell her like this. There were too many questions to be answered before he knew if he'd reenlist or not. He didn't want to rush her, but his reenlistment decisions were beginning to involve her. Certainly within the next month he'd be asked for his decision. If he were to be transferred to another base, either out of the country or within the U.S., it would take time. "How about another cup of coffee?" he said in an effort to draw her into the kitchen where they could be alone.

"Sure," she said, standing. "Uncle Mac?" Kenneth hoped Mac would stay where he was.

"No, not for me, thanks anyway," the older man said from behind his paper. "It's getting too hot for coffee."

"Iced tea?" Sharon offered. Kenneth wished she'd leave well enough alone and just come out to the kitchen where they could talk in private.

"Maybe later," Mac answered. Kenneth was relieved and, taking her by the hand, led her quickly into the kitchen before she could get distracted.

"Sharon," he said, spinning her to face him once the swinging door closed behind them, "I want to talk to you."

Pulling out a chair, he motioned for her to sit down and he took a seat on the opposite side of the table.

"Don't you want some coffee?" she said and started to scoot her chair from the table and stand. Kenneth reached across the small table and caught her arm.

"Please, Sharon," he said, "will you just sit down?"

Kenneth didn't know how to begin. "I've been up a good part of the night," he said. "I've been thinking and even praying about how to say this." Looking in her eyes, seeing her beauty, all the pain and the innocence captured there in spite of everything she had endured, Kenneth felt his heart ache and then quicken with his growing love for her.

"Kenneth?" she said softly.

"It's difficult—please, you'll have to bear with me. Just don't say anything until I'm done, okay?"

"Okay."

"Sharon, I'm thirty-two years old. I've been through college and this is my third term in the military."

"Third?"

"Once for four years, then two three-year enlistments."

"Oh."

"In all that time, I never came close to feeling this way about anybody before. Not even . . ." He paused and searched her eyes once more.

"Not even . . ."

"I was engaged once," he said. "After my first tour. Her name was Michelle. We went to college together. Dated some. We wrote while I was stationed in Florida. She came to see me a few times. We discussed marriage."

"What happened?"

"Life, I guess. I wanted to wait until I had already served overseas and would be able to stay stateside before I got married. She got tired of waiting and married somebody else."

"Oh," Sharon said.

"She forgot to tell me, however, until after the wedding. Just a minor detail."

"I'm sorry," Sharon said.

"There you go again." Kenneth wanted her to stop apologizing for everything that ever went wrong in everyone's lives. "You can say, 'That's too bad' or 'Good for her,' but please don't apologize for something somebody else did."

"I didn't know I was doing that," she said.

"You do it all the time." Kenneth felt his emotions tightening. This wasn't at all what he wanted to say. "Never mind," he said, trying to bring the conversation back on track. "It's beside the point." Kenneth stood, walked to the coffeepot. Shaking it he discovered it was nearly empty.

"I can make more," Sharon said, coming to stand beside him.

"Sharon," Kenneth said, overlooking her offer, "I have to say this. Please, listen to me." He put the coffeepot back on the unlit stove and pulled her into his arms. "Sharon," he whispered into her hair, "I think I've fallen in love with you." He felt her stiffen. "Is that such a surprise?" he said, pulling back just enough to look into her eyes.

She stepped away, turned her back to him, and walked toward the table. Kenneth stood still, his feet frozen to the floor. When she turned, he could see the tears welling up in her eyes. "Kenneth," she whispered, "I don't know what to say."

"Say you return the feelings!" he said almost angrily.

"I'm not sure I can."

"Can? What do you mean you're not sure you can? You mean you're not able or do you mean you don't want to?"

"It's not that," she said. She began to cry. "It's just that my life is so complicated."

"You mean because of that . . . because of Richard?" Kenneth struggled to keep his voice down.

"Not just that. It's my kids too. I can't just follow my heart any which way and forget that I have responsibilities that have to come first."

"You think I'm not considering them?" He forced his feet to close the distance between them. "You think I wouldn't?" He felt as if a knife pierced his heart when she drew away defensively. "Honey," he said, lowering his voice to a hoarse whisper, "please don't pull away. I'm not going to hurt you." He raised his hands in a gesture of surrender. Sharon flinched. "He really did a number on you, didn't he?" Kenneth asked bitterly.

Sharon wiped her tears from her cheeks with the palms of her hands. Stepping back to his side of the table, Kenneth lowered himself slowly into a chair. "Sit down, Sharon," he pleaded. "Please?"

Once she had slid into the chair opposite him, Kenneth decided to try another approach. "Look, I'm not going to rush you," he said. "I'll go back on duty, get busy, and in a few weeks we'll talk again."

"A few weeks?" The panic in Sharon's eyes gave Kenneth the encouragement he needed.

"How about two?" he suggested. "More than likely, I'll have weekends off. How about going out on a date with me two weeks from this weekend?"

"Well," she said slowly, "I guess it would be all right." Kenneth had no way of knowing that Frances Mason's words were flooding Sharon's mind. All he could tell was that something had clouded her beautiful features.

"What's wrong?"

"It's the kids. I don't know. Going out on a date while—"

"If they're back from Big Bear by then, my mom would love to watch them, you know that. You'll still be staying upstairs at night. The kids will be fine." He was suddenly struck by a thought. "Sharon, don't you ever go out and leave the kids?"

"No, I guess I don't."

"Why not?"

"It never really crossed my mind."

"Well, get used to the idea, okay?"

"I'll try," she said.

Shortly after five, Kenneth put his things in his rental car, and while he said good-bye to Mac and hugged his mother, out of the corner of his eye he watched Sharon. Finally he took her by the hand and she walked beside him. Meg tactfully shooed Mac inside the house to give them a last few minutes of privacy.

"Sharon, I love you," he said with his face barely two inches from hers.

"I know," she said. Kenneth wished for more but decided to be grateful that at least this time she didn't push him away.

CHAPTER THIRTEEN

*Y*ou really ought to take Jen up on her offer." Meg's voice surprised her in her workroom one morning just before lunch. "Otherwise we're going to have to build a room addition just to accommodate all these lovely creations."

"Do you think anyone would really buy one of these?" Sharon asked, grateful for Meg's interest and a momentary diversion from her own confusing thoughts.

"I think you ought to put them in Miller's Home Furnishings and find out. What can it hurt?"

"My pride," Sharon said, shrugging. "What if I cart them all down there then have to bring them all home again later? What if—"

"Enough of that," Meg interrupted. "If I lived my whole life governed by what if's, I would never have married, had children, or—"

"I get the picture, Auntie Meg," Sharon teased. "Okay, okay. I'll give it a try. Goodness knows I have to find something to do with them. Look in there," she said, pointing to a small alcove draped with a canvas. "I have over sixty pots in that spot alone."

"No one can ever accuse you of being nonproductive, Sharon," Meg laughed. "Have you ever thought of showing at one of those art shows?"

"Art?" Sharon still smarted from Mac's insult nearly a month ago. "Better not let Uncle Mac hear you say that."

"I don't think your Uncle Mac would know a piece of art if it walked up to him on the street and smacked him across the face." Even in criticism, Meg's voice overflowed with affection for her husband. "He's not the refined type, haven't you noticed?"

"Come to think of it, I have," Sharon laughed.

"That's more like it," Meg said, sliding her arm around the younger woman's shoulder. "It's good to hear you laugh."

Sharon welcomed the affection of the older woman she loved as "Auntie Meg" and now as Kenneth's mother. She loved her own mother, of course, but lately she found more in common with Margaret McKenzie. Sharon dismissed thoughts of her mother and turned her attention back to Meg.

"You haven't been off the place for nearly a week," Meg said.

"No, I guess I haven't."

"How about going to the store for me this afternoon? My concord grapes are ready, and I'll be busy all day in the kitchen making juice and jam. I'd go myself, but on these hot days, when that fruit is ready . . ."

"Of course I'll go," Sharon said without hesitation. "Make me a list. Maybe I'll go to Redlands and drop a few of these off while I'm at it."

After lunch, Sharon changed into a clean sundress, then pulled her long hair back on one side and fastened it with a brightly colored barrette. Slipping into her leather sandals, she looked into the mirror only long enough to smooth a touch of lipstick on her mouth. Arriving downstairs she overlooked Mac's admiration, grabbed Meg's list from the counter in the fragrance-filled kitchen, and let the screen door slam behind her carelessly. Going to town without one or both of her children in tow was a rare treat. Jen and Dan were still vacationing in the mountains, but she was sure someone would help her put her pots in the store's back room until they returned.

Half an hour later, Sharon pulled into the alley behind Miller's Home Furnishings and noticed for the third time a dark luxury sedan. Trying to remain calm, she pulled as close to the back door of the store as possible, and relieved to find it open, rushed inside. Turning quickly, she shut the door soundly and slid the large slide bolt easily into place.

"Hey there," one of Miller's friendly salesmen greeted her with a quizzical smile. "Most of our customers use the front door," he said, still smiling.

"Oh," Sharon said apologetically, "I'm not a customer. I'm Sharon Potter."

"I think I've met you before. You're a friend of Jen's, aren't you?"

"I'm a potter," she said.

"So you said. Sharon Potter, right?"

"No!" she said still leaning against the safety of the locked door. "Yes! I mean, I'm also a pottery person. You know, I make pots."

"I see." The man was obviously amused. "Sharon Potter, the potter."

In spite of her anxiety, Sharon had to laugh. "I never thought of it that way before."

"Well, what can I do for you, Sharon the Potter?" the good-natured man asked.

"Jen's been after me to get some pots down here, so I brought some. They're in my car."

"Well, then," he said, moving toward her, "if you'll just move over, I'll unlock that door and we'll—"

"No, wait!" she said too quickly. Taking a deep breath, she forced herself to lower her voice to a calmer tone. "I think someone may be following me."

"Really?" the friendly man teased. "Now you're the mysterious Sharon the Potter."

"I'm not kidding, please." Sharon felt the tears welling in her eyes against her will.

"I can see that." The man dropped his smile. "Well, then, better let me have a look." Sharon stepped aside and waited while the man opened the door and peered outside. "Nobody out here. This little VW your car?"

"Yes," she answered.

"Come on then," he called to her, "I'll give you a hand."

On the third trip to the car, Sharon noticed the large dark car slowing as it passed the alley. "There," she nodded with her head toward the end of the alley. "See? There is it again."

"Okay," he said. "Go ahead and lock up your car. Let's get these in and then we'll decide what to do next."

Sharon's hands began to shake as she fumbled with her keys. Once inside, she leaned against a large table in the store's back room.

"You okay?" the man beside her asked gently.

"I think so."

"Any idea who might be following you?'

"I'm afraid so."

"Good taste in cars, I'll say that for him."

"Him?" Sharon's head flew up and her frightened eyes found those of the salesman's. "Did you see him?"

"No, not really. I'm assuming it was a man, that's all."

"What should I do?"

"We need to get the license number," the man said.

"How am I going to do that?" Sharon's voice edged with terror.

"Not you," he said, "I said *we*. By the way, my name's Bob. Bob Abernathy, at your service." He bowed toward her, sweeping his hand in a ceremonial gesture of gallantry. "It's not every day I get to help a real damsel in distress."

"I'm sorry, Mr. Abernathy," Sharon started to say.

"Bob," he interrupted. "Your partner in mystery and crime."

"I hope not," she said, frowning.

"I've overdramatized. I'm known to do that. Pay me no mind whatsoever."

A few minutes later, Sharon straightened her shoulders and tried to act as nonchalant as possible while Bob walked her to her car. Then they waited to see if the familiar car would pass by again.

"There, don't look," Bob said as he stepped away from her car. "I'm sure he saw us. Now, pull slowly to the end of the alley. Give him time to come around the corner and pull out. Then drive around to the front of the store and park. There's plenty of spaces right in front. I'll be at the window, and I'll get his number."

Sharon nervously did as she was told. Glancing back into her rearview mirror, she was grateful to see Bob standing there as he agreed until he saw her pull into traffic.

She waited momentarily until she saw the large dark sedan round the corner and head slowly in her direction. She quickly pulled into traffic and the car sped up slightly. She reached the corner just as the light turned green. Once she rounded the corner, she found a parking spot in the front of Miller's Home Furnishings and waited. The sedan drove slowly by and she could feel the driver looking at the back of her head. She forced herself to sit still without turning around. Instead she stared straight ahead into the window of Miller's where Bob was writing hurriedly on a slip of paper. He motioned her to come in.

"Got it!" he said triumphantly as she entered the store. Then he rushed to take her arm just as her knees buckled. "Here," he said helping her to an overstuffed rocking chair. "You better have a seat."

"Call Jeff Bennett," Sharon said. She put her hand on her chest in a futile effort to slow her racing heart.

"Are you all right?" Bob asked.

"My goodness, Sharon!" It was Sarah Jenkins. "You look like you've seen a ghost, dear. What's the matter?"

"Sarah—" Sharon, grateful to see someone she knew and trusted, could no longer hold back her fearful tears. "Sarah," she repeated.

"You two know each other?" Bob asked.

"Sure," Sarah said gently. "We're good friends."

"Sarah, what are you doing here?" Sharon could barely believe her eyes. Never in her whole life could she remember needing to see a familiar face as much as this moment.

"I'm filling in while Dan and Jennifer are in the mountains. Jeff tried to call you this morning before he left. It was a spur of the moment thing. He decided to take the day and drive up too. Just for the day, though. He'll be back tonight. I think Cari's decided to stay at least for a few more days. They wanted you to go along."

Sharon stared into the face of the trusted woman. "Sarah, I think Richard's back. Somebody's been following me." With sheer determination, Sharon kept her voice under control.

"Come with me, dear," Sarah said. "Come into the office. Stephen's here. He's doing some work for Dan. I think we'd better tell him. He knows how to reach Jeff."

"First," Stephen Bennett said after hearing Sharon's story, "we'll call this license number in to the police. And while they're checking that out, we'll call Jeff. Then I'll get you home." Sharon felt safer with Stephen in charge. Bob Abernathy was nice, but somehow with Jeff's brother involved, Sharon knew Richard wasn't the threat she had felt he was just a few moments before. She listened to Stephen's side of the conversation with Dan Miller. "They haven't arrived yet," Stephen said, replacing the receiver carefully on its cradle.

"I heard," Sharon said. "I'm sorry to be such a bother."

"You're no bother," he said. "Richard Potter—now he's a bother."

Sharon got in her car while Stephen pulled his up to the curb and waited. She kept a close watch on him in her rearview mirror all the way home. This time she was glad she was being followed.

Meg poured tall glasses of iced tea while Stephen filled her in on most of the details. Before he could finish the whole story, Jeff called.

"Sure thing," Stephen said to his brother on Meg's kitchen phone. "Good idea." After a few more short comments, he turned to Sharon. "Get a few of your things together. Jeff wants me to take you up to the cabin."

"But I . . ."

"Just for a few days, dear," Meg encouraged her. "It'll do you good. Besides, the kids will be thrilled to see you. Go on now, gather up your things. I put a suitcase in that back closet last spring. Do you need anything from your house?" Meg bustled around, shooing Sharon toward the stairway. "Let's turn on that fan. My goodness it must be over a hundred degrees up there."

"But Uncle Mac—" Sharon hesitated. "Shouldn't I tell him?"

"He's glued to that darned TV right now. President Johnson made some sort of important announcement about the war. He's not about to hear you right now anyway. Get your things ready, then we'll tell him."

"You're going where?" Mac said when Sharon was about to leave with Stephen. "Aren't you overreacting, Sharon?"

"I don't think she is, sir," Stephen answered for her. "Jeff said—"

"Well, if Jeff knows about this and he—" Mac interrupted.

"It was his idea, sir." Stephen wasn't about to let Sharon tangle with her uncle after finding out that the car following her this afternoon had been reported as stolen. Stephen parked Sharon's VW in plain sight of the road, then threw her suitcase in the back seat of his car, and opened the door for his passenger. "Here you go," he said gently. "We'll be on our way."

Settling in Stephen's car, Sharon suddenly felt very tired. It would be a two-hour drive, at least. *Kenneth,* she said silently, *I won't be there when you call tonight.* Disappointment now filled her breast where fright had crowded out and almost crushed her earlier. *Oh, well,* she told herself, *this is reality.* One thing Sharon Mason Potter had learned to accept in her brief life was harsh reality. Disappointing, sad, and sometimes frightening, reality was something she had never learned how to escape.

CHAPTER FOURTEEN

*T*ired, hot, and hungry, Kenneth reached for the phone the minute he came back to his quarters. Hoping Sharon would answer the phone, he was disappointed to hear Mac's booming voice.

"Is Sharon there? This is Ken."

"Sorry, Ken," Mac said. "You missed her."

"Missed her?"

"She left this afternoon for the mountains."

"I see." Kenneth ached for more information. "Was this a sudden decision?"

"I think so. Ran into Stephen in town this morning, I guess. They up and decided to go early this afternoon."

Kenneth knew the extent of Mac's information had been covered. "Well, Mac, tell Mom I'll call a little later, will you?"

"Sure thing. Hey, I've been watching the President all afternoon. Made some pretty big steps toward winning the war if you ask me. Have you heard about it down there yet?"

"We're on alert status here, Mac. I was going to tell Sharon, but you can pass it on if you'd like. I've been working twelve-hour shifts for several days and now with the news out, I'll be working straight through the weekend. I was planning on coming up. Sharon and I had a date. Looks like I won't make it."

"Sort of makes your decision a bit easier, doesn't it, Son?"

"My decision?"

"Whether or not to stay in the service."

"Yeah," Kenneth said, wishing he were talking to Sharon instead of Mac. "It makes it easier."

"Then you'll be reenlisting." Mac's certainty infuriated Kenneth.

"No, Mac, I won't." Ken was surprised to hear the calm resolve in his own voice. "The President is making decisions I can't agree with. I don't know who's giving him his advice, but he needs to get somebody else."

"It's not your place to demand the commander in chief agree with your position, boy. He's the one in charge, the responsibility is on his shoulders."

"He may be in charge, but I can tell you that the responsibility isn't on his shoulders alone, Mac. They're sending eighteen-year-old boys out there to die. They bear some of it on their shoulders too." Kenneth's patience was wearing thin.

"Well, now, that's what war's all about. If we want to win, and if the cause is important enough to fight for in the first place, then we ought to go out there and get the job done."

"What job is that, Mac?" Kenneth plunged headlong into a conversation he really didn't want to have with anyone, especially not with Jack McKenzie. "What job are we going in there to do—win the war, or save Johnson's popularity in the polls?"

"Now I've heard enough. No president is going to escalate war just to get votes. Besides, the election is more than three years away."

"If you ask me," Kenneth said, knowing very well that Mac would be enraged by his next comment, "L.B.J. isn't escalating this conflict for anything other than his own personal reasons. He's going in deeper because he simply doesn't know how to get out. Listen to me, Mac." Kenneth let his pent up emotions and his opinions merge. "Johnson is risking lives to save his own hide, and I don't want any part of it."

"So you'll quit then?"

"Quit?" Kenneth's anger snapped. "Is that what I'm doing? I've been in ten years, Mac. Ten years!" He was shouting and no longer cared. "How long did you serve— three, four years?"

"I stayed until the end."

"I'd be an old man by then, Mac. If I survived. I've been there twice, for heaven's sake. I'm not going back. I can get my discharge in December. That's what I plan on doing."

"Then what?" Mac asked angrily. "Go back to regular life, whatever that is, when you know that the country needs you?"

"Ten years, Mac. I've already given ten years." Kenneth's voice dropped. It was no use. Mac refused to consider Kenneth's point of view. "I'm not a national hero. Sorry I let you down." Without waiting for Mac's response, Kenneth dropped the receiver back on its hook. He hadn't wanted to talk to Mac in the first place. Disgusted with himself, angry at Mac, and irritated with Sharon, he headed for the shower.

"Who was that on the phone?" Meg asked, coming in before Mac hung up.

"Kenneth."

"Ken? I'm sorry I missed his call."

"It wasn't you he wanted," Mac said angrily. "He was looking for Sharon."

"Well, did you tell him about what happened to Sharon this morning?"

"I told him she went to the mountains with Stephen," Mac said.

"And that's all?" Meg took a deep breath and tried to keep her voice even and calm. Nothing clammed Mac up quicker and tighter than a spat. "Didn't you tell him about, you know, Sharon being followed?"

"Come on, Meg," Mac pleaded, "we don't know that for sure. I think everyone's overreacting, don't you?"

"No, I don't," Meg said flatly. "I'm worried about her and the kids. Jeff called a while ago. The license number on that car—well, he said it's a stolen car."

"When did you find this out?"

"Before I left to gather the eggs."

"And when were you going to tell me about this?"

"I tried, Mac." Meg was starting to lose her temper. "I tried, but you were glued to the TV set. All I got out of you was grunts and uh-huh's. I'm not in the habit of talking over the TV."

"I was watching the President," Mac defended himself.

"I know," Meg busied herself around the kitchen. "And, you've been watching him over and over again all afternoon. Honestly, Mac, there is life besides . . ." She didn't finish her sentence. She was in no mood to fight with her husband tonight. There was enough turmoil going on inside her mind and heart without adding stress with Mac too.

"What did Kenneth have to say?" She purposely tried to keep her tone warm and friendly.

"Not much," he answered. "Did you pick up the mail?"

"Over there," she said, pointing to a small stack of envelopes on the counter.

"The paper?"

"In the dining room. Kenneth all right?"

"He's fine. Tired, I guess. A little on edge." Meg held her breath while Mac busied himself with the day's mail. "Says he's working overtime a lot. Seems the base is on alert status. No wonder with the President's announcement and all."

"Announcement?"

"He's sending more troops. They've already started shipping out. Keeping everybody busy down there, I guess."

"He still coming home next weekend?"

"Nope."

"Sharon will be disappointed."

"No, she won't." Mac's voice was matter of fact.

"She won't?"

"He says he's getting out in December. That should make her happy."

"He's what?" Meg's temper flared again. "You said he didn't say much."

"He didn't," Mac said, picking up an envelope that interested him and ripping it open. "He said he wanted to talk to Sharon. I said she wasn't here. He said he was not going to reenlist and that he'd be out in December. Said he was working long hours and he wasn't going to make it next weekend. That was it. Like I said, he didn't say much."

Meg wanted to scream at Mac. Instead she turned to the familiarity of her kitchen cupboards and occupied her hands with dinner preparations. Her father often said that eating a good home-cooked meal kept a man's body and soul together. "And preparing it often saves a man's life," her mother would respond. Busying herself with peeling potatoes, Meg smiled, understanding the comment more than ever before.

"Maybe I should call him back," Meg wondered aloud.

"Give it a while, he wasn't in the best of moods," Mac advised.

"After dinner then," she decided.

Before Meg finished cleaning the kitchen after dinner, the phone rang and Jeff Bennett asked to speak to Mac. Meg could hear the concern in his voice.

"No kidding?" Mac said into the phone. "You don't say." Pause. "Didn't catch him though."

Meg fussed with the dish towel she still held in her hand.

"I'll be," Mac said. Meg stepped closer to her husband. "She's up there with Dan and Jen? Your brother called, I see." Pause. "I agree with you one hundred percent. She might as well stay a while." Mac turned to Meg, "Get me something to write with, will you? He'll give us the phone number where Sharon and the kids are. Yeah," Mac said back into the phone, "I'll tell her." He quickly jotted the number on the pad Meg provided. "Sure thing. Give me a call, anytime."

"How about that?" Mac said turning to face his wife. "The car that was following Sharon this morning—stolen in the Redding area a month ago. They found it this afternoon in a side street in Riverside. Potter's finger prints all over it. It was him, all right. He was following Sharon."

Meg felt her knees weaken and the blood drain from her face. Finding a chair nearby, she steadied herself on the table and sank slowly into the seat. "Oh, my goodness." Meg said. "He's been here too, hasn't he?"

"That's what Bennett thinks. I guess I have to agree with him on this. Didn't want to admit it, but it looks like he's back."

"Didn't they find him—I mean, if they found the car . . ."

"Abandoned, I guess. At least he wasn't in it when they found it. The license number helped identify it. One of Miller's salesmen wrote it down this morning."

"Now do you think we're all overreacting?" Meg lashed out. Her temper snapped. "Now will you listen to me?" She leaned forward and with both elbows on the table buried her face in her hands and sobbed out her hurt, anger, and fear.

"Meggie, darlin'," Mac whispered, leaning over his wife protectively. "Hush, now. It'll be all right. Margaret, please don't cry."

"Don't come tryin' to make me feel better now, Mac. You've dismissed this whole thing as some figment of our imagination. Sharon knows. She felt it. You gave in because of Jeff Bennett. You'll listen to him and you won't even listen to your own flesh and blood. She knew, Mac. She knew!"

"I'm sorry, Sweetheart. I just didn't want the whole family upset, that's all."

"Well, for your information, the whole family has been upset for some time. Except for one, that is. You're the only one who's not been upset. It wasn't the family you were watching out for, Jack McKenzie. It was you. You didn't want to be upset. You know something? We've all be trying to take care of you in this whole mess. We've been trying to play down our fear, our awful fear, for your sake. It's time you started thinking of Sharon, Mac. She's the one he's after—not you. And like it or not, the whole family is upset. And you might as well face it, your life is upset too."

"Meg, honey," Mac said soothingly, pulling her to stand in his strong embrace. "I'm sorry. It's just that I'm not very good at this family stuff. I was an old confirmed bachelor when you came into my life. I've not had much practice where this is concerned. Please, Meg."

"Well, you better get in practice. Like it or not, this is a family you have here, Mac. And we're depending on you to listen to us. Sharon needs you to listen to her and believe her when she talks to you. She's not one to make up stories or exaggerate, you know that."

"I know, Sweetheart," Mac said, and Meg thought the apologetic tone of his voice was genuine. "I'm sorry."

"There, now that's a word I understand. Hold me, Mac. Tighter. It'll help me forgive you."

"My pleasure," Mac said into the soft hair of his wife. "I love you, Meg. I don't know what I'd do without you."

"And our family?" she asked, her voice muffled against his shoulder.

"And our family."

CHAPTER FIFTEEN

*K*enneth fumed at the traffic on his way to work the next morning. Camp Pendleton was a small city in its own right, and the President's orders escalating the war in Vietnam had caused a flurry of activity and tension. Sharp military salutes had become even sharper. Orders were given in the clipped official style as usual, but they seemed less human than ever. Waiting for a traffic light to change, Lieutenant Kenneth James Matthews recalled with anger his phone conversation with Mac.

"So convinced he knows everything about anything," Kenneth said aloud. He thought about others he had known who affected him the same way. What did they have in common? "Closed-minded, arrogant—" He stopped. This was getting him nowhere.

"Somewhere, somehow I have to find common ground with Jack McKenzie. For Mom's sake," he added under his breath, "and for Sharon's and the kids' too. We're a family, for crying out loud," he scolded himself. Somehow the thought of being in the same family with Mac didn't thrill him, not this morning anyway. But like it or not, Mac was not only Sharon's second cousin, he was Kenneth's stepfather. *Thanks, Mom,* Ken thought. *If my future turns out to be with Sharon,* he realized, *he'll practically be my father-in-law as well.* Kenneth checked his rearview mirror and then surveyed the traffic snarl ahead. *After all,* he returned his thoughts to home, *Mac is the closest thing Sharon has to a father.*

Just as the light turned green, military police entered the intersection and held Kenneth's lane of traffic back for a convoy of large military trucks to pass through.

Kenneth thumped his thumbs impatiently on the steering wheel. *There's got to be a way to break through to him,* he thought. "But where do I start looking?" he asked aloud. He glanced at his image in his rearview mirror, checking to see that his short brown hair was slicked back and neat. His attention was drawn to the reflection of his own eyes. Somewhere deep within his heart he heard, "Start there, Son. Why not start with you?"

Ken recognized the voice. It had been a familiar one in the past, but he hadn't taken the time to listen for it lately. He'd been so busy being frustrated, nursing his anger, and looking for reasons to leave the military, he had lost touch with his real reason for being there in the first place. As a young man Kenneth felt God call him into the military just as if he had been called to missions or ministry. Kenneth Matthews was convinced beyond a shadow of a doubt that he was in the Marines because God had sent him there. No wonder he was unable to meet on common ground with Mac; he had lost touch with not only himself, but his purpose and calling.

"Dear God," he prayed, "I left you out of this decision—out of everything lately haven't I?" Kenneth's mind drifted back to Vietnam. As surely as he knew anything, he knew God had protected him that one awful night—a night he tried unsuccessfully to forget. How many other times had God spared him? He had no idea. *But why not the others?* The unwelcome thought invaded once again. *Why me?* He shut his eyes against the pictures of his buddies flooding his mind. Some wounded, some dead. Others shaken so deeply at what they witnessed that, though they bore no visible wounds, they would carry emotional scars their entire lives. He thought of those who died in a massacre the day he was supposed to go but at the last minute was pulled out of the ranks to work on a generator problem that no one else seemed able to fix. *But what about Scottie?* the inner voice came back. "Scottie," Kenneth said. "Yeah, Scottie. If I hadn't fixed that hospital generator, he wouldn't have made it. Even the docs said so."

"But, God—" Kenneth leaned forward, resting his forearms on the steering wheel of his car. "You must have some reason ..." His voice trailed off. Why was this prayer so hard to pray? "Dear God, You know my questions are too deep for words. Help me out here, okay?"

Breathing deeply, Ken forced himself to relax against the seat. And right there in the middle of a hopeless traffic jam, he opened his heart to God. "Heavenly Father," he whispered, "I want your will. I've been struggling trying to find my own way through this mess. I'm up against it, Lord. I need you as much today as I did back there in Nam."

Closing his eyes against the tears that threatened to blur his vision, Kenneth knew peace for the first time in months. Sharon's face loomed in front of his mind's eye, and with her Kenneth saw Richie too.

"I needed you there," the Lord seemed to say into Kenneth's heart. "Now I need you here. It's time to go home."

The sound of a loud horn behind him brought his attention back to the congested traffic. An impatient MP blew his whistle and waved for him to drive on. Just as traffic began to move, Kenneth breathed a deep sigh of relief. *Home*, Kenneth said to himself, *and hopefully, to Sharon and the kids.*

Somewhere in the San Bernardino mountains, Sharon woke to the happy sound of children's laughter and the aroma of fresh-brewed coffee. She had no idea where she was for a moment, and hearing the sounds of her children happy and safe, she didn't care.

"Hey, Matthews!" a fellow corpsman yelled across the noisy repair shop. "The CO is calling for you. He wants to see you in his office on the double!"

Ken replaced the tools he was using in the bin, washed his hands, and glanced at his reflection in the mirror. He tugged at his fatigues, shrugged his shoulders, and walked to his car. The drive across the base took less time than it would have several hours ago. The hustle and bustle of the early morning seemed to have eased a bit.

"Lieutenant Ken Matthews reporting, sir," he said when shown in to the CO's office.

"Matthews," the older man said, "it has come to my attention that you're coming to the end of your current tour of duty. Your reenlistment papers are here; you will see they are all in order. You can put in a request to be stationed here in the states—your second tour in Vietnam entitles you to that. However, in light of the President's latest announcement, I would strongly urge you to request this base, Lieutenant. We could use a man of your caliber here at Camp Pendleton."

"Thank you, sir," Kenneth said. "However—" Ken took a deep breath and blurted out his decision. "I've decided not to reenlist."

"Sorry to hear that, Matthews," the officer said seriously. "This is an important time in the history of our nation. Important indeed. We need every available man we can get with your talent. From what I read here, there's not a machine or motor you can't fix. You were an invaluable asset to your command over there. You've been recommended for a commendation. And, with your reenlistment, a promotion as well. A decorated combat veteran can go far in the military. I would be remiss in my duty if I didn't ask you to reconsider."

"Yes, sir," Kenneth said respectfully. "I already have, several times."

"We hate to lose men like you, Matthews."

"Thank you, sir." Kenneth stood erect and motionless as his commanding officer rose slowly and walked to the window. He turned his back to Kenneth and looked at the activity outside his window.

"Have any idea what you'll be doing after you're discharged?" the older man asked after a few moments.

"Not completely, sir. I'd like to have a shop of my own."

"Are you sure you've given this enough consideration?"

"Yes, sir," Kenneth said confidently. "I have."

"I see," the older man said. "Well, we'll send your papers through then. Again, I'm sorry to hear you won't be reenlisting. I had you pegged for a career man."

"I thought so too, sir." Kenneth hoped he wouldn't press the subject further. "If there's nothing else, sir?"

"You understand that you'll be working almost straight through to your discharge. We're still on alert, and you're still in the Marines."

"Yes, sir," Kenneth said.

"That'll be all, Lieutenant."

Kenneth snapped to attention and sharply saluted the senior officer. When the salute was returned, he spun on his heel and walked quickly out the door.

"It's done," Kenneth said barely above a mumble. "I'm going home."

"You know, Sharon," Jen said after Dan had taken the three children out to chase butterflies, "I'm really glad Jeff insisted you come. I'm sorry about all this stuff with Richard, but I'm so glad we're here to see to it you don't have to face it alone."

Sharon fought back pent up tears, "Jen, I . . ."

"Listen, my friend." Jen pulled a kitchen chair alongside Sharon and slipped her arm around her shoulder. "We don't say it often enough, but you and me and Cari, we're friends. Good friends, okay? You and she have so much in common it's not funny. We aren't just thrown together because of some difficult circumstance, you know."

"No?" Sharon wiped her eyes with a napkin off the table.

"I heard," Jen said. "God always seems to put that woman in the right place at the right time, doesn't He?"

"Does He really do that?" Sharon asked.

"Do what?"

"Put people in the right place at the right time?"

"How else do you think Dan and I would have gotten together?" Jen asked, her face beaming with joy. "My goodness, with all the trouble I gave them both—well, it had to be God. Believe me."

Shoving a long, auburn curl behind her ear, she once again sat close to her friend. "I'm praying for you, Sharon."

"Thanks," Sharon said as tears once again filled her eyes. "I really need it."

"Dan is too," Jen said. "We're not only praying about this situation with Richard, but somehow we feel impressed to pray for more. We're not sure if we're praying because we're being led by the Lord to do so, or if it's just because we want everyone to be as happy as we are."

"I don't understand," Sharon said.

"Well, let's just say we think it's time you met someone as special to you as Dan is to me. Someone like Jeff or Stephen. We want someone to come along for you. Not just anyone, mind you. Someone perfectly suited for you—and of course, a wonderful daddy for Richie and Frannie. Honestly, Sharon, I don't know how you do it alone."

Sharon dropped her eyes and shyly avoided looking directly at Jen.

"Wait a minute!" Jen nearly squealed. "There *is* someone, isn't there? Look at that! You're blushing."

"I'm not," Sharon said.

"Come on, girlfriend," Jen prodded, "tell."

"Tell what?" Sharon asked innocently.

"A name, details—all the juicy details."

"There aren't any details . . . well, not very many at this point."

"In on the ground floor, am I?" Jen seemed elated.

"Jennifer," Sharon said with a low moan. "It's too soon to—"

"Nonsense! Come on. Want me to start guessing? Let's see, who have you seen lately? No kidding!" Jennifer jumped to her feet with sudden revelation. "I know who. Why didn't I guess this before? Oh, Sharon, this is wonderful. Wait until I tell Dan."

"Jen, you don't know anything," Sharon argued.

"You don't think I'd recognize something as plain as the nose on my face. This is great! Want me to say his name? Or will you?"

"Jen!" Sharon protested.

"It's that sharp Marine, isn't it? Meg's son?"

"You're hopeless," Sharon said, laughing out loud.

"I'm right, aren't I?" Jen wouldn't let up. "Auntie Meg is about to become Mother McKenzie. You've taken a liking to her son—what's his name? I only met him a time or two. It's him, isn't it?" Jen was relentless. "I know, Kenneth something or other. Let's see, what was Meg's name before she married Mac?"

"Matthews."

"Sharon Matthews," Jen said dreamily. "That has a nice ring to it, don't you agree?"

"I haven't thought of it," Sharon lied.

"I wasn't asking you," Jen said. "I was asking Him," she laughed as she pointed to the ceiling. "Now we have a name to work with. We're getting somewhere finally."

Sharon stood, moving slowly, thoughtfully, and took their empty cups to the kitchen sink. She needed to talk to someone about Ken, but didn't know whether or not she really should.

"Uh-oh," Jen said from her chair near the table. "I see some dark clouds forming over there."

"Jen—" Sharon searched for the right words as well as the courage to share her heart with the vivacious young woman across the room. "I need to ask someone some questions."

"Shoot," Jen said confidently. "I've had my two cups of coffee, I'm ready for anything."

"I'm serious," Sharon admitted.

"I'm delirious," Jen said smiling. "No, really, I'm serious too. It's just that I'm so happy for you. In the middle of this whole mess with Richard, God is—well, I can't really say for sure what God is doing. He's checked me from time to time for reporting to everyone what He's up to. I'm not His spokesman, per se, it's just that I have a hard time controlling myself when I see Him at work this way."

"Jen, I've been married before," Sharon said bluntly.

"So?" Jen popped a grape into her mouth from the fruit bowl in the center of the table.

"So, I've read the Bible, Jen. It says that a man who marries a divorced woman commits adultery with her. I don't want to do that to anyone."

"Hold it right there," Jen said, sitting up straight in her chair. "I'm no expert on the Bible or theology or doctrine or any of that stuff, but I *am* an experiencer of God's mercy. Are you really going to tell me those verses apply to you? Do you honestly think that you fit in that category?"

"I am divorced," Sharon said. "I was married to Richard Potter and I have two children by him."

"You shouldn't have ever married that jerk if you ask me," Jen said impulsively. "Oh, Sharon, I'm sorry. I'm trying to learn to think before I speak, but as you can tell, I've got a long way to go."

"It's too late to think like that, Jen. Don't you see? What I should have or shouldn't have done then has no bearing on now. Now I'm divorced. I can't explain or excuse that away. It's a fact. Plain, though not so simple, I'm divorced. I've made my peace with that. I've been happy at Uncle Mac's. The kids and I—well, the kids at least—are very happy. If I had only them the rest of my life, I would be . . ."

"Lonely," Jen said before Sharon could finish her sentence. "Face it, Sharon. Raising two kids, even with Mac and Auntie Meg so close by, you're still doing it alone. Even with your sculpture—"

"Sculpture? You mean my pottery."

"Nah, you're only getting started. This is only the beginning for you Sharon, I know that." Sharon started a modest protest, but Jen stopped her. "You wait and see. These pots of yours are wonderful, but there's more in there," Jen said pointing at her friend. "Give it time and the freedom to come out, will you?" Jen stood and walked the short distance to stand beside Sharon at the sink. "Know what I think?" Before Sharon could respond, she said, "I'll tell you what I think about this whole divorce thing." Jen took Sharon by the arm and escorted her to the living room, where they settled at opposite ends of a comfortable sofa.

"Listen, Sharon," Jen said, reaching for the Bible that sat on the coffee table. "I bet if you looked in here, you can also find verses that pertain to Richard's part in this whole thing. Isn't there something about a man staying faithful to his wife, respecting her, loving her as his own body?"

"Yes, I've read those verses," Sharon said. "But it only says clearly that under those circumstances she's free to divorce. It's not so clear that she's free to remarry."

"Don't you wish you could get God on the phone sometimes and ask Him to give a straight answer?" Jen said, pouting.

"I never thought of it quite like that before." Sharon had to smile at Jen's simple, straightforward manner. "But you know, it would sure make things easier to understand, wouldn't it?"

"Somehow God hasn't made it His priority to cater to my every whim and demand," Jen said with a smile.

"You've got Dan to do that, right?" Sharon ventured a gentle teasing of her own.

"You got that right," Jen responded, recapturing her newlywed glow. "And he does, too."

"I—" Sharon began, then hesitated. Jen waited. "Jen, I'm glad I could come here with my children. I . . . well, this is hard for me to say, but I like you, Jennifer Miller."

"And I like you Sharon Matthews—I mean Mason—I mean Potter."

"Jennifer, you're hopeless!" Sharon exclaimed.

"No, Sharon, hopeless is one thing I'm not." Jen beamed knowingly at her friend. "And you're not either, just you wait and see. Come on," she said, pulling Sharon gently by the hand, "let's plan dinner. Jeff will be coming back and I thought we might cook something on the grill. I've got a ton of food out there. Let's get really creative."

CHAPTER SIXTEEN

*T*here's a good chance he's headed for Mexico," Jeff told Sharon and the others after dinner. "It seems he made some contacts in prison. One of the convicts he was close to was released just about the time Richard broke parole. Their fingerprints were in the car found in Riverside, and apparently the police have some reason to believe they picked up another guy and headed south. My guess is that he wanted to see you before he left. Or, perhaps—"

"Richie," Sharon finished his sentence. "Somehow I think he wanted to see Richie."

"I hope that's all he wanted," Cari joined in. Sharon turned quickly to face the other woman who knew the full force of Richard's temper and will.

"What do you mean?"

"We can't dismiss the bragging he did while he was in prison, Sharon," Jeff said. "You might as well face it. He said nobody would keep his son from him. It seems no one took him seriously. Chalked it up to all talk, you know, to sound big and tough. He didn't get along very well inside. Men who abuse women and children find themselves on the other end of the stick when they come up against those who are doing time for hard crimes, such as armed robbery and even murder. There's a code inside, believe it or not. Sort of a pecking order. Wife beaters and child abusers start at the bottom and usually stay there. Even among criminals Richard didn't find respect." Sharon knew Jeff was minimizing the abuse Richard may have suffered at the hands of those who looked down on him while he did his time. She was also convinced that those Richard held responsible for sending him there would not escape revenge if he could find a way to get even. That included both Jeff and Cari. And in Richard's twisted mind, it included Sharon too.

No one understood Richard's strange way of thinking and rationalizing the way Sharon did. Even then, she was at a loss to explain his behavior. After all, she believed him at one time. *How could I have ever thought he would change just because we got married?* she thought. Mac had been the one to convince her that, as Mac put it, "when a man has a wife and family, he often settles down."

"Sharon?" Jen stood at her side. "You seem lost somewhere."

"Just thinking," Sharon said. "And remembering."

"Sharon," Cari said, moving to sit on the sofa beside her, "don't. You're not to blame for any of this."

"How did you know what I was thinking?" Sharon asked, reaching to take Cari's outstretched hand.

"I've been there, remember?"

"I almost forgot. I've felt alone for so long, it's hard to keep in mind that I'm not the only one who Richard hurt." Sharon searched Cari's dark eyes and found understanding she could find no other place.

"Past tense. We *were* hurt, Sharon, but not any more. We're not going to take anything from him ever again."

"You know," Dan Miller joined in, "seeing the two of you sitting together is such a reminder of how much we who belong to Christ belong to each other. What would we do without that bond?"

"I can't imagine," Cari said.

"It's for you, Sharon, " Jennifer said a few days later when the phone rang. "I think it's Kenneth."

As Sharon took the receiver, Cari had to force Jen from the kitchen so she could talk in private.

"Well hello at last." Kenneth's voice sounded good to her, but she could tell he was tired.

"Hi," she said timidly. "You found me."

"Yeah, but it wasn't easy. Mom gave me the number. Mac wasn't about to, that's for sure."

"He'll get over it," Sharon said.

"You sound like Mom." It was good to hear him laugh. "You all right?"

"I'm fine," Sharon said. "I'm getting spoiled. Coffee every morning when I come downstairs."

"How are the kids?"

"Fine."

"They having fun?"

"Loads. Richie and Dan have become fast friends," she said.

"Men have to stick together in a house with all those women."

"That's what they say." Sharon's heart lurched with longing for him.

"I miss you," he said. Sharon's heart beat faster.

"That's what I was thinking," she said.

"Sharon, Mom told me about the other day. I'm sorry I wasn't there."

"Now who's apologizing for no reason?" she teased.

"I mean it," he said. His tone of voice was unmistakably serious.

"You couldn't help it," she said. "Even if you were there . . ."

"Don't you get it, honey?" Sharon closed her eyes and swallowed the lump in her throat at his tenderness. "He doesn't bother you unless you're alone. He's a coward."

"I can't be watched over every minute," Sharon said.

"I'd like to try," he answered.

Not knowing how to respond, Sharon said nothing.

"You still there?" he asked after a moment of silence.

"Right here."

"I wish I knew exactly where you were," he said.

"Me too."

"Pardon me?" Kenneth was puzzled.

"I have no idea where we are. I relaxed and Stephen drove. I lost my direction after about the tenth curve. You'd need a map to get in here."

"So I've heard. By the way, who's Stephen?"

"Jeff's brother."

"Anybody I should worry about?"

"Kenneth," she said.

"I guess I don't have the right . . . do I?"

"You don't have to worry about Stephen."

"Anybody else?"

"Just Richard."

"I'm not worried about him. I'm concerned about you, though. Listen, this is all going to turn out all right. I know it. Can you believe that?"

"I can hope," Sharon said.

"Yes, you certainly can," Kenneth said. "And so can I."

"I'm sorry about our date," Sharon said. As the full realization that she was not going to get to see Kenneth as they had planned finally hit, her stomach tightened.

"Well, I am too." She could tell he was as disappointed as she was, and it helped just to know that. "But, as you probably have heard, everything's a royal mess down here. The ships that are going out are leaving from here. Large cargo planes are taking off right and left. It keeps us pretty busy."

"Kenneth," she interrupted, "what are you talking about?"

"You haven't heard then," he said. "The President announced the other day that he's escalating the war in Vietnam."

"Oh no." Sharon feared what this escalation might mean for Kenneth.

"I know what it's like to be over there and not have the right parts to fix things when they break down. I've been assigned to the area that ships parts. Since I just came back, I have a pretty good idea of the importance of this job."

"I see," Sharon's heart stood still. "Does this change your plans?"

"Sharon—" Kenneth began soberly. She held her breath, fearing what he was about to say. "I've been doing a lot of thinking and, in fact, some heavy-duty praying as well." She waited without comment. "My CO called me in a few days ago and offered me a promotion if I'd reenlist. He had the papers for me to sign right there on the spot. He said I could be stationed here, he'd see to that." Kenneth paused and Sharon waited without comment. "You still there?" he asked.

"I'm listening," she said, not wanting to influence his decision one way or another.

"He was very complimentary," Kenneth said. "But not his usual self. He was even a bit subdued, now that I think about it. Makes me wonder if the President has all the support he thinks he has. Oh, well. It's his decision, not mine. He's the one who'll have to live with it, not me."

"What do you mean?"

"Sharon, I told my CO I wasn't going to re-up."

"Re-up?"

"I'm coming home," he said quietly. "I'm leaving the Marines."

"Ken—" she said, barely able to speak as she choked back her tears.

"I want to put this all behind me—the service, the war." His voice grew quieter and Sharon could barely hear him. She pressed her ear into the receiver and covered her opposite ear with her hand.

"What did you say?"

"I want to get on with the next phase of my life," Kenneth said. "Whatever God has for me, I'm ready to move on."

"I don't know what to say," Sharon said.

"Don't say anything yet. This is my decision. I've prayed about it and I'm sure it's the right thing to do."

"Okay," she said, smiling into the phone. "Have you told your mother?"

"No," he said, "I wanted to tell you first."

"Do you have any idea when?"

"I wish I knew when it was actually going to happen," he answered. Sharon put her hand on her stomach to try to calm the excitement that was beginning to grow inside. "It's funny. I thought that I'd be a Marine for as long as . . . well, as long as they'd let me. Now I can't wait to get out. This change really takes me by surprise."

"So," Sharon said, groping for the right words, "I guess we'll be seeing you soon then."

"Can't say for sure. The military works on its own sweet schedule. When the paperwork goes through, I guess. My three-year enlistment is up in December, but I stayed on in Nam for a few months and I'm supposed to get some time reduced because of that. I wish I could be more specific, but I can't. The worst part of it all," he added, "is that with the base on full-alert status, all my weekend passes have been canceled. We're all working long shifts, round the clock. It could be that way for a while. And if the President actually declares war—"

"Oh, Kenneth, is that really bound to happen?"

"Well, not bound, I guess. They keep calling it a conflict or some other term short of war. But let me tell you, for the guys out there it's . . ." Kenneth didn't finish his sentence. He no longer wanted to think about Vietnam. The nightmares he experienced there were something he wanted to put far behind him and away from what he hoped would be a happy future with Sharon and the children. "Listen," he said, suddenly changing the subject, "tell Richie I said hi and give Frannie a hug for me, okay?"

"I will," she said.

"I wish I was there with you," Kenneth admitted. Sharon wrapped her arm across her ribs.

"I do too," she said.

"Promise me something, okay?"

"What's that?"

"You stay safe. Do what Jeff and Dan tell you to do. Stay as long as necessary, okay? Hopefully they'll catch this jerk and then—"

"If they do."

"*When*," Ken corrected. "*When* they catch him."

"When," Sharon said. "I'll go home as soon as I can."

"Good," Ken said. "I want to be able to picture you in your own little house when I talk to you. Or at least at Mom's."

"Ken?" Sharon said, her eyes once again filling with tears.

"I hear you, honey," he said. "I hear you."

CHAPTER SEVENTEEN

I talked to Sarah yesterday afternoon" Jen said. She tells me some mighty important news."

"Oh?" Cari asked over the rim of a steaming cup of coffee.

"She tells me Sharon's pieces are moving very nicely. First American Bank has inquired as to the name of the artist. It seems they like to do a feature display every fall of a local artist's work. They'd like to see more of Sharon's work." Jen continued the conversation as if Sharon weren't in the room. "And if that's not enough, Old Man Jepson, the realtor, is redoing his offices and wants to talk to the artist *personally* to contract a few custom pieces as well as select a few existing ones for the less important people in his firm. And—"

"And?" Sharon gasped. She could barely believe Jen wasn't teasing. "There's more?"

"And," Jen continued as if Sharon hadn't spoken at all, "the Saganaugh Gallery is interested in handling a few pieces on consignment."

"The Saganaugh Gallery?" Cari asked.

"Victoria Saganaugh is only the most important member of the Friends of the Fine Arts Association in Laguna Beach. She came into the store herself. It seems she was up for a weekend in Palm Springs and stopped by to do a little slumming in our dinky little town."

"Hey, wait a minute," Cari protested. "Redlands isn't a dinky little town."

"Not to us, it isn't," Jen said. "But to Victoria Saganaugh, it is. She travels worldwide. Even Carmel would be a step down for that lady."

Sharon's head throbbed with the impact of what Jen was saying. *A display of my own at First American Bank? A commissioned job for Mr. Jepson? A few pieces on consignment in Laguna?* Surely she must have misunderstood!

"Jen," she cried aloud, "you've got to be kidding!"

"I'm not," Jen said with pride. "Didn't I tell you your work was wonderful? Victoria," Jen exclaimed proudly, "even bought a piece for her own personal collection."

"She probably wants it to put pencils in it," Sharon laughed, trying to downplay the importance of this last bit of information.

"I doubt that," Cari said. "Did Sarah say what she bought?"

"Who wants to know and why?" Jen teased.

"Because, that's why," Cari retorted.

"So you can get your hands on one for your own personal collection?" Jen asked, putting on exaggerated mannerisms of sophistication.

"So I can get hold of one before you mark up the prices," Cari shot back.

"What did she buy?" Sharon asked.

"One of those darling pots with the holes cut out and the piece sort of twisted—you know the one."

"The jasmine pot," Sharon said, holding her hand to her mouth. "Can you believe that?"

"Jasmine pot?"

"I made it for . . ." Sharon blushed as she let her sentence drop unfinished.

"Come on, Shar," Jen prodded. "Did you have special inspiration for that piece that we don't know about?"

Sharon's eyes once again brimmed with tears. Overwhelmed with the fact that someone had actually liked the pot she had created for Kenneth that night in the shop, and that others were interested in showing her work, Sharon could barely believe how happy she felt at that moment. In fact, she couldn't ever remember feeling happier or more hopeful in her entire life. Even the threat of Richard's invasion into her life was forgotten for the moment—but unfortunately, only for the moment.

"Who would do such a thing?" Meg asked tearfully while Mac stood close by for support. "And why?"

"I can only think of one person." Mac's voice broke with emotion and anger. "And who knows his reasons?"

Mac stepped carefully through Sharon's work studio and surveyed the damage. "Looks like he took a baseball bat to the place."

"Isn't there anything left at all?" Meg cried.

"Not by the looks of it," Mac growled. "What's behind that canvas?"

"Oh, my goodness, maybe he didn't see that area," Meg said hopefully as she stepped toward the little alcove where Sharon had been storing her pots. "Look, Mac! They're okay!"

"But look at this mess out here," Mac said. "He must have bashed several dozen of her largest things. How's she gonna feel about this?"

"We both know the answer to that," Meg said. "Maybe I should clean it up before she gets home."

"Don't touch anything," Mac barked. "I think the police should have a look at this first. I wonder why Major didn't put up a ruckus. Surely, even as deaf as he is, he would have heard this."

"I haven't seen him this morning. And besides, why didn't *we* hear something? And why didn't Sam hear anything? You talk to him, Mac. Maybe he was sleeping on the job."

Mac hung his head and Meg saw the angry flush flood his features. "Mac," she said, "what on earth—"

"He wasn't here last night, Margaret," he confessed. "I sent him home. Seems he had some sort of headache. I thought he might be coming down with something. I let him go just after eleven."

"Didn't they send someone else to take his place?" Meg referred to the security company they hired.

"I didn't think it necessary," Mac admitted defensively. "My gosh, Margaret, it's been weeks since that day—"

"Jack McKenzie—" Meg was obviously upset and angry. "Will you ever learn? What if he had decided to take a bat to us while we were sleeping in our beds, then what?"

"I didn't think he'd try a stunt like that."

"Did you think he'd do a thing like this?" She was nearly yelling.

"I didn't think—"

"Of course you didn't," she shouted. "Of course you didn't think! Why should I assume anything else?"

"Meggie," Mac tried to plead with his wife.

"Don't 'Meggie' me," she retorted. "I'm as angry with you for this as I am him!" Meg turned and left Mac standing in the ruin of Sharon's workshop.

"Meg wait!" he said suddenly, turning to follow after her. His long strides made it easy to overtake her. "Meg, please," he begged.

"Call the police, Mac. I've got my eggs to tend to. I don't want you even near me while I work on them, do you hear me? I'm so mad I'll be surprised if this morning's gathering doesn't look like that mess back there before I'm through. I'm telling you, McKenzie, stay clear of me for a while. Go on now, call the police, better they get here and get their job done before Sharon and the others get back. I'm

expecting them sometime around noon. Get on with you—"
Mac reached for his wife and she stopped him with both
hands firmly planted on his midsection. "I mean it, Mac.
Let me be."

As Meg expected, Sharon and the kids arrived at the
ranch right before lunch. Meg pasted on a smile and invited
the Bennetts and the Millers, who had come with them, to
join them for tuna salad sandwiches.

Shortly after lunch, Sharon finally addressed the obvious
tension between Mac and Meg. "Okay you two, I can tell
something's wrong."

"You going to tell her or am I?" Meg snapped at her
husband. "Go on, no use putting it off any longer."

"Sharon," Mac dropped his eyes to his plate. "I owe you
a deep apology," he paused.

"Get to it, Mac," Meg ordered impatiently.

"I'm trying. This isn't easy for me, woman!" His defeated
tone indicated that Meg had the upper hand in this situation. "Sharon, someone broke into your workshop last
night and . . ."

Sharon felt her heart freeze. "And what?"

"Well, it's a mess out there," he said.

"How did this happen? What happened?"

"Things are pretty smashed up," Mac said hoarsely. Un-
accustomed to tears, Mac wiped his eyes with the backs of
his rough hands.

Sharon stumbled toward a kitchen chair and sat down
with a thud. "Can someone start at the beginning and tell
me what happened?" Then, standing quickly, she bolted
toward the door. "Never mind. I'll go see for myself!"

"Wait," Meg said gently as she caught Sharon's arm. "The
police have asked us to leave everything just as it is until
they can come."

"The police?" Sharon felt her knees buckling. "I don't understand . . . how did this happen? I thought the night watchman was here to prevent something like this." She turned to Mac. "How did he get past the night watchman?" She saw the pain of guilt crease Mac's tanned forehead. "There was a night watchman, wasn't there?"

"Sharon, I'm sorry," Mac said.

"I can't believe you'd let him go. Didn't you think Richard would . . .? I mean, what were you thinking, Uncle Mac?" Fear gripped Sharon's heart, and for a moment she thought she might throw up. "Uncle Mac?" She didn't fight the tears that streamed freely down her face. "Uncle Mac, whatever he did out there, I can't even bear to imagine what it might be. But what if I had been out there? What if you had been? And what about Major? Where was he all this time?"

"We've not seen Major this morning, dear," Meg said quietly. "I'm almost afraid to think . . ."

"Oh, my gosh," Sharon said, coming slowly to sit once more. "Oh, my gosh."

Jeff and Cari had been listening without saying a word. Cari busied herself taking care of the children. She settled them in front of the TV to watch *Lunch with Casey*. Just as she left the kitchen to check on the kids, Jeff finally spoke.

"We've got a real problem here, don't we, Mac?"

"Looks that way," Mac said in a hoarse whisper.

"Are you finally going to admit that this man is someone you can't take lightly?"

"I guess so," Mac said.

"You guess so?" Sharon's anger rose and she didn't try to conceal it. "You guess so? You haven't been on the end of his fist or his boot, Uncle Mac. I tried to tell you, but would you listen? I'm leaving here," she announced decisively.

"Where will you go?" Mac asked and Sharon could hear hurt in his voice.

"I have no idea," she said. "But you can't expect me to stay here, can you?"

"Sharon," Meg pleaded. "Honey, please don't do anything too hastily. Please, Sweetheart, for your own good— and for the children. We've already called the security company, they're sending out someone else right away. Mr. Sampson got sick, your uncle let him go home. He assumed that since we hadn't heard or seen any evidence of Richard in weeks, one or two nights without security wouldn't be dangerous."

"Auntie Meg's right, Sharon," Jeff said. "With stepped-up security, I can't think of any place that you'd be safer than right here. I'll work on a couple of things this afternoon. I think it would be a good idea to get some perspective on things before you go running off. He didn't do anything as long as the guard was on duty. Who knows if he'd follow you? We'll just have to pressure the police into stepping up their efforts. You and the kids can stay upstairs, okay? We've got to keep our heads, now more than ever. Come on, Mac." Jeff motioned toward the man who looked so defeated. "Let's have a look."

"Do you think Sharon could tell us just how much damage is here? I mean, do you think she even knows how much of her inventory has been destroyed?" Jeff asked after surveying the rubble.

"Inventory?" Mac asked. "I'm not sure this could be considered inventory. After all, it's more of a hobby than anything else."

"Then you haven't heard," Jeff said, stepping back out into the afternoon sun. "I thought she'd rather tell you herself, but it appears as though Sharon's work has made quite an impression in town. You know she put several pieces in at Miller's before she went to the mountains."

"Yeah, I know." Mac pulled the damaged door closed as far as he could.

"She's being commissioned to do several pieces for a large real estate firm in Redlands, and First American is interested in displaying her work in the fall. A high-class art gallery in Laguna Beach has inquired about handling a few pieces on consignment and perhaps commissioning a few more. You've got a very talented young artist in there, Mac, and the sooner you know it the better. The damage in there can no longer be calculated in materials only, but in lost sales." Jeff turned and walked a few feet away, shoving his hands in his pockets. He studied Mac's reaction out of the corner of his eye. "I think," Jeff said after a few minutes of silence, "you had better get used to the idea, Mac. What you have judged as a hobby could very well become a full-time career for Sharon. And no one deserves it more, wouldn't you agree?"

"Well, she does have a break or two coming, that's for sure. Life hasn't been easy for her."

"And," Jeff said as they began their walk back toward the main house, "I think you need to understand that Potter's behavior is no longer just considered a nuisance. If this is his doing—" Jeff stopped and faced the older man. "If this is who we both think it is, he's crossed the line to criminal behavior now. With breaking parole, stealing a car, and now this, he will be facing prison again once he's apprehended."

"So what do we do in the meantime?" Mac asked.

"Be careful. That's one thing you *can* do, Mac," Jeff laid his hand on the shoulder of the rough man. "And, I've already filed for a restraining order. All Sharon has to do is sign it."

"Where will all this end?" Mac asked as they approached the back steps.

"I wish I could say for sure. But for now, we've got to protect our girls, right?"

CHAPTER EIGHTEEN

*N*o one was surprised to see James and Sarah Jenkins pull in the driveway just as supper dishes were being finished.

"Jeff told us what is happening here," James said to Mac.

"We want to help," Sarah added.

"That's so thoughtful," Meg said, her voice thick with emotion. "But I really don't know how you can."

"Well," Sarah said, putting her arm around Meg's shoulders, "we have an idea or two. Will you listen while we tell you what we're thinking?"

Meg nodded and poured tall glasses of iced tea, and the four friends gathered around the kitchen table. Mac glanced at Meg, who shot him a warning look, and he allowed his wife to take the lead in dealing with the Jenkinses.

"It's almost canning time," Sarah said. "We've always canned together before. So that won't change. What is changing is that we realize that Sharon has her work cut out for her if she's to take full opportunity of the offers she's being made."

"That's where I come in," James said gently. "I'd like to come along and take over the egg gathering and sorting for a while—while the women get their canning done and Sharon gets caught up."

"I don't think—" Mac started to protest.

"I think," Meg said, interrupting Mac with both her voice and her hand firmly on his arm, "I think that would be wonderful. Our egg production was down during that hot spell, but with the cooler weather we've been having, it's picking up a bit. You know, Mac," she said sweetly to her husband, "it might be nice to have James and Sarah on the place. I can't help but think there's safety in numbers."

"That's just what I told Jeff," James said, then turned to Mac. "It doesn't appear that Richard Potter is brave enough to come out in the daytime. Or at least, when there's anyone except women or children about. I thought you might feel better about it all out there on your route if you knew there was a man here on the place. Not that I'm really needed for protection. But a deterrent never hurts, is my guess."

"And," Sarah said, encouraging her husband, "tell them the rest, James."

"You'd be doing us a favor in return," James said. "We've decided it's time to fix up our old house a bit. Sarah isn't as well as she could be," he said, reaching to gently pat his wife's arm.

"Sarah?" Meg said with concern.

"It's nothing, Meg," Sarah said, trying to minimize her situation. "It's just that old asthma kicking up again."

"The doctor says we might want to consider getting rid of that old carpet, and you know how it goes, one thing leads to another. Subflooring needs replacing, kitchen needs rewiring. I thought being up here a few weeks while the work was being done on the house would be good for her. I can't even think of having her in the dust and mess of remodeling right now."

"Perfect!" Meg exclaimed. "Just what we all need, then. You and James could stay out in Sharon's house while she and the kids stay here with us. We'll just have to move a few beds and we'll be all set."

"We're more than glad to do this," Mac said. "But you don't have to work it off. We're more than happy to help."

Meg and Sarah exchanged knowing looks. *How does James manage,* Meg wondered, *coming to offer to help us out and we end up thinking we're doing him a favor.*

Sharon could hear the voices of the two older couples conversing in the kitchen and decided to slip out the front door once the children were tucked in for the night. It was all she could do to stay away from the workshop, now that the police had been here and their reports were finished. She waited until the children were settled so that Mac and Meg could have some time with James and Sarah. Shutting the front door as quietly as possible, she descended the front steps, walked on the grass alongside the gravel driveway and made her way toward her workshop.

Smashed, she said to herself. *Uncle Mac said he smashed things up a bit.* She first surveyed the damaged door. Carefully, slowly, she opened it, then closed her eyes for a moment before stepping inside. In the semidarkness of twilight, she could sense more than see the latest blow of destruction at the hand of Richard Potter.

"Will it never end?" she cried, falling to her knees amid broken pieces of her handiwork. "When will it stop?"

Kenneth hadn't taken the time to call ahead when his twenty-four-hour pass came through. He had been away from Sharon far too long to spend the extra minutes on the phone explaining. Noticing an extra car in the driveway, he decided to go directly to Sharon's house, hoping she would be there by now. When he didn't find her, he headed for the main house, then on an impulse, decided to check the workshop instead.

He stopped a few feet away. He listened, trying to interpret what he was hearing. "Sharon?" he said quietly. "Sharon?"

"Dear God," he heard her praying, "somehow, someway, You have to help me. I can't take this anymore," she said between deep, heart-wrenching sobs. "Please, Father, please, help me."

Kenneth opened the slightly ajar door before he noticed its damage. The late sunset sky let in only enough light for him to see her sitting amid the pieces of smashed pottery.

"Sharon," he whispered, immediately kneeling and pulling her inside his arms. "Sharon, baby, what happened here?"

She turned and buried her face in his chest. He could feel her small body shaking uncontrollably. Tightening his arms around her, he squinted in the darkness, trying to survey the damage. "Oh, Kenneth," she cried, "I'm so glad you're here."

"Come on, honey," he said pulling her to her feet. "I can help clean up this mess. Can you tell me what happened?"

"Richard," she said angrily. "Richard is what happened."

"Are you sure about that?" Kenneth suddenly felt his heart pounding and his temple throb. "Are you all right? I mean, he didn't hurt you, did he?" He reached for the light switch and immediately the room was flooded. "Wow," Kenneth said with a low whistle. "He didn't pull any punches, did he?"

"He never does," she blurted out. "You can't imagine—" Sobs choked off her words.

"Mac know about this?"

"Yes, and the police and Jeff and Cari. Jen and Dan Miller too."

"Who's there?" Mac's voice called from a safe distance away.

"It's me, Mac. Sharon's out here too."

"I didn't hear you drive in," Mac said curtly, swinging open the damaged door.

"I saw you had company," Kenneth explained. "I thought I might find Sharon out here, but I certainly didn't expect to find this." He gestured toward the vandal's work. "Potter?"

"Probably," Mac said. "Police didn't find any evidence linking him, though. No fingerprints. Gloves probably took care of that."

"What'd he use, a bomb?"

"A baseball bat," Mac said, nodding toward a wooden implement tossed carelessly to one side. "Looks like he used Richie's bat."

"Come on, honey," Kenneth said, taking Sharon by the arm. "Why don't you go up to the house and let me clean this up."

"Your mother and I were planning to start on it in the morning," Mac said.

"Would you mind if I got a head start?" Kenneth asked, trying to stay on Mac's good side.

"Not in the least," Mac shrugged. "Have at it with my blessing."

"Thanks, Mac," Kenneth said, reaching to shake hands with the older, gruff man.

"I want to stay," Sharon said. "Please, Ken. I want to get to my wheel. I can't tell if it's damaged or not."

"We've got some things to talk about," Mac said, referring to James and Sarah's plans. "But there's plenty of time later. I'll tell your mother you're here," Mac said to Kenneth. Then he turned and walked out into the evening shadows.

Picking up a broom, Sharon started sweeping the pieces of her smashed pots into a dusty pile in the center of the room. Kenneth disappeared, then quickly reappeared with a flat-nosed shovel and a large battered garbage can.

Sharon restrained him before he could scoop up the pile of debris at her feet. Searching her eyes, Kenneth felt his heart break with the pain he saw there. "It'll be okay, baby," he said softly.

Sharon didn't try to stop the tears flowing freely down her dusty cheeks. "It's like all my hopes and dreams have been smashed in to a million pieces." Her voice was thick with sad emotion.

"No, Sweetheart," Kenneth corrected her gently, "no. He's attacked your studio, I won't deny that. But your dreams and hopes aren't in these pots," he said. "Your hopes and dreams are in there." He pointed to her heart. "And they are safe, Sharon."

"But all my work," she said, pointing to the debris at her feet.

"Your talent is in your hands, not these pots. These were only the beginning," he said confidently. "Sharon," he said, slipping his arm around her slender waist, "he may have meant you harm. He may have wanted to make you fearful, even terrified. But I can't help but think God can bring good from this somehow. We can't see it right now, but isn't that what He does? Can't He bring good from whatever bad we give to Him?"

"Can He?" Doubt tinged Sharon's voice with a tone that scared Kenneth more than Richard's vandalism.

"If we let Him," Ken said softly. "Don't try to do it now. Give it time. After this mess is cleaned up, pray about it, okay?"

Sharon shrugged. It wasn't agreement, but it wasn't resistance either, Kenneth noticed.

When the shop was swept clean, Kenneth made a cursory examination of the motor on Sharon's wheel and announced that the rest of the cleanup could wait until morning. "I've got something to tell you and Mom," he said. "And it sounds like they might have something to tell us."

On the way to the house, Kenneth threw back his head and laughed. "What's so funny?" Sharon asked, slapping her leather work gloves against his midsection.

"I was just wondering what in the world they might have to tell us," he said. "Maybe Mom's expecting!"

"Don't even say that," Sharon said in dismay. "My gosh, she's in her sixties!"

"She's too old?" Kenneth asked. "You better not let her hear you say that."

"Kenneth," Sharon scolded, "you're not being very funny."

"And what about you, my little pretty," he teased, pulling her around to face him. "Do you think you're too old?"

"For what?" she said shyly, blushing under the light on the back porch.

"For adding to your little family." Suddenly his tone was seriously tender.

"No, but I'm getting there fast," she quipped.

"Can't you slow it down a bit?"

"Nope," she said. "Some things we can't control."

"Well, then," he said triumphantly, "I guess we'd better—" Kenneth stopped short of asking her to marry him right then and there. Looking deep within her eyes, he could barely control the beating within his chest.

"Maybe we'd better," she said softly. "But I have to warn you. You'll have Uncle Mac to deal with." Kenneth relaxed when he heard her laugh.

"And a not-so-nice-guy ex-husband," he added.

"Oh, yeah, that," she said. The look on her face made him wish he hadn't made the comment.

"Don't you worry about him," he said. "We'll find a way." Kenneth wanted Sharon to know she wouldn't have to face this alone. "I promise you, we'll find a way."

CHAPTER NINETEEN

*R*ichie's bloodcurdling scream to full consciousness jerked him fully awake. Bolting upright in the small bed in Sharon's house, he listened. Almost deciding it was a bad dream, he vacillated between getting up and investigating and lying down and pulling a pillow over his head. Then he heard it again. This time there was no mistaking the sound. Richie was screaming from somewhere on the other side of the main house.

Kenneth jumped into his clothes, and jamming his sockless feet into his military-style shoes, he bolted for the door, crossed the patio, and closed the distance between him and the small boy's voice.

"Mommy! Mommy!" he heard Richie screaming.

"Richie!" Sharon's voice called from behind Kenneth.

At least she's all right. Kenneth drew a breath of relief without taking the time to turn around to see her.

"Where are you, Richie?" Kenneth called.

"Mommy, Mommy!" The boy's terrified voice had also reached Meg and Mac. Every routine job on the ranch stopped dead as the panic-stricken family converged on the frightened little boy sitting under the large overgrown willow tree alongside the front porch. "Mommy," he sobbed as Kenneth reached him. "Kenny," he wailed when Ken forced his way between the thick green branches. "Kenny, he's dead!"

Ken's heart lurched with pain and nausea gripped his middle at the sight of the six-year-old cradling the blood-soaked head of Mac's longtime companion in his lap.

"Let me have him, Son," Kenneth said, reaching for the stiffened carcass. "Come on, Richie, I'll take care of him now." Ken signaled Sharon to keep her distance. "You go be with your mother, okay? Papa Mac's on his way. Come on, it's okay."

"He's dead, Kenny," Richie cried, burying his face in the thick fur of the dead dog. "Somebody hurt him real bad and he's dead."

"He doesn't hurt anymore, Richie. Come on, guy, your mama's here. We don't want her to see this, do we? No, I didn't think so," he said when Richie shook his head. "You go take care of her, okay? Papa Mac and I will take care of Major. Go to your mama and little sister."

Richie slowly released his tight grip on the old dog and scooted silently on the seat of his pants until he was a few feet away. Only with additional coaxing from Kenneth did he finally struggle to his hands and knees and crawl through the dense greenery to where Sharon waited.

"What's going on?" Mac's voice boomed from close range.

"Mac," Kenneth yelled, "I don't think you should come in here."

"It's Major," he heard Sharon say. "He's gone, Uncle Mac."

"Somebody hurt him real bad, Papa Mac," Richie started crying again. "He's bled everywhere."

Ken crawled his way from under the old tree. "Mom," he said to Meg, "can you find me a tarp of some kind?"

"What happened to him?" Mac growled.

"I can't tell for sure. Sharon, you better take the kids back in the house. I'll take care of him."

"I want to know," Mac insisted.

"It looks like somebody got to him with a club or something," he said when he was sure the children couldn't overhear.

"An old harmless dog? Who'd do—?"

"Mac," Ken said, examining the dirt alongside the house, "looks like he made it back to this old spot on his own. Look." Kenneth pointed to what appeared to be dried blood spots in the dirt.

"I'm going in to him," Mac said, lunging toward the sagging willow branches.

"He's a mess, Mac. And it looks like it's been some time. Are you sure you want to see him like this?"

"I've had him since he was a puppy, Ken. I'll take care of him now," Mac said as he parted the branches and stepped within the cool, shady hollow near the willow's trunk.

"I'll wait for him, dear," Meg said, taking Kenneth's arm. "Go to Richie, will you? I can't imagine what that little boy must be thinking. See if Sharon needs your help."

As Ken walked away from the terrible scene, he paused as he heard Mac's low moan and muffled sobs. Wiping his own tears on his shirt sleeves, Kenneth went to be with Richie.

"How is he?" Sharon asked a little later when Meg came through the kitchen door.

"He loved that old dog," Meg said. "We wondered why we didn't hear—" She stopped when she saw Richie's haunted eyes.

"I didn't do it," Richie cried, moving to stand as close to Ken's mother as he could. "Honest, Auntie Meg, I didn't kill him."

"I know that, honey. Nobody thinks you did that awful thing. You loved Major just like Papa Mac did. We're glad we know where he is. Papa Mac was worried sick. At least he's not sick or someplace where he can't get home. He died in his favorite place, didn't he, darlin'?" Richie nodded.

"Where's Mac?" Ken asked.

"Out back, he's burying him out back."

"I think he could use some help," Kenneth commented.

"I'll do it," Richie said. Straightening his shoulders and standing as tall as his six years would allow, he walked with a determined stance toward the door. "I loved Major, too," he said.

"Richie," Sharon said, trying to stop him.

"Let him go," Kenneth suggested, restraining her with a gentle tug on her arm. "A man's gotta do what a man's gotta do—even a very little man."

Mac slumped into his favorite old wicker chair on the back porch after a somber family supper. No one felt like eating very much and Richie claimed his stomach was still a little sick. Sharon put the kids to bed, staying upstairs longer than usual to make sure both children were sleeping soundly.

Meg said very little as she cleaned up her kitchen. Kenneth knew that her way of dealing with difficulties often meant paying close attention to details such as cleaning the stove or scrubbing out the scum collected at the base of her kitchen faucets. As long as she kept her hands busy, she had often stated, she could keep her imagination in check.

"Mom," Kenneth said finally. "Can't you sit down a while?"

"Can't help it," she said. "I can't help but think of the pain that poor animal must have suffered. How could any one be so cruel?"

"Sit down, Mom," Ken said, motioning to the chair opposite his.

"Let me be a while, Ken," she said softly. "I'll be finished soon enough."

Ken shrugged and walked slowly toward the back door. He could hear the soft squeak of Mac's porch rocker.

"Well, Ken," Mac said as he approached. "Just sitting here thinking back about that old dog of mine. Pull up a seat. Can't even remember how old he was for sure. Good old dog, that one. Smart too. You know he . . ." Mac's voice broke.

Kenneth sat down without a word.

"He had a streak of meanness in him, though," Mac continued. "No one really knew it but me. Came out when he thought somebody he loved was in harm's way. Had a man try to hit me over the head with a wrench once. Before I could even turn, Old Major jumped him, knocked him to the ground. Brought blood on the poor fool's arm. Thought I shorted him on his pay check, I guess. I fired him on the spot. Gave Old Major a raise though—right then and there. He had two bones that night."

"Did you look him over?" Ken asked.

"Yeah, he was beat up pretty bad. I figure it could'a been the same bat used out in Sharon's shop. Major must have heard the ruckus. Probably mosied out to see. He could bare them sharp old teeth and make you think he could still tear a body limb from limb. Mostly bluff though. All somebody'd have to do is whistle and take the time to find out his bark was a lot worse than his bite. Gentle old dog. I'm sure gonna miss 'im." Mac wiped his nose on a red bandanna hanky pulled from his back pocket. Stuffing it back in his pants, he turned to Kenneth. "You send the boy out?"

"Nope," Ken said. Then turning his eyes to search the autumn night sky he added, "That was his own idea. I was about to come out and help you dig the hole. But then he said he was going to do it. I saw his determination and let it be. I thought the two of you might need to be together right then. I didn't want to interfere."

"Thanks, Son," Mac said. He placed a firm grip on Ken's shoulder. "Thanks."

When Sharon came out, Mac excused himself. "I'll let you kids . . . I'll say good night," he said. Then, pausing, he turned. "Glad you were here, Ken."

"Thanks, Mac," Ken said. "Me too."

"Do you have to go?" Sharon asked quietly as Kenneth embraced her.

"I'll be late as it is," he answered.

"What'll they do to you?"

"What can they do? I'm already working almost round the clock. But I'm sure they'll think of something."

"Bad?"

"It's all relative, honey. After you've been in Vietnam . . . well, let's just say it can't be all that bad."

"Did you tell your mother you were leaving?"

"In a minute," he said pulling her closer. He tenderly covered her lips with his own.

Driving the many twists and turns of the back roads through Live Oak Canyon, Kenneth almost didn't see the dark figure walking along the road. Only after his headlights reflected on the buckles of a familiar looking duffel bag did he impulsively slam on the brakes.

"Hey, buddy!" he called out the window. "Need a lift?"

"How far you goin'?" the dark-haired man asked.

"Camp Pendleton," Ken answered. "How about you?"

"Hey," the man smiled, "that'll do just fine."

"I barely got a twenty-four-hour leave. I'm pressing my limit. How about you?"

"Twenty-four hours, huh?" The man slouched in his seat and, reaching into his pocket, withdrew a pack of cigarettes. "Smoke?" he said, offering the pack to Ken.

"No thanks." Suddenly Ken thought his mind was playing tricks on him. The unkempt man had a familiar odor about him. His mind wandered to Billy Carlson. *He was high when he went out this morning,* someone told Ken when they carried Billy's body back in a bag. *He didn't feel no pain.* But Ken knew better. Billy's pain didn't come when the grenade went off at his feet but in the days of endless waiting before they went out.

"Mind if I do?" Ken's passenger asked, lighting up without waiting for Ken's answer. "I'd be walking all night if you hadn't happened along." Ken forced his mind back to this side of the ocean and the stranger sitting in his car.

"In the service?" Ken asked, wondering how long it would be before the marijuana cigarette had its effect on the man.

He answered with a nondescript shrug. "How about you?" the stranger asked.

"Marines," Ken said.

"See any action?"

"A little," Ken said.

"No kidding?"

"Vietnam. How about you?"

"Nope."

"Where you been stationed?"

"Me?" The man almost laughed. "Up north."

"Frisco?"

"Near 'bouts." His eyelids dropped heavily, and his speech was even more relaxed than when he first got in the car.

"I was thinking about putting in for the bay area myself. But I've decided not to reenlist." Ken tried to keep the conversation light and friendly. He adjusted the wind wing to scoop in as much of the fresh night air as possible. *Thank goodness it's warm enough to keep the windows down,* he thought.

"I don't blame you none." The stranger put his head back on the seat and took a slow drag on his cigarette. "Sure you don't want none?" he asked, shoving the smoldering cigarette toward Ken. Ken shook his head. "How long you been in?" the man asked.

"Ten years, this fall."

"Ten years? No kiddin'. You volunteered for ten years?"

"Yeah. How about you?" Ken kept his eye on the highway ahead.

"Two," the man said.

"Drafted then," Ken said.

"Well, I sure didn't go of my own free will," he quipped. "Hey, mind if I play the radio? I'm not much for conversation."

"Sure, go ahead," Ken said. Already sorry he had picked the man up in the first place, Ken thought the radio would be a relief.

Ken watched as dirty fingers spun the shiny radio dial first one way then the other. A dark spot between his thumb and index finger looked permanent. Ken glanced and noticed the man was obviously a habitual nail biter. His stomach lurched slightly at the thought of anyone sticking such a filthy finger in his mouth. Finally the man settled on a rock and roll station, and Ken winced as Jerry Lee Lewis's voice boomed through the speakers in the dashboard.

After a few minutes Ken noticed the man nodding from side to side. Reaching toward the radio dial, Ken paused, not wanting to disturb him, and then turned the volume knob slowly to a more tolerable level.

"Hey, buddy," Ken said an hour later. Shaking his groggy passenger gently, Ken pulled to the curb just outside the military base's gate. "This is as far as we go."

"Oh, yeah," the man said sleepily. "Much obliged."

"Where you headed?" Ken asked.

"Mexico."

"That right? What's in Mexico?" Even with his dark, wavy hair, Ken knew the stranger wasn't Mexican.

"A woman, maybe two," the man said, and Kenneth recoiled from the evil grin that spread across the stranger's face. "I'll be back, though. I'm not down there permanently."

"You're from up around Riverside, Redlands then?"

"Somewhere near there."

"You go back and forth often?"

"As often as necessary."

"Well, then, maybe I'll see you sometime," Ken said, trying to be friendly. "I drive up as often as I can."

"Yeah, sure," the man said. "I go up to see my wife and kids once in a while."

"I see." Ken tried to think of a way to end the conversation.

"Well, she doesn't," his passenger said angrily. "But then a man's got a right to see his own son, don't you think?"

"She doesn't let you see—" Kenneth didn't finish his question.

"Not yet, but she'll come around. She takes special handling, if you get my drift. So far I've just let her know I'm in town." Again the disturbing grin split his face. "But soon, she'll know more than . . . Hey, man. Thanks for the lift," he said as he stepped unsteadily from the car and hoisted his dingy bag to his shoulder. Kenneth watched the man walk away, trying to identify the sick feeling within his stomach.

The dark figure walked slowly along the road. Without even turning to face the traffic, he lifted his thumb to signal his need for a ride.

Suddenly Kenneth remembered something Jeff Bennett had said. *He's been bragging that no one will be able to keep him from being with his son.* "Dear God," Kenneth said aloud. He looked down the darkened highway just in time to see the retreating figure step into still another vehicle headed south.

CHAPTER TWENTY

*S*ir?"
Ken barely noticed the uniformed MP bending toward the window of his car.

"Excuse me, sir?" the young man repeated.

Ken glanced back toward the darkness that covered his passenger as he hitched another ride down the highway toward Mexico.

"Are you all right, lieutenant?" the MP asked.

"Oh," Ken said, yanking his attention from the incredible thoughts whirling inside his head. "I'm sorry, I . . ." his voice trailed off as a panicky nauseous feeling swept over him.

"Lieutenant Matthews, sir, are you ill?"

"I'm all right." Ken's voice was barely above a whisper.

"I'm sorry, sir, but you're five hours, thirty-seven minutes late. Are you aware of that, sir?" The young man spoke with respect.

"Yes, I'm aware."

"I don't have any choice but to file a report, sir."

"I know."

"Sir, are you sure you're all right? You look like you've seen a ghost."

"Maybe I have," Ken responded.

"You know, sir, if you had a good reason, maybe—well, you know, like a death in the family or something I could put down here."

"A death in the family," Ken repeated mechanically. His mind filled with pictures of Richie and Mac's poor dog.

"Major," Ken said softly. "File your report, officer. I'd like to pass now. I'm on duty in a few hours."

"Yes, sir," the young man said, saluting smartly. "Proceed."

After just a few hours of fitful sleep, Kenneth pulled on his work fatigues and headed out into the still dark early morning. "Three A.M.," he mumbled under his breath. "Don't even feel like eating this time of the night." But more than the early morning hour, what was robbing Kenneth of his appetite and sleep was the idea that he might have actually given Richard Potter a ride in his car. And if it wasn't Richard, Kenneth imagined it was somebody just like him. *I think I'm going to be sick,* he thought as he got in the car which still reeked of smoke and body odor.

"Jeff?" Kenneth said into the phone just before noon. "It's Ken Matthews here."

"Ken," Jeff said heartily, "what can I do for you?" Ken heard him rustling papers, then giving instructions to someone obviously standing nearby. "When are you going to be in town? Old L.B.J. keeping you plenty busy down there?"

"Too busy," Ken said. "I came home day before yesterday."

"Then you're in town! Great!" Jeff's voice was enthusiastic, and Ken sensed a genuine warmness in his voice.

"No, I'm not," Ken said. "I had a twenty-four-hour leave. I'm back on duty already."

"That's too bad," Jeff said. "We were hoping you'd make it for a weekend real soon. The girls would like to plan a get together of some kind. Let us know, will you?"

"Sure," Ken said. "But that's not why I'm calling."

"What's on your mind, Ken?" Jeff's voice became instantly serious. "Is this about Sharon?"

"In a way, I guess it is." Ken hesitated then plunged into the entire account of Major's death and Richie's harrowing experience of discovering his body.

"How awful for that little guy," Jeff said. "I bet this has hit Mac hard as well."

"It was a tough day all around." Ken rubbed his throbbing temples. "But there's more. I can't believe it myself. That's why I'm calling you." As best he could, Ken recalled the encounter of the evening before. "I tell you, when it hit me that this might well have been Potter in my car—well, I still can't believe it myself."

"Have you ever seen a picture of Potter?" Jeff asked.

"No."

"I'll see what I can do about that," Jeff said. "You know there are several warrants out for his arrest. Seems he left a trail of trouble all the way from up north. Have you touched your car since?"

"Drove it to work this morning, that's all." Ken began massaging the back of his neck, hoping a nagging headache wouldn't develop much further.

"It is locked?"

"Of course."

"Sit tight, will you? I think someone should have a look at it. Maybe we can tell if it was Potter. Did he leave anything behind that might help identify him?"

"I don't know. He wasn't the most careful person I've ever met, but I don't think so. Just a cigarette butt. It's still in my ashtray."

"You're on duty now?" Jeff said.

"Until seven tonight. We're all pulling doubles."

"How could someone find you if they came to the base?"

Ken left instructions with Jeff; they said their good-byes, and Ken returned to work. Within an hour Ken was summoned to the front of the machine shop.

"Matthews?" A man in civilian clothes stepped forward and extended his hand. "I'm Charlie Duncan with the FBI." He shoved an identification wallet toward Ken.

"FBI?"

"We're working on a federal case possibly involving someone you might have come across last night. Mind if we take a look at your car?" He motioned toward a couple of other investigators waiting outside the door.

"Help yourself," Ken said. "I'm glad to see you guys, but the FBI?" Stepping toward the door, Ken held it open for the agent.

"We'd like to dust it for prints. Would that be all right with you?"

"Fine with me. My prints are on file with the Corps."

"We know," the humorless man said. "We're getting them now."

"Looks like a perfect set here," another agent called from the passenger side of Ken's car. "The lab is sending someone over—they should be on their way."

"Ever see this man before?" Duncan asked.

"Never."

"Can you describe him?"

"Dirty, unshaven. Dark hair and eyes."

"Any scars or other identifying marks that you saw?"

"No. Well, there may have been a small cross tattooed between his thumb and index finger. His sleeves were long and his hands dirty. I'm not sure whether I saw the tattoo, or if I just wouldn't have been surprised to see one. Know what I mean? He certainly was the type."

"How was he dressed?"

"Dark clothing. Almost didn't see him at first. He was carrying a dark canvas duffel bag. That's why I picked him up. Thought he might be a soldier on leave or something."

"This duffel bag—black, olive green, what?"

"Couldn't say for sure. He tossed it in the back seat of my car, and I didn't pay any attention after that.

"Anything strange about his behavior?"

"Everything about his behavior was strange. He lit his cigarette then—well, let's just say I had to put it out in the ash tray."

"Is the butt still there?"

"Sure," Ken said.

"Keys?" the agent said, reaching his hand toward Ken, palm up.

Ken placed his keys in the man's hand and watched as the agents took a careful look inside his car.

Ken answered as many questions as he could. No, he didn't know exactly where the man was headed. Sorry, he didn't mention any names. And, yes, without a doubt, he'd know him if he saw him again.

"Hey, man," Ken said at the end of their conversation, "what's up? I mean I called Jeff Bennett's office in Redlands and within an hour the FBI is combing my car and asking all kinds of questions."

"He's your lawyer, right?"

"Bennett's my friend. He's a friend of the family."

"I'm not at liberty to discuss the case. Sorry, Matthews. What made you call Bennett about this?"

"It's my girl. She's being harassed by her ex-husband. He spent some time in prison and recently jumped parole. Ever since then, strange things have been happening around her house. After the conversation I told you about, I thought this guy might have been him. Guess I was wrong, huh?"

"Know his name?"

"Potter, Richard Potter."

"Well, Lieutenant, you might be more careful who you pick up from now on."

"It was him, wasn't it?" Ken felt his knees weaken beneath him, then a surge of anger swept through his chest and his head began throbbing again. "It was him!" he spat through clenched teeth.

"The prints will tell us the whole story. Somebody as popular as he is shouldn't go around laying his entire flat hand on a shiny fender like that." Duncan nodded toward the technician at work near the front end of Ken's car. "Even doped up, he's usually not this careless."

"I can't believe—I just hate the thought that—"

"Well, Matthews," Duncan said, "look at it this way. Tell your little lady to rest easier for a little while. We don't know where he is exactly, but at least we know he's *not* in Yucaipa at the moment. That should give her some relief, even if it is only temporary."

When Ken finally returned to work, his superior officer came to his side. "You in some kind of trouble, Matthews?"

"No, sir," Ken said respectfully. "I picked up a hitchhiker on my way in last night. Seems he's a fugitive from justice."

"No kidding," the officer said. "How'd they trace him here?"

"There was something about him that just didn't set right with me, sir. I called a lawyer friend and asked him about it. The rest you saw." Kenneth didn't want to go into the full details of his personal life.

"I received word that you reported late last night. Five and a half hours late. Is that report accurate?" The officer pulled a form from his clipboard.

"Yes, sir."

"It says something here about a death in the family?"

"Major," Ken said without thinking.

"A military man?" the officer asked.

"No, sir, the family dog."

"I see. Breed?"

"Pardon, sir?"

"What kind of dog was it, Lieutenant?"

"Shepherd, sir."

"I'm a German shepherd man myself."

"How old was he?"

"Nearly fifteen, sir."

"Good old boy. Longtime family friend then."

"Yes, sir."

"Died of old age, then?"

"No, sir. Murder."

"Excuse me?" The man looked up from the forms in his hand.

"Somebody clubbed him to death."

"Anything to do with this incident here?"

"We don't know, for sure. There could be."

The man circled "death in the family" and scribbled his initials at several appropriate places on the form.

"My condolences, Matthews."

"Thank you, sir," Ken said gratefully.

"I can't very well give you time off for a funeral. But you look like you could use some sleep. I'll sign you off until tomorrow morning at O-three hundred hours. Get some rest, soldier." He turned without waiting for Kenneth's salute, then turned back to say, "I'm really sorry to hear about the Major, Son."

"Thank you, sir," Kenneth said, staring openly after the retreating officer. Of all times to discover the military had a heart buried somewhere beneath all its inhuman policies, unwavering regulations, and endless red tape!

CHAPTER TWENTY-ONE

*W*hat time is it?" Kenneth asked sleepily.

"Did I wake you?" Jeff asked.

"Oh, no, that's all right, I had to get up to answer the phone anyway."

"I think there's something you need to know."

"Oh?"

"Richard Potter is wanted for questioning in connection with a murder in the Los Angeles area."

"No kidding?"

"Seems he's gotten mixed up with some pretty heavy-duty people over there. Undercover cops have been trying to break a drug smuggling ring for some time now. Seems some dope is making its way either from Mexico or through there. Anyway, some guy was found with a gaping hole in his stomach a week or so ago. Seems Richard Potter is connected in some way. Did you see a knife or a weapon of any sort when you picked him up?"

"Then it was him," Ken said, feeling the same nausea return. "I had a feeling it was."

"My contact in L.A. seems to be pretty sure it was him."

"Jeff, this whole thing caught me completely off guard. First there was the thing with Sharon's workshop, then Major being killed like that, then dealing with Richie most of the day—let's see, was that only yesterday? Seems like a week ago. Then I give a ride to the one person in the whole world that I'd like to see . . ." Ken was afraid to finish his sentence.

"You had quite a twenty-four-hour leave, didn't you?"

"Like no other, that's for sure."

"You tell Sharon?"

"I can't," Ken admitted. "Not yet at least. I have to give it some more time to sink in first. I know she'd feel better if she knew he was out of town."

"I'll call her."

"Don't tell her, about, well, you know. I'm not sure I want her hearing that from anybody but me."

"Sure thing. I'll just tell her we have good reason to believe he was headed for Mexico."

"Make her believe it, Jeff. I don't think any of us realize how much terror she lives with on a daily basis."

"So, Matthews, tell me—are your intentions toward our lovely blond friend honorable?"

"Most certainly. But I don't want to rush her. She's got an awful lot to deal with until this Richard Potter thing is completely behind her. I get out in a few weeks, then I plan to court her in a very old-fashioned way."

"With Jack McKenzie watching your every move."

"He may be more of a challenge than Potter!" Ken said jokingly.

"Did you know James and Sarah moved their things up to the ranch today?"

"Already?"

"With this latest thing, James thought they shouldn't wait. He's really a stable man. Just having him on the ranch will bring peace of mind to everyone."

"How long are they planning to stay?"

"When did you say you'd be discharged?"

"The paperwork's being processed now. It's a day and a half project—let's see, in military time, that means a month or six weeks minimum."

"Well, it's my guess that's about how long they'll be staying then. They're having a little work done on their house while they're up there, but it's not more than a few weeks' worth. I think we've got things covered for a while anyway. This weekend Dan Miller plans on moving the rest of Sharon's inventory to a back room at his store. James will begin repairing the shop door just as soon as he can."

"She's a remarkable young woman, isn't she?"

"That she is," Jeff said. "I'm glad you noticed."

After a few more pleasantries the two men ended the conversation. Kenneth understood that Jeff was offering not only a gesture of friendship, but approval of his relationship with Sharon. Leaving the military and going to Yucaipa were beginning to feel more and more like going home and to Sharon and the kids.

Ken lay back down on his bed and turned out the lights. Letting his mind drift, he thought of her. As he rubbed his temples, he discovered that his headache was completely gone. He wondered what she was doing at that very moment.

"Thanks for calling, Jeff," Sharon said as she turned to face the puzzled expressions on Meg and Mac's faces.

"What was that all about?" Mac insisted.

"Mac," Meg warned, "Sharon will tell us if it's any of our business." Then Meg turned to Sharon. "Well, dear? Is it any of our business?"

Sharon tried to identify the sudden surge of laughter that rose unexpectedly in her chest. "Richard has been seen heading for Mexico," she said. "I can't tell you how relieved I am."

"Are you sure?" Mac asked.

"Jeff talked to somebody who saw him. He's pretty sure it was Richard. Seems the police are after him for something or other, Jeff didn't say. But they picked up his fingerprints on some car they found down there. A witness saw him get into another and head down the highway to Tijuana. At least for now, we can breathe a little easier." She didn't need to explain the tears that blurred her vision.

"For now," Mac grumbled. "But he'll be back. We both know that. It's just so irritating that a man can come in here and do what he did and then just catch a ride to Tijuana like nothing ever happened."

"But," Meg interrupted, trying to add a positive note to the conversation, "at least we have this time to put things back together again—for Richie's poor little heart to mend a little."

"He's having bad dreams again," Sharon said. The fresh memory of Richie's fitful night dampened her spirits. "I thought that was over."

"Oh, my dear," Meg said. "That poor child. What can we do to help?"

"Nothing, really," Sharon said gratefully. "He cries for Major. He loved that old dog and to find him like that . . ."

"No use going' over it again," Mac said, wiping at a moist eye with the back of his hand. "He's gone and nothin' will bring him back again."

"Sharon," Meg said standing by the kitchen sink. "Look over there, dear."

Sharon looked in the direction Meg was indicating. There in her small house, lights were shining at every window.

"See how friendly and warm your little place looks when there's life inside. That's the way it looks to Mac and me when you're over there. Feels good to know James and Sarah are on the place, doesn't it, Mac?"

"Guess so," Mac grudgingly admitted before going in the living room to watch the news.

"How do you stand him?" Sharon asked with exaggerated disgust.

"Stand him?" Meg asked innocently. "I love him."

"You'd have to," Sharon said.

"That's what I told the Lord before I married him. I said that if I didn't love him enough to stand him day in and day out, I needed to know before it was too late."

"And?"

"I fell more madly in love in those few weeks after praying that prayer than I had already." Meg laughed. "I get mad at him sometimes. But all in all, I don't know what I'd do without him."

"And I don't know what we'd do without you, Auntie Meg."

"Think you'll ever call me anything else?" Meg asked shyly.

"What did you have in mind?" Sharon teased.

"I know I could never take the place of your own mother," Meg started. "But then, I wouldn't even try. But you know, Sharon, if you and Kenneth . . ."

"If Kenneth and I ever—well, we'll let you know in plenty of time, Grandma McKenzie." Sharon laughed more freely than she had in months.

"We'll negotiate the name, okay?"

"Maybe." Sharon threw her arms around the older woman in a tight embrace. "And maybe not."

CHAPTER TWENTY-TWO

*W*ith her inventory safely moved to Miller's Home Furnishings in Redlands, Sharon set about helping James install a new door frame and hang a new, stronger door in her workshop. Afterward, James installed a dead bolt then checked over her kiln for damage. When he was satisfied that her workshop was secure, he left her to clean and arrange her work space while he put in the necessary wiring for better outside lighting.

Except for Mac, the entire family seemed to adjust to having the Jenkinses' company and help around the ranch. Finally when James agreed to let Mac have a hand in installing the subflooring in his house in Redlands, Mac's mood began to lighten.

"He sure misses that old dog of his," Meg told Sharon and Sarah one afternoon.

"He ought to get another one," Sharon said.

"That's what I told him," Meg said. "But it wouldn't be the same. He knew old Major wasn't going to last much longer. But when it ended this way—well, it's too terrible to even think about."

"He'll come around," Sarah said. "Time and patience."

Jen called several times each week to chat with Sharon about the children, her workshop, and the growing interest in her work. As fast as Sharon could complete a few pieces, James or Mac carted them down to Miller's.

But, it was Ken's calls that Sharon looked forward to receiving almost every evening just before ten. His work shifts had been shortened to twelve hours, and working from seven in the morning until seven in the evening suited them both just fine. It helped the time move a little faster for Ken and took the worry off Sharon that he might be working too hard. Working seven days a week hadn't allowed him another visit, but they both looked forward to the day of his discharge.

School seemed to be the distraction Richie needed to keep his mind occupied most of the day. Even so, the teacher's most recent note inquired about his frequent dark moods.

Frannie, however, was as bubbly and bright as ever. Somehow in all the noise and confusion, she had escaped seeing the old dog or understanding exactly what had happened. School for her meant making new friends, wearing new clothes, and picking up a new attitude of independence.

"Not for you," Meg said to Mac one night after Richie had cried himself to sleep again, "for him."

"I said I'd think about it, and I will!" Mac said gruffly before switching off the light and turning his back to his wife. But Mac knew Meg was right, and he had already given it some thought. He'd make some inquiries tomorrow, he decided. It wouldn't be easy, but he'd do it for the boy. *And,* he admitted to himself, *because it will please you, my precious wife.*

"I love you, Jack McKenzie," he heard her whisper before she kissed him on the shoulder. "I married myself a fine man, I did."

Mac felt the tension and resistance drain from his body. "You married an oaf," he said aloud into the dark room.

"But I do love you, Margaret. It scares me to think how much."

"Why is your back to me, then?" she teased.

Before long, James set about making cabinet doors to replace the cotton curtains hanging on the cupboards in Sharon's kitchen. He was a master at finding odd jobs to do while everyone else was occupied elsewhere.

Sharon spent the very early morning hours at her wheel, loading and unloading her kiln. She was back in the main house in time to kiss her children good-bye and walk them to the bus stop.

Richie protested that he was old enough to make it without her escort, but Sharon overruled his objection with an offhand comment that belied her fear that while Richard was away at the present he might return any moment. She needed to see her children safely on the bus and know that they were under adult supervision until they came home.

The favorite time of Sharon's day was when Meg and Sarah would poor fresh coffee, cut a freshly baked coffee cake, and open their Bibles together for their morning study and prayer time. Early on they had invited Sharon to join them and she eagerly accepted.

"Sharon, Meg," Sarah said thoughtfully, "I came across this passage of Scripture the other day and it seemed to be so familiar I just, well, you know, breezed right on by. But then something caught my attention and I read it again. Here, let me read it to you," she said. "It's right here as plain as the nose on my face, 'Then shall the righteous answer him, saying, when saw we thee ahungered, and fed thee? Or thirsty, and gave thee drink? When saw we thee a stranger, and took thee in? Or naked and clothed thee? Or when saw we thee sick, or in prison, and came unto thee? And the King shall answer and say to them, Verily I say unto you, Inasmuch as ye have done it unto one of the least of these my brethren, ye have done it unto me.'" Sarah closed her Bible and looked at the two women across the table. "That was Matthew, the twenty-fifth chapter. But my thoughts are these: I was captivated by the words, 'inasmuch as ye have done it unto the least of one of these, my brethren, ye have done it unto me.' I can't help but think that when someone does one of God's children harm, he's touching not only one of God's children, but God himself. I can't help but pity poor Mr. Potter."

"Pity him?" Meg controlled the anger Sharon saw snapping in her eyes. "Pity *him?*"

"That poor old fool has no idea who he's messing with," Sarah said matter-of-factly. "God's been patient with him so far, but you know I have a feeling that patience is about worn out. He's not going to let that man go on harming us forever. And when the mighty hand of God moves, whatever he has done to you and the children, Sharon, will pale in comparison. Now that's only my opinion, mind you. But these days I've been holding this verse up to God, sort of like a reminder. All I've been telling God is that one of his little children is being troubled. And I've gotten pretty brave in my old age. I've asked God to bring a swift and sure justice."

"Can we do that?" Sharon asked, her eyes glistening and wide. "I mean, can we actually ask God to do something so specific?"

"Oh, honey," Meg laughed, "the Bible also says right here—I underlined it so I could find it easier—'Be careful for nothing; but in every thing by prayer and supplication with thanksgiving let your requests be made known unto God.'"

"Where is that?" Sharon said, trying to see Meg's Bible.

"Philippians 4:6," Meg said, turning her Bible so that Sharon could see it better.

"Is it all right to write in your Bible?"

"You bet it is," Sarah said, fanning the pages of her old worn volume. "My Bible is so marked up it doesn't make any sense to anyone but me. Except, of course, the Lord. He's made me so many promises from this old book, I'd have a hard time keeping track of them all if I didn't mark 'em."

"So then, I can ask God, specifically—I mean really spell it out—what I want from Him."

"And we'll agree," Sarah laughed.

"Agree?" Sharon asked.

"We'll study that another day," Meg said, joining Sarah's laughter. "But for now, let us just say that when we are in agreement, the request is in God's will, and you pray in faith, we'll see some changes in the situation. No doubt about that, is there, Sarah?"

"I sense the Lord's presence with us," Sarah said. "I think we should stop jabberin' about prayer and start praying!" She bowed her head and closed her eyes. "Dear Lord," she began softly, "I know you are here with us, for your precious word promises us that when two or three of us meet together in your name, you are here too. So, precious Savior, here we are. And we've got something specific to ask, something impossible to us, but possible for you. We lift Sharon and her wonderful little children to you right now. You know the trouble she's been having lately."

"Yes, Lord," Meg said from across the table.

"We ask in the name of Jesus that something be done."

"Something permanent," Sharon whispered.

"What was that, dear?" Meg asked. "Go ahead, pray right out loud. Sarah and I are here, too. Tell the Lord what it is you want."

Sharon squirmed slightly in her chair. "Dear Jesus, I need you to do something once and for all to let the children and me be free of Richard's abuse and mistreatment. I'm not asking so much for me—I made the mistake of marrying him—but none of this is the fault of my children. Please, Lord," she said as tears flowed freely down her cheeks. "Please, Lord, forgive me for marrying him, and please, God, help me get him out of my life for good."

"And, Father," Sarah joined in, "just as you sent Moses to lead your children out of bondage, we pray now for a deliverer for Sharon. In Jesus' name we pray, Amen."

"Amen!" Meg added enthusiastically. "Amen!"

"Word has it he's back," Jeff told Dan and Jen one evening while playing cards. "I got the call just before I left the office this evening."

"No kidding?" Jen's face revealed how she felt.

"No kidding." Jeff laid his cards down on the table and reached for Cari's hand. "Don't worry, honey. So far he hasn't even made a move toward you or the kids. He'd much rather prey on Sharon. He's not really interested in tangling with us again."

"When will Kenneth be home?" Dan asked.

"I'd certainly feel better if I knew he was on the ranch. But I haven't heard lately. Thought I'd give him a call later tonight. Last I knew he was expecting the paperwork to come through any day. With Johnson's escalation of the war—"

"Conflict," Dan interrupted.

"Pardon me?"

"We're not at war, haven't you heard? We're only in a 'conflict'."

"Whatever they choose to call it, it's really put everything in an upheaval. I have a feeling there are more guys like Kenneth who thought they'd be in for as long as the military would have them but now would just as soon return to civilian life."

"Is he—well, how do I put this? Is he running away just when his country needs him most?" Dan asked.

"He's been there twice," Jen said. "I think that's plenty of time to spend in a nonwar war, don't you?"

"Besides," Cari joined in, "we have our own little domestic conflict going on right here. I think the lieutenant is needed on the homefront."

"Uh-oh," Dan said, laughing. "I smell a conspiracy."

"Not at all!" Jen protested. "But why go half way around the world to fight for our country, when you could battle for something as wonderful as a wife and a family right here on home territory?"

"Does this make sense to you?" Jeff asked Dan good-naturedly.

"Of course," he said with exaggerated seriousness. "Besides, if we don't agree, we'll be in a war zone ourselves."

"So what are they doing about it?" Cari asked.

"The fact that he's back?" Jeff asked. Cari nodded. "What can they do? Wait, I guess. I don't know that the police or even the FBI have even spotted him. Who knows, it may just be rumor."

"I hate him," Cari said angrily. "I know I'm not supposed to, but I can't help it. I forgave him for what he did to me, but for heaven's sake, he never stops hurting Sharon and her kids. You saw them, all of you—aren't they a wonderful little family?"

"Yes, honey," Jeff said, patting his wife's arm, "they are indeed. And, we'll have to continue to love and pray for them everyday just as we have been. God's got to be in charge here, Cari, not us. He's bigger and more powerful than all of us combined—even with the help of the FBI. If we know things can't continue going on like this, we can be assured so does He."

"Makes trusting God a whole new concept, doesn't it?" Jen asked.

"Tests our faith, that's for sure," Dan agreed.

"And poor Sharon!" Cari said. "If it's hard for us, think how it is for her."

"Does she know?" Dan asked.

"Not yet," Jeff said. "I wanted to talk to Ken first."

"Oops," Jen said, hiding the bottom half of her face behind her cards. "Could this be a conspiracy I smell here?"

Jeff's smile mischievously pulled one side of his mouth into a boyish grin. "He made me swear to call him first—I had nothing to do with it."

"I bet," Jen chided. "Jeff Bennett, always the innocent one."

CHAPTER TWENTY-THREE

*A*s soon as he finished talking to Jeff Bennett, Kenneth looked at his watch. Barely three-thirty. He quickly dialed the number to the CO's office for an appointment. He needed some answers, and perhaps a favor or two.

On his way to see the CO he recalled the conversation with Jeff. *He's back,* Jeff had said. Kenneth's insides tightened as he thought of the implication this information had for Sharon. *Does she know yet?* Ken glanced at his watch. Jeff and Cari would be at the ranch by now.

Ken slowed his car and eased it into a parking spot a few spaces from his destination. *Dear Lord,* he prayed silently, *please protect Sharon. Give her the courage and strength she will need until this is over. And,* he added as he got out of his car, *let it be over soon.*

Walking into his commanding officer's office, Ken resolved to get some answers about his discharge.

"You know these things are out of my control," the older man said when Ken addressed the issue head-on.

"I know, sir, but I thought you might be able to track it down and see where I stand. I was scheduled for discharge in December and promised an early out if I stayed on in Vietnam."

"I'm aware of that, lieutenant," the man snapped. "But things have changed, you know that."

"There's a situation at home, sir," Kenneth said respectfully. "I need some news about my discharge. Have you had any information?"

"What's the problem, Matthews?"

"I want to go home, sir."

"So do a few hundred thousand other soldiers."

"I've been in ten years, sir."

"So what's your hurry? A month or two either way—"

"I want to get married, sir."

"Well," the man said, a smile spreading across his face. "Well then, Marine, congratulations. But why not stay in the Corps, Matthews? You've already been stationed overseas. You could end up on this post with a good steady job, serving your country as well. A Marine's life is a good one. Ask my wife," he said confidently.

Kenneth hesitated, not wanting to be rude.

"Well, Lieutenant, you have something to say?"

"Yes, sir," Ken said knowing he shouldn't.

"Then say it."

"Which one, sir?"

"Which one, what, soldier?"

"Which wife?" Ken relaxed his stance a bit and looked directly into the officer's penetrating gaze. "I'm sorry, sir, but if what I have heard is true, a Marine's life may be a good one, but it's not always so good for his wife."

Kenneth thought he saw the hint of a pained expression cross the older man's face. He hoped he hadn't pushed too far.

"You're definite about this, Matthews?" the man asked sternly.

"Yes, sir," Kenneth said. *And I told you so the last time we met,* he wanted to add.

"You've thought this through? A change of career, not just some girl at home who can't stand the thought of being a military wife?"

"I've thought it through," Ken said.

"Well then, if you're sure there's nothing I can say to change your mind, I'll go ahead and sign the paperwork and send it back through channels. You'll hear something definite within a few weeks."

"Will all due respect, sir," Ken said carefully, "it's October. I was promised a few months in return for an extended tour in Vietnam. I'm hoping the Marine Corps will make good on its word, sir."

"I'll see what I can do, Ken." The man's tone was surprisingly humane. "In the meantime, would a weekend pass help?"

"Somewhat," Ken said.

"How about if I arrange for a change in your work schedule to let you off by noon Friday and then switch you to graveyard on Monday. That would not require you to return to the base until twenty-three hundred hours on Monday."

"Thank you, sir."

"Is there anything else?"

"May I check back with you next week, sir?"

"That won't be necessary, Matthews. I'll make a note on my calendar. You'll be hearing from me. You have my word on it," he said, extending his hand toward Kenneth. "I like you, Matthews," the man said quietly and with well-trained decorum. "I always have. I recognize the military is losing a good man when you leave us. I had hoped your decision would be different. But then, we really can't expect much more from a man than he spend three tours, and two of those in a conflict area." The man walked toward the window and stared out into the street. "I'll see what I can do."

"Thank you, sir," Ken said, taking the man's hand in a firm grip. "I appreciate it, sir."

With a quick salute, Ken turned and walked from the meeting. "Where's a phone I can use?" he asked the corpsman at the desk.

"Around the corner, sir," the young man replied as he indicated the direction.

"Hi," Ken said when he heard Sharon's voice on the other end of the line.

"Hello," she said. Ken could tell by her tone she had already heard the news of Richard's reappearance.

"I'm coming home Friday," he said. "After I get off duty."

"Oh, Ken, that makes me feel better. Even with James and Sarah here, it's nerve-wracking to know he's back."

"I know, honey. But didn't Mac get a night watchman again?"

"He did. He also added someone to be here during the day. The only time we don't have a guard at the front drive is during the evening when James and Mac are both home. Honestly, Kenneth," she said softly, "it's beginning to feel like a fortress here."

"How are the kids?" he asked. As sorry as he was that she was feeling penned in, Ken was glad she was being protected.

"They're fine."

"Do they have any idea what's happening?"

"I don't think Frannie does," she said. "But it's hard to tell with Richie. He's so quiet. He's keeping a lot to himself, I think. And he's started having bad dreams again."

"Again?"

"He hasn't had them for a long time," Sharon said. "It was really bad for a while, until we came to live here with Uncle Mac close by. But even having him right downstairs doesn't seem to help right now."

"He knows something's up," Ken said. "I wonder if we should tell him. You know, come right out with it all and then tell him we're protecting him and the family as best we can."

"We have to do something," Sharon said. "He's afraid for Frannie to go out and play. And, he hasn't been back out front under the tree since . . ."

"I don't blame him," Ken said. "I don't think I would either."

"It was his favorite place. He called it his secret fort."

"Somehow we have to find a way to let him have it back," Ken said.

Sharon was silent for a moment. "Ken?" she said finally.

"Yes?"

"When you say *we*, I want to understand what you mean."

"I mean we, Sharon, you and me." Ken didn't want to ask her to marry him just yet—and certainly not on the phone. On the other hand, he wanted her to be able to depend on how he felt about her and the children.

"Oh," she said simply.

"Sharon, someday really soon, you and I are going to have a very serious conversation about our relationship. I'm in your life, Sharon. I don't see myself as being out of it any time very soon, if ever. Please, depend on that, will you?"

"I want to," she said.

"Good," he said, wishing he could take her in his arms and get it settled once and for all. "I love you, honey," he said. "And, I love the kids. Will you try to get used to that idea?"

"I'll do my best," she said. Ken could almost see her bright smile.

"Until I get there, please, please promise me you won't take any unnecessary chances with . . . well, just promise me you'll be extra careful, okay?"

"Okay."

"Have you made arrangements with the school?"

"The school?"

"Do they know to be careful with Richie and Frannie?"

"Jeff said we needed to do that," she paused. "I'll go up tomorrow and talk to the principal."

"Don't go alone," Ken said.

"I won't," she returned. "Jeff said he'd go with me."

"That's good."

"What time will you be home on Friday?"

"Just as soon as I can get away after my shift." He didn't tell her his shift had been changed. "Not one minute later than absolutely the soonest minute I can get there."

"Then you be careful," she said. "I couldn't bear the thought of anything happening to you."

"Then don't even think about it," he said, dropping his voice to a low whisper. "Just think of being right there when I get home. I want to think of you waiting for me."

"I am already," she said. Ken felt his heart beating faster. "I'd better go, now. Your mom is calling supper."

"I love you," Ken said.

"I know," she answered. "I'm glad."

Ken reluctantly hung up the phone, wishing he had heard her say the same words. But he had the assurance of the Lord's leading him toward home and Sharon and the children. "You'll say it soon," he said to the receiver where he had heard her voice only moments before.

On Friday Kenneth managed to get home just as the family was sitting down to supper. Sharon's heart jumped to life, and without thinking she flew into his arms. Frannie leaped off her chair and hugged Ken's leg. Sarah and Meg quickly moved to set another place while James retrieved an additional chair from the dining room. Mac and Richie sat quietly.

"You made good time, son," James said as soon as the commotion would allow. "We didn't expect you until later."

"I was all prepared to keep your supper warm in the oven," Meg said.

Ken held Sharon's chair with one hand while she sat down and he scooped a squealing Frannie up into a big hug with the other.

"We were just about to ask the blessing here, Ken," Mac said without emotion. "Maybe you'd like to put that young lady in her place and sit down." He motioned toward Kenneth's place, hastily set next to Sharon.

"Oh, sure, I'm sorry, Mac," Ken said, dropping Frannie into her chair from behind and quickly sitting.

"James," Mac said, "would you return thanks?"

"Dear Father," James began. "Your mighty works and wondrous blessings toward us never stop. How can we ever thank you for all you do for us? The rich and wonderful food you provide for our bodies, the friends and family you have given that enrich our very souls. Truly, dear Lord," he said with emotion straining his voice, "you are much too good to us. Please, please don't stop now," he said with a genuine friendly tone to his voice. "We appreciate all you do for us, and we thank you in Jesus' name, Amen."

"Amen!" Meg echoed enthusiastically.

Amid happy chatter and with Ken by her side, Sharon thought she'd burst with happiness. She stared at her empty plate, a smile spreading her full lips.

"What are you thinking about?" Ken whispered.

"Us," she said quietly.

"Good," he said, dumping a large portion of Meg's tamale pie on her plate. "Just hold that thought."

"I will," she said, smiling up at him.

"Sharon," Mac growled, "do you mind passing that casserole this way?"

After supper, Sharon offered to do dishes and Ken enthusiastically offered to help while Richie complained that he needed help with schoolwork.

"I'll give you a hand there, little guy," James offered.

"I want Kenny." Richie's mouth puckered into a pout.

"Well, Ken," James laughed, "seems you're the most wanted guy in the house tonight."

"Excuse me," Mac said bluntly, scooting his chair back noisily over the kitchen floor. "I'll catch the news."

As soon as Meg, Sarah, and James left, Ken pulled Sharon to her feet, then into his arms, and kissed her in full view of the children. Frannie hid her mouth behind her hand, stifling a high-pitched giggle. Richie moaned and put his head on his arms on the table. "Mush!" His muffled muttering barely reached Sharon's ears.

"Is not!" Frannie yelled, hitting her brother on the head with her spoon.

"Ow!" Richie hollered. "Stop it!"

"You take it back!" Frannie screamed.

"No!" Richie yelled. "Mush, mush, mush!"

"That's enough!" Sharon corrected firmly. "Frannie, don't hit your brother. Richie, don't tease her."

"Hey, big guy. Where's that schoolwork? Let's get to it, shall we?"

"What about the dishes?" Sharon pouted.

"I'll help you, Mommy," Frannie offered cheerfully.

"See?" Ken said, holding out his hand in mock surrender. "I've been replaced. Hurry up, Richie," he said. Sharon noticed his eyes twinkling with triumph. "We'd better get to it."

Sharon turned her attention to the small, curly-haired blond looking up at her. "Can I wash?" Frannie asked. "I'm a big girl now. I can wash, can't I, Kenneth?" Frannie turned from her mother, obviously hoping to get him to override the expected objection.

"Better not," Ken said. "I don't think I like little girls with dishpan hands," he said teasingly.

"But what about Mommy?" Frannie asked innocently. "What if she gets dishpan hands?"

"I said I didn't like *little* girls with dishpan hands. Mommy's a big girl."

"Ain't I a big girl?"

"No, missy, you're not. But you know what I do like?" Sharon turned to hear what Ken was about to propose to Frannie. "I like little girls who know how to stand on the kitchen stool without falling, and who wipe the silverware and put it in the right places in the drawer."

"I can do that," Frannie asserted.

"Without help from anyone?" Ken teased.

"All by myself." She tossed her curly head and squared her shoulders confidently.

"Oh, brother," Ken said to Sharon. "Have we a challenge ahead of us with this one."

"Are you going to wrap around her little finger, like Uncle Mac does?" Richie said.

"Richie!" Sharon scolded.

"Well, that's what Auntie Meg said. She said Uncle Mac—"

"I know what Auntie Meg said," Sharon interrupted. "But I don't think Ken—"

"Probably," Ken said, winking at Richie. "But I'll let you in on a little secret sometime, Richie. It's about women and that little finger stuff. We'll talk about it when there are no girls to hear what I'm going to say. I'd say we need a guys' hangout."

"Hangout?" Richie said. "What's a hangout?"

"A secret place. Someplace where girls aren't allowed to come unless we invite them. Think we could find a place like that?"

"Sure!" Richie said enthusiastically. Then pain clouded his usually clear eyes, and they glistened under the kitchen light. "No, I guess not."

"Hey," Ken said, placing his hand on the shoulder of the small boy, "I bet you and I could find a neat place. Let's think a minute."

"Under the tree," Frannie said from her perch on the kitchen stool.

"No!" Richie cried. "Stop it! Mommy make her stop it."

"He's talking to Richie, honey," Sharon told Frannie. "It's not polite to butt in to other people's conversations."

"But it's true, Mommy." Frannie lowered her voice to a loud whisper and leaned toward her mother. "He always went to the tree."

"Mommy," Richie pleaded, "make her stop."

"Richie," Ken said quietly, "don't you go to the tree anymore?"

"No," Richie said, dropping his sad eyes to the flash card in his hand. "Not since . . ."

"Since Major?" Ken asked gently.

"Somebody killed him, right there in our secret place." Richie's eyes brimmed with tears.

"I don't think so," Ken said, occupying his hands with the various cards on the table.

"But you saw him yourself. He was dead, Kenny." Richie was openly crying now. "You saw the blood and everything."

"Yuck!" Frannie said disgustedly.

"Frannie," Sharon warned, "are you being polite?"

"Well, I can hear everything, Mommy."

"Mind your own business, Frances." Sharon's voice was warm, but firm.

"I don't think he was killed there, son," Ken said. Sharon's heart warmed hearing Ken refer to him that way. "I know he died there. But you see," Ken said, rubbing his chin and staring at the ceiling for a moment before continuing, "I don't think that whoever did that to him followed him to the tree. I think they thought he was already dead out there by your mama's workshop. But Old Major, he wasn't dead. No sir, he only pretended to be dead. Then, when no one was looking, he decided he was hurt too bad, probably would die anyway, but he wasn't going to let anybody keep him from dying in his favorite place. He was like an old soldier, Richie—you might be able to knock him down, you might even be able to strike a mortal wound—"

"What's a mortal wound?" Frannie whispered to her mother.

"Frances," Sharon said in a tone that Frannie knew meant business.

"Like I said," Ken began again, "you might be able to strike a mortal wound—you know, hit somebody so hard they'd die—but when it comes to old soldiers like Major there, well, he'd pick the place he'd die."

"Do you think anyone saw him go there?" Richie asked, his eyes wide with eager anticipation of Ken's answer.

"Old Major was a lot smarter than to let anybody see him go there," he said. "He knew that was your spot too. He wasn't going to let someone else know where it was. No siree—" Ken lowered his voice and his face to Richie's nose to nose. "I bet he waited until he knew the coast was clear, see? Then, when he knew he'd not lead anyone who shouldn't know where your secret spot was, he went there to die in peace. In his favorite spot. Thinking of you. He probably knew you'd be the one to find him even. He didn't know how messy his face was. Otherwise he might have done differently."

"Dogs don't know everything," Richie said seriously.

"Exactly. All that was smart enough, don't you think?"

"Yeah, smart enough for an old dog. I miss him," Richie said tearfully.

"I'm sure you do," Ken said, surrounding the grieving boy with his arms, then pulling him into his lap. Richie snuggled into Ken's body, and Sharon could see only his dark hair over Ken's shoulder.

"Well, Rich," Ken said, "know what I think?"

Richie shook his head.

"I think that if Old Major would have thought you wouldn't go back there anymore, he would have picked another place to die. But I think an old soldier like Major should be able to die where he chooses. What do you think?"

"Can I go back there tomorrow?" Richie asked sitting up and staring deeply into Ken's compassion-filled eyes. Sharon tried to hold back her own tears. Frannie dropped knives, forks, and spoons noisily into their proper places.

"Sure thing," Ken said.

"Will you go with me?" the boy asked.

"I'd be honored," Ken said.

"You were pretty convincing in there," Sharon said after the kids were in bed and she and Ken settled on the back porch.

"My mama taught me you never have to convince anyone of the truth," he said with a grin as he reached for her hand and tucked it in his.

"Are you trying to tell me you believed all that?"

"Every word," he said, smiling.

"Right," she said.

"Even Mac agrees with me."

"I find that hard to believe."

"That he'd agree with me?"

"On anything," she said. A frown creased her forehead.

"Well, it's true," Ken said. "We noticed that there were no marks indicating that the poor old dog had been dragged there. We have no idea how long—"

"Don't think about it, then," she said. She didn't want any troubling thought to cross the mind of the man she considered no less than a miraculous addition to her life. "Let's not think about anything unpleasant, okay?"

"Okay with me," Ken said. "We don't have to say a word if you don't want to."

"Only one," she said, hoping Ken wouldn't see her blush in the dim light of the October evening.

"What's that?"

"*We,*" she said nervously, "It's become my favorite word in the whole world."

"Enjoy it," Ken said.

"I am," she said.

"I won't be rushed, sweetheart, I won't be rushed." Sharon's protest was smothered by his kiss.

"Mac?" Meg said softly into the darkness of their bedroom.

"Hmm?" he answered.

"Have you made up your mind what to do about Richie?"

"Yeah," he said.

"And?"

"I'll take care of it," Mac said.

"When?"

"Tomorrow," he answered. "Now let me sleep. I'm bushed."

"Go right ahead," Meg whispered and kissed her husband on the shoulder.

"Then let me be," he said. "And stop kissin' me like that."

"You gonna make me stop?" she whispered.

"No." Mac turned over to face his wife and pulled her tight against him. "You are the most frustratin' woman on the face of the earth," he said hoarsely.

"I know," she said. "I love you too."

CHAPTER TWENTY-FOUR

*E*arly Saturday morning, Ken opted to leave Sharon alone in her shop while she worked on a piece already sold to Mr. Jepson. Instead, he climbed the stairs to the guest room and gently shook Richie.

"Shh!" Ken put his finger across his lips to keep the small boy as quiet as possible. He pointed at sleeping Frannie, and Richie nodded in agreement.

"Where are we going?" Richie asked when they reached the main floor.

"First, you need some breakfast. Then we've got business outside. Come on, now, what shall we eat?"

"Auntie Meg always makes oatmeal," Richie said. "But I don't like it very much."

"Me either." Ken rummaged around in the cupboard and found a box of Cheerios.

"Can I have two spoons of sugar?" Richie asked.

"What does your mother let you have?"

"One," Richie said in a defeated tone.

"Okay," Ken said. "You put on one and I'll put on one."

"Neato," Richie said, perking up.

"But just this once."

After they ate their cereal, Ken took Richie by the hand and walked him toward the kitchen door. "Now, young man, I think we need to make a memorial to Old Major. You know, a special marker to put in the spot where he died."

"A what?"

"A memorial. I saw one once in Gettysburg. That's back east. A famous soldier fell and died in a war and they put a special marker right on the spot."

"No kidding?"

"People come from all over the world just to visit the place where he died. I thought we could do something like that for Major."

"Uncle Mac already put a big rock on the grave out back."

"That's a grave marker. I'm talking about a memorial."

"Oh," Richie said. "What's it look like?"

"You'll see," Ken said. He led Richie toward the tool shed. "We'll think of something really special."

"What's going on?" Sharon asked, walking toward them. Intent on their project, Ken didn't see her coming.

"Oh, good morning," he said.

"We're making a memo—what's it called again?"

"A memorial," Ken said.

"To Major," Richie added proudly. "We're going to put it where he died. Want to come?"

"No," Sharon said, "you go on. Sounds like something for men only."

"You're right," Ken said. "See you later?"

"I'll be inside."

"Half an hour," Ken winked. "I haven't had my coffee yet."

"Is that an order, Lieutenant?"

"A request, ma'am."

"Let's go, Kenny," Richie pulled at his arm. "Don't mush with her again."

Richie pulled back the long graceful wisps of willow branches and crawled between them. "It's in here," Richie whispered reverently as if he were entering a chapel.

"Let's see," Ken whispered back. "Can you remember where he was when you found him?"

"Sure," Richie said. "Right here." Inside, near the trunk, Richie was able to stand up. Mac had cleared the lowest branches away, hollowing out a green cave.

"Where are the rocks?"

"Here," Richie said, producing the tin can.

"Okay, stack them up carefully. There, put them in a circle like this first," Ken instructed. "That's right."

"Now his bone, right here on top?" Richie asked in a low, quiet voice.

"Wait!" Ken had a sudden thought. "First we'll say a few words of tribute."

"Tribute?"

"You know, about how good Major was and all."

"Good old Major," Richie said respectfully. "He always liked to play with me, or just sleep here by me when I came in here to hide from everything."

"In tribute to an old faithful friend and companion, Old Major. May he rest in peace," Ken said dramatically. "A hero fallen in the line of duty."

"And died in his favorite place," Richie said.

"Let these stones forever mark the place," Ken added.

"And his bone," Richie said, ceremoniously adding it to the top.

"We salute you, Major," Ken said, placing his hand across his heart.

"Salute," Richie said, mimicking Ken's motion.

Ken looked at the solemn boy now grown suddenly silent and still. He knew he was crying. "We'll miss you forever," Ken said hoarsely.

"Forever," Richie whispered.

"You'll come back here and remember him, won't you, Rich?"

"Can I?"

"It's your special place, isn't it?"

"Yeah."

"Then whenever you miss Old Major, you can come right out here to this place. A memorial is a place where we can come and remember the one who's memorialized."

"Uncle Mac goes out to the grave," Richie said.

"Do you?"

"No—I don't want to."

"Then you don't have to," Kenneth said.

"I'll come here, though."

"That'll be good."

"I used to talk to Major. Now I'll just talk to the rocks."

"That's okay." Ken smiled down at the small boy sitting next to him in the dirt. "Whenever you want."

"Okay, I will," Richie said, wiping his eyes on the backs of his hands.

"Hey, listen," Ken said. "Is Mac calling you?"

Scurrying out of the willow shaded spot, Richie ran in the direction of Mac's voice.

"Come here, Richie, I want to show you something," Mac said gruffly.

Ken followed at a distance, curious what Mac had in the large box by the back door.

"Oh, Uncle Mac!" Richie said, jumping backwards when he opened the flap. "Kenny! Come here!"

"Go ahead, boy, take him out," Uncle Mac said. "He's sure anxious to get out and run around a bit."

"Can I have him?"

"He's all yours," Mac said. Ken noticed the first smile on Mac's face since Major's death.

Once lifted from the box, the exuberant puppy ran circles around the boy, wagging his tail enthusiastically.

"Great idea, Mac," Ken said, coming up behind the older man.

"It was your mother's idea," Mac said. "She can be pretty persuasive at times."

"Where'd you find him?" Ken asked.

"Local man here in town. He's a mix. Collie and shepherd. He's going to have a real coat of hair, that one. Should be a good dog for the boy, though."

"What's his name, Uncle Mac?" Richie said, holding the wiggling puppy near his face.

"That's up to you," Mac said.

"What'll we name him, Kenny?" Richie asked, innocent of the fact that he should be discussing it with Mac.

"I think that's between you and your Uncle Mac, don't you?"

"Come on, Kenny," Richie called as he let the puppy down to run again. "Let's teach him how to fetch."

"Sorry," Ken said as he sensed Mac's mood changing. "I'm going in to have coffee with your mother."

"Come on, Uncle Mac," Richie called over his shoulder. "You don't have to have coffee do you?"

"No," Mac said. But Ken could tell the older man was already hurt. "Come on then," Mac said, glaring at Kenneth. "Let's find him a stick."

Sharon had observed the entire situation along with Meg from the back porch. Both Meg and Sharon could see the frown creasing Kenneth's forehead as he opened the screen door.

"Don't you worry, Ken," Meg said. "Mac is just having a hard time. He was the only man in any of our lives for so long. He'll adjust. Give him time, okay?"

"I don't mean to get in his way," Ken said apologetically. "But it seems that no matter what I do . . ."

"He'll learn," Meg said confidently. "I know my husband."

"She has more confidence in him than anybody I've ever known," Sharon said, coming to stand next to Ken. "It's not you, personally," she said. "Any man coming into our lives would be a threat to him, don't you know that?"

"I don't mean to take his place, Sharon," Ken said.

"I know you don't. But some of it's bound to happen."

"Time will help," Meg said, coming to stand on his other side. "And of course, I'll do my best to help him along."

"Poor Mac," Ken winked at Sharon.

"Poor Mac?" Meg asked innocently.

"He said you could be pretty persuasive," Ken laughed.

"He hasn't seen anything yet," Meg said.

After coffee, Ken excused himself, saying he had a few errands to take care of in town. He slipped out the front door and quietly backed his car out of the driveway before Richie could notice.

"Where's he going?" Sharon asked Meg.

"He may have a thing or two to take care of, but I think he's mainly giving Mac and Richie some time alone."

"He would do that, wouldn't he?"

"I'm very proud of him," Meg said, her eyes glistening with love and pride.

Later that afternoon, James and Mac found places in the shade while Richie and his dog romped in the grass nearby. Only after intensive begging did Sharon give in and let Richie go to the crying puppy on the back porch during lunchtime. The only time Richie stopped playing with the dog all day was when the poor little creature was too exhausted to go on. Then he sat in a grassy spot, and the dog slept either on his lap or draped across his foot.

"You decided on a name yet?" Ken asked when he returned just before dinner.

"I'm going to call him Samuel," Richie said, proudly petting his sleeping puppy.

"Samuel?"

"Yes, 'cause I want him to come when I call him."

"Pardon me?" Ken looked up at Sharon with a puzzled expression.

"Don't you know the Bible story 'bout Samuel, the boy who heard God call his name?"

"Oh," Ken said as the realization struck him. "Of course."

"So when I call his name, he'll come."

"What else did Samuel do?" Sharon asked, coming to join them.

"Obeyed," Richie said. "I'll teach him to obey. I call him Sam for everyday though. You know, like my name is really Richard, but you sometimes call me Rich for short."

Sharon smiled at the boy recalling the few times when Ken referred to him as Rich and ignoring an entire lifetime of being called Richie by everyone else in the family.

"Sam," Ken said admiringly. "Good name."

"Where have you been all day?" Sharon asked as they climbed the steps to the back porch.

"Business," Ken said without explanation. "Where's Frannie?"

"Stringing buttons with Sarah. She's felt pretty left out all day. She thought you went away without telling her good-bye."

"I got her a present, is that okay with you?"

"Sure," Sharon said. "But you better be careful, she's in a pretty foul mood."

Sharon watched as Ken presented the pouting child with a book of brand new paper dolls and some blunt-nosed plastic scissors. Sarah breathed a visible sigh of relief and nodded her approval so that Sharon could see.

"I thought you went away," Frannie whined. "And that you would never come back."

"I told your mother I had business in town," Ken said, resting his chin on top of her soft blond curls. "She knew I was coming back."

Ken sat on the sofa and Frannie crawled up in his lap, clutching her present. "You didn't say it to *me*," she complained.

"I'm sorry, sweetheart," he said, placing his cheek next to hers. "But you, sleepyhead, were still upstairs in bed. I couldn't wait all day." Ken touched the palms of her hands then frowned over the top of her head at Sharon. "You feel all right, honey?"

"I don't feel good," Frannie said. "My tummy hurts."

Sharon soon learned that her daughter was running a fever, and a few telltale spots were beginning to peek through on Frannie's tummy and back.

"Uh-oh," Sarah joined the consultation. "Looks like pox to me, little girl."

"Pox?" Ken asked excitedly. "Should we call the doctor?"

"Not yet," Sarah said calmly. "She's got three really good doctors right here in the house."

"Don't worry, Ken," Sharon reassured him. "It's probably just chicken pox. A notice came home from school last week. It's going around."

"My froat hurts," Frannie whined.

"Funny, she didn't complain all day." Sharon smiled at Ken. "Not a word until you came home."

"Jell-O," Ken said ignoring the implication of Sharon's comment. "Mom always has Jell-O."

"And sherbet and ice cream," Sarah said. "Sweetheart, you'll be eating Popsicles for breakfast even. Won't that be fun?"

At supper, Ken sat with Frannie limply draped across his lap. He spoon-fed her crushed ice and tiny bites of cherry Jell-O.

"You were gone quite a while, son," James said offhandedly.

"Yeah," Ken said. "Well, I went to speak to Bob."

"At the machine shop?" Meg asked.

"I wanted to ask your advice, Mac," Ken said addressing Sharon's uncle. "I was hoping to wait until later, but now that the subject's been opened, I thought I might get a job there."

"He's thinkin' of retirin' soon. I doubt if he'd be interested in takin' on any help right now."

"That's what he said. But he told me he'd be glad to keep the shop open if I wanted to work it. You know, see how it goes for a while. Then he thought I might be able to buy him out in a year or two."

"That right?" Mac said, almost interested. "What'd you tell him?"

"Told him I wanted to talk it over with you."

"What'd you tell him that for?" Mac growled in response.

"Because I do," Ken said.

"Why?" Mac pressed.

"Because—" Ken paused and took a deep breath. Mac made being his stepson difficult at best. "Because it's a big step and I thought I might need—"

"I don't have any money," Mac said flatly. "If that's what you had in mind, you can forget it. Everything your mother and I had we sunk into this place."

"I don't want any money," Ken said, wishing this conversation wasn't being witnessed by the entire family.

Meg scooted her chair back and shot Mac an angry look before rising and turning her back to the table. At once, James and Sarah excused themselves and quietly left the table and went out the back door to the guest house. Sharon tried to take Frannie from Ken's arms, but gave up when Frannie started crying and clinging to Ken's neck.

Standing, Ken adjusted Frannie's weight and walked toward the door connecting the kitchen to the rest of the house. Before he left the room he paused.

"Advice, Mac. I was hoping to get some advice."

"Advice is cheap," Mac remarked.

"Not around here it isn't," Ken said softly, then left the room.

Sharon sat motionless, fighting back tears and anger.

"Can I go out and check on Sam?" Richie asked.

"You didn't ask to be excused." Sharon tried to keep her tone even when she addressed her son.

"Excuse me, please."

"That's better," Sharon said gently, even managing a smile. "Make sure James is out there, too."

"Okay," Richie said, bounding out the door and slamming the screen on his way out. "Samuel," they heard him call. "Sam!"

Sharon sat still until she heard James's voice join Richie's in the yard. Finally she turned and stared directly at her uncle.

"What's the matter?" Mac asked defensively.

"You don't know?" Sharon said angrily. "You actually want me to believe you don't know?"

"All I said was—" Mac began innocently.

"*All* you said was presumptuous and rude," Sharon stated flatly.

"Listen to your big words, will you?" Mac retorted.

"Better than your picky, petty ones," she shot back.

"Stop it, both of you," Meg said tearfully. Sharon hastily left the room to tend to Frannie and Kenneth. "Mac," Meg said tenderly, "you'll drive them out of the house and away from us. Don't you see that?" She put her hand on her husband's rough, suntanned forearm. "My darling husband, these are our children. Ken's had a ten-year career in the military. He's a decent, thrifty young man, always has been. If you had taken the time to know him better, you would have realized that. Didn't you even notice he bought himself a good, decent used car, not a new one? Haven't you seen how carefully he plays with the children? He's my son, Mac. Don't you know you drive a stake through my heart whenever you strike out at him? What has he ever done to you, Mac? He's my son, and he loves Sharon—how much more perfect could that be?"

"I just meant that we didn't have—"

"That's just the point, Mac. You didn't even know what he was going to say before you blurted that out. Nobody is after what little we have, honey. Least of all Ken."

"I didn't think, I guess," Mac finally admitted.

"It's a frequent problem with you, Mac. Sharon and I overlook it many times. But you'll not get away with it with Kenneth. He'll meet you man to man. He wants to ask your advice; he must respect what you'll have to say. Can't you at least hear him out before you jump to conclusions?"

The screen door squeaked open, and James scooted Richie inside.

"Sam's all bedded down for the night," James said.

"We made him a bed in the big box. Uncle James put in a old rug and a clock."

"A clock?" Meg asked.

"Just an old windup with a loud ticker," James explained. "Thought he might like the company his first night away from his family."

"He was whining, Auntie Meg. Can't he come sleep with me?"

"No, young man, he can't. That dog will soon be the size of Old Major, and he's not a house pet. He's a farm dog. He'll sleep right out there where he belongs."

"Okay," Richie moaned, hanging his head as he moved through the kitchen toward the front of the house.

"Upstairs with you," Meg said. "Your mama's up there with Frannie already. Get along now."

"Where's Kenny?" he asked curiously.

"Upstairs with your mother and Frannie," she said. Turning back to Mac, she could see the look of disapproval on his face.

"You're doing it again, Jack McKenzie."

Before Mac could answer, Ken slowly opened the door and walked into the kitchen. Placing both hands on the back of a kitchen chair, he leaned forward thoughtfully. "I'm sorry, Mac," he said, "I didn't mean to give you the impression that I needed to borrow money. I should have made myself clearer."

"Sit down, Kenny," Meg said sweetly. "Your stepfather wants to talk to you. Isn't that right, McKenzie?"

CHAPTER TWENTY-FIVE

*S*arah's offered to stay home with Frannie so we can all go to the picnic," Ken said, appearing for breakfast on Sunday morning.

"I can't let her do that," Sharon said. "I'll stay."

"I think she'd really like to," Ken offered. "I'm not sure she feels up to going for an all-day event."

"I think he's right," Meg said. "Sarah's not feeling quite up to par these days. Besides, you can all come back here for ice cream later."

"You mean after we go to a church picnic we should all come back here and eat some more?" Ken teased his mother.

"Good excuse as any," she countered. "If that's what it takes to get you all in one place."

"Will she be all right all day alone?" Sharon asked, feeling the old familiar fears for the first time since Ken came home.

"I think James will be coming back after church. I thought I'd stay home this morning," Meg said.

"And, besides," Ken laughed, popping half a cinnamon roll into his mouth, "Sam's on duty!"

"Right," Sharon scoffed.

Once Mac announced he planned to keep Meg and Sarah company until James returned from church, Sharon began looking forward to an entire day with Ken and their friends from church. This would be the first time Sharon and Ken would be attending a church function as a couple. Sharon felt as excited as if she were attending a high school prom.

After church, Ken proudly held her hand and walked among the lighthearted church crowd gathered at Sylvan Park. Sharon smiled and blushed appropriately as well-wishers pressed them for details and teased them about setting a wedding date.

"Hey!" Ken protested good-naturedly, "I haven't even asked her yet."

"Just don't make it a New Year's Eve wedding, will you?" one older man complained.

"Yeah," another joined in, "he stayed up for Jennifer's last year—that's once in the past twenty-five or so."

Laughter filled the reserved area and friends who were more like family teased and played together as easily as they worshiped together each Sunday.

"Feels good here," Ken said. "Like home."

"It is," Sharon said. "Isn't it wonderful?"

"So are you," he said admiringly.

Sharon felt the too frequent blush creeping up her neck again.

The afternoon was everything Sharon had hoped it would be. Richie and Kenneth fell down during a three-legged race, and Sharon cheered from the sidelines as Ken jumped his way to the finish line in a gunny sack. A water balloon toss left both Ken and Richie soaked through to their skin, but Richie resisted Sharon's suggestion that he change into something dry.

"Nah," he said. "We're tough, we can take it. Right, Ken?"

"Right," Ken laughed in return, then turning to Sharon, "besides I'm hot. This feels good. See?" He grabbed her and gave her a wet hug. Both Ken and the onlookers were delighted when she screamed and struggled to get away from his grasp. Just then Jennifer Miller secretly slipped her a squirt gun. As soon as she could manage to get a few feet away, Sharon turned to blast Ken in the face. He ducked just in time to let the cold stream fly past and hit Jeff Bennett squarely in the forehead.

"Hey!" Jeff yelled. "Who did that?"

"She did!" Ken pointed at Sharon. "She's the guilty one!"

The ensuing battle spared no one; even Meg wiped water from the front of her cotton dress. "Children," she ordered, "behave yourselves!"

Suddenly Ken grabbed both Sharon's arms while Jeff pulled Richie toward her. "Come on you guys," Sharon pleaded. "I've had enough for one day." She struggled to get free and Ken pulled her close enough to speak directly into her ear.

"Take Richie into the rest room, and do it now," he said with unquestionable authority.

"Ken, what in the world?"

"Come on, everyone, see Sharon get her head dunked in the drinking fountain," he called. Then he turned to her and spoke in a serious tone that was a stark contrast to his jovial expression. "We have visitors," he said without taking his eyes from hers. "Take Richie into the bathroom."

"I don't want to go in the girl's bathroom," Richie whined.

"Just this once," Ken said, scooping him up and carrying him to the door before handing him to Sharon, who followed close behind. Immediately they were joined by Cari and Jen.

"What's going on?" Jen asked, coming to stand beside her two friends in the women's room.

"I think we're being watched," Cari said, quietly hoping Richie wouldn't overhear. Nodding toward the window, Jen took her signal and tried to peer above the half-opened frosted pane.

"Mama, I don't want to be in here," Richie said, nearly in tears.

"I know, sweetheart," she said, stooping to look him in the eyes. "But Ken said we have to wait here until he makes sure we're safe, okay?"

"Mama, I'm scared," he wailed.

"I know, honey," she said into his dark hair while holding him close. "Me too."

"Jen!" It was Dan's voice from outside the bathroom door. "Jen, you in there?"

"Go ahead," Cari said. "We'll be all right."

Immediately Jen returned and checked the stalls. "Anyone else in here?" she asked.

"I don't think so," Cari said.

"We're alone," Jen called.

Dan Miller's tall frame soon filled the women's public rest room. "Sorry girls, I know Richie and I don't belong in here, but it couldn't be helped."

"What's happening out there?" Sharon asked.

"Ken and Jeff are handling it," he said. "Seems we had a party crasher and he brought along a few friends." Dan's eyes told Sharon more than his comment.

"Did Jeff call—"

"He's doing that now." Dan broke off Cari's question before she could mention the police. "Meg and Mac are packing up to go home. As soon as it's all clear I think we're all headed up to your place.

Once they were in the car and headed up the highway toward the ranch, Sharon looked several times at Kenneth questioningly. He merely glanced out the rearview mirror and into the back seat where Richie was dozing off.

"He'll get his second wind once we're at home. It's been quite a day for him, hasn't it?" he asked.

Sharon could wait no longer. "Ken, what happened back there?"

"I think you were followed," he said, giving her a look that communicated more than he was willing to say.

"Are you sure?"

"All I can say is that once a black and white showed up, four men got back into a car and drove carefully away."

"Oh, my gosh," she exclaimed quietly. "How in the world does he know where I am?"

"You're not too hard to spot, baby, believe me. I'd know where you were if I wanted to badly enough." He smiled at her. "I don't know what he expected to see when he came back, but believe me, Sharon, I'm convinced you far exceed his expectations."

"Kenneth," she said modestly.

"I know you do mine." He reached across the seat and tugged gently on her arm until she slid across the seat.

"I love you, Sharon." Ken spoke without taking his eyes from the highway. "I can't tell you how much."

Once the children had played with the puppy, eaten their fill of Sarah's peach ice cream, and settled down in the living room to watch TV, the adults indulged in another cup of coffee and gathered around Meg and Mac's dining room table.

"How can you be sure it was him?" Mac asked for the third time.

"I'm sure," Ken said.

"How can you be so sure?" Sharon asked. "You've never even seen him. Maybe you guys were mistaken." She glanced up in time to see Jeff and Kenneth exchange knowing looks.

"Ken?" she asked. "You've never seen him, have you?"

Suddenly the room fell silent, and no one knew exactly what to say.

"I certainly have," Jeff said, trying to cover Ken as best he could. "And he wasn't with those—"

"Ken?" she repeated insistently.

"I may have," he admitted reluctantly. "Once."

Sharon stared straight into her coffee mug. "I'm listening," she said.

Captivated by Ken's account of the night he gave Richard Potter a ride south, no one noticed Richie inching away from the other children , edging his way to the end of the sofa nearest the dining area. When Ken finished, silence fell among those gathered around the table.

"Mommy," Richie said quietly from his place on the sofa. Sharon saw his eyes, filled with fear, rivet on her face. "Mommy," he cried softly. He had heard every word of Ken's story.

"Richie," she said. "Come here, sweetie."

He cried into her shoulder as she held him as tight as she could. "He's going to kill us, isn't he, Mommy."

"No, Richie," Sharon said, but her friends saw the doubt and fear in her own face. "He won't."

"Just like Major," Richie sobbed. "He's going to beat us 'til we're dead."

"Rich," Ken said, squatting and encircling both mother and young son within his arms, "we're not going to let that happen. Uncle Mac and Uncle James are with you every minute. And when they're not home, the guard is out front. You're as safe as you can be," Ken said.

Mac cleared his throat and Meg's eyes filled with tears, as did Jen's and Cari's.

Sharon sat perfectly still, cradling Richie close while the Millers and Bennetts gathered up their things and said simple good-byes.

"We'll get the kids ready for bed," Sarah said, nodding to James. "You keep each other company as long as you like."

Carefully, James coaxed Richie away from his mother and carried him upstairs while Mac lugged a spot-filled Frannie.

Ken pulled his chair nearer Sharon's as she folded her arms on the table and slowly lowered her head to rest on them before she gave way to her deep inner fears and sobbed.

"Sharon," Ken said after letting her cry for a short while. "Honey, listen to me." Gently, he pulled long strands of her honey-colored hair away from her tear-stained face. "If he does what he has done in the past, he's long gone from here by now. Certainly those men were up to no good. They saw the police drive up and they didn't hesitate to leave. They know we saw them. Who knows, maybe they're looking for him too. He's not going to stay around. That's not his way."

"Why didn't you tell me you had seen him?" she cried. "Dear God, Kenneth, why didn't you tell me?"

"Can you imagine how I felt when I figured out who it was?" Ken recalled the nausea that swept over him at the moment he realized. "I couldn't believe I had done it. I felt as if I'd betrayed you."

"But you didn't know," she said, defending his actions.

"No, but somehow I thought I should have."

"You've never even seen a picture of him," she said.

"No, and now I don't need to. I'll never forget the look in his eyes. Drugged, drunk, or whatever, I swear he could look right through me."

By this time, Mac had taken to pacing back and forth in front of the drawn dining room draperies.

"I'm so glad you were there," Sharon said. "I can't believe that I was actually planning to go to the picnic without you. Can you imagine what would have happened if Cari or I had noticed those men first?"

"I think that's what they were hoping for," Ken said. "For the life of me, I can't believe why, but somehow I think maybe they were actually hoping one of you would spot them first."

"I would have been scared out of my wits," Sharon admitted.

"Well, I was there," Ken said. "I'm glad I was. Jeff knew immediately when I made eye contact with him. He's got good instincts. I don't know," Ken continued, "maybe they wanted to send a message of some kind. To Richard, to us . . . who knows."

Mac cleared his throat.

"Mac," Meg said, "you want to say something."

"Yeah," Mac said barely above a whisper. He cleared his throat again. "Thanks, Ken. I'm not sure I would have known exactly what to do. I—"

"Well," Meg said standing to clear away the coffee cups. "Give me a hand here, will you McKenzie?"

"Wait a minute, Mom," Ken said. Then turning his attention to Sharon, he asked, "Would you mind, honey? I want to talk to Mac—alone."

"Well, Mac," Ken said after they were alone and James and Sarah had said their goodnights. "I still need that advice."

"I thought I told you the other night," Mac said with new admiration for the young man sitting across the table from him.

"It's not about the machine shop," Ken said. "Well, yes it is. No—" He groped for the right words. "It's really about Sharon and me, first—then the machine shop."

Mac grinned at the attractive son of his treasured Margaret. "I figured as much," Mac said.

"I plan to ask her to marry me, sir. If that's all right with you."

"That's up to Sharon," Mac said.

"Your approval is important to her—and to me, Mac."

The two men locked eyes across the wooden table polished to a high shine by Meg's loving hands. "You hurt her, Matthews—" Mac's warning echoed in his deep, searching eyes. "And you'll answer to me. You understand that?"

"Yes, sir," Ken said, smiling. "I certainly do."

"Although," Mac said, backing down some, "after the way you handled the situation today, I'd guess I'd not be much of a match for you."

"I won't hurt her," Ken promised, extending a hand across the table to his stepfather, uncle-in-law to be.

"Make her happy, Ken," Mac said, his voice breaking with uncharacteristic emotion.

"I'll do my best," Ken promised.

"I can't ask more than that I guess." Mac stood and stretched. "It's been a long day, I think I'll turn in."

"Sir, could I ask an extremely personal favor?"

"You're not through?"

"I'd like to check on them, if you don't mind. I'll leave the door open. You could stand at the bottom of the stairs the whole time. I'd just feel better if I knew she was all right. It's been quite a day for all of us."

"Well—" Mac glanced toward the ceiling. "I suppose it wouldn't hurt nothin'." He shoved his hands in his pockets and went toward the kitchen door. "Go on," Mac said, "I trust you."

CHAPTER TWENTY-SIX

*K*en?" Sharon could barely make out his face as he stood above her. "You scared me."

"Honey?" he whispered.

"What time is it?"

"I have no idea," he said.

"You asleep?"

"I think so," she moaned.

"Can we talk?"

"Here?" she said, suddenly fully awake.

"I'll sit right here," he said folding his frame to sit cross legged beside her bed. "How're the kids?"

"Frannie's fine. Richie had a little trouble going to sleep."

"Ken?" Richie's sleepy voice came from the other side of the small room.

"I'm right here, pal."

"You sleeping with us?"

"Not tonight," he laughed quietly. "I'll stay a while though. I want to talk to your mama."

"Oh," Richie said before turning over and flopping his head back on his pillow.

"That okay with you?" Ken whispered. Richie didn't respond.

"He's out," Sharon said. "Don't you want me to come downstairs?"

"You want to leave him?"

"Not really," she confessed.

"Uncle Mac knows I'm here," Ken said, hoping that fact would make her more comfortable.

"He does?" Sharon leaned on one elbow and pulled the light blanket high to her chin. She was glad she had on her cotton pajamas, knowing she was more than adequately covered. "What'd you do, hog-tie him?"

"No," Ken said. "Not quite."

"What are you doing here?" she asked.

"We need to talk," he said.

"Now?"

"Right now."

"What's so important that it can't wait 'til morning?"

"Nothing," he said. "Good night."

"Ken!" she whispered loudly. "Don't do that."

"Sharon," he said simply. "I love you."

"I know," she said happily.

"And whether you say it or not, I know you love me."

"I think you're right."

"Will you marry me?"

"What?" she said out loud, sitting straight up in her bed.

"Shh. You'll wake the kids!" he warned.

"What did you say?"

"I said you'll wake the kids."

"Not that, before that."

"Oh that," he said. "Please, Sharon, marry me. For pity's sake if nothing else."

"Okay," she said simply.

"Good," he said. He fought and subdued an almost uncontrollable urge to pull her into his arms. Standing upright and towering over her he walked quietly to check on both of the kids.

"Well, I'd better get downstairs before Mac comes looking for me."

"Kenneth?" she whispered softly.

"Don't, honey. I'm using all the self-control I can manage. We'll talk more in the morning, okay?"

"Okay," she whispered back.

"Good morning, all," Ken said the next morning as if nothing had happened the night before. Richie was finishing up his oatmeal while Mac was sipping a cup of coffee and reading the paper. Meg was bustling around the kitchen as usual.

"Hi," Sharon said, pouring herself another cup of coffee.

"You look bright and chipper this morning," he said.

"I do not," she complained. "I look awful. I didn't get much sleep, as you probably know."

"I slept like a log," he said. Then taking a seat next to Richie, he addressed the boy. "How about a ride to school this morning?"

"All the way?"

"Yep," Ken said. "Frannie could go too, but she's got those nasty spots."

"She'll be out another week at least," Meg said.

Sharon sat across the table as if she hadn't made the most important decision of her life the night before. "Ken, he can take the bus as usual. You don't have to drive him," she said.

"I'm going to take him this morning," Ken announced.

"Suit yourself," she grumbled.

"I will," he said, grinning at her tousled appearance. "This is a pleasant side of you I've never seen before," he remarked.

"This is my morning side."

"Every morning?" Ken asked.

"If I don't get my sleep," she answered.

"I'll remember that," he said.

After Richie fed and watered Sam, he stopped in front of Sharon for a last minute inspection before heading off to school. Before going out the door, Ken stopped by and quickly gave Sharon a casual peck on the cheek. "Be right back," he said cheerfully.

"No hurry on my account," she said.

"Mom, will you be here when I get back?"

"Of course," Meg said, smiling up at her grown son. "Where else?"

"Eggs in?" he asked.

"I'm free until around ten. Sarah's been helping me wash and sort. Then we women have Bible study. You're welcome to join us if you'd like."

"Maybe not," Ken said.

"Good move," Mac finally said from behind the morning paper.

"I'd like to have a look at that old feed mixer," Ken told Mac. "Sounds like the motor's a little tight to me."

"Good idea." Mac grinned without taking his eyes off the paper.

The back door slammed behind Ken and Richie as they left. Sharon winced. "Don't they ever learn to shut a door quietly?"

"Some do," Meg said affectionately, nodding in Mac's direction. "Most don't."

"How'd you make out last night?" Mac asked without considering how his question sounded.

"Uncle Mac!" Sharon's shocked tone brought his eyes from the newspaper to her.

"Mac," Meg scolded. "Don't put it that way."

"Well," Mac said, "did you two talk?"

"A little," Sharon said, picking at a piece of toast. She wished Ken would return and help her face his mother and Mac.

"I see," Meg said.

"Well, what happened?" Mac said. He laid the paper in his lap. "Do we have to pull it out of you?"

"Not much," Sharon said.

Relieved when she heard Ken's cheerful call to James, Sharon tried to stay calm. Mac would press Kenneth now, and she was sure they wouldn't be able to keep their news from the family any longer.

"Mom," Ken said, pouring himself another cup of coffee, "Sharon and I—well, we have something to tell you."

"If you mean that you went up to her room last night, Mac already told me. What I want to know is what were you doing up there."

"I asked her to marry me," Ken said matter-of-factly.

"Oh?" Meg asked, looking from one face to the other.

"I said yes," Sharon said as if they were discussing the weather.

"Glory be!" Meg screeched. "Praise the Lord!"

Ken and Sharon stared at each other across the table, slow grins spreading across their faces. Finally both leaped to their feet at once. Walking around the table toward each other, they met and locked their arms tightly around one another.

"Hallelujah!" Meg said softly as she wiped tears from her eyes with the corner of her apron. "It's an answer to a mother's prayer, that's what it is."

"What's all the hoopla about?" James said, coming in with Sarah walking closely behind.

"A weddin'," Mac said. "Say, James, see the weather report?"

"Go on," Meg said. She yanked the paper from her husband's grasp. "You can act like this isn't important to you all you want to, Jack McKenzie. But I know better!"

Sarah hugged Sharon while James pumped Ken's hand. "Congratulations, son."

"Thanks," Ken said sheepishly.

"Oh, honey," Sarah said, holding Sharon at arm's length. "Last year at Jen's wedding, I just knew it wouldn't be long before the Lord brought someone special your way. I just knew it."

"Women!" James said. "First they go about tellin' the good Lord how to do His business, then they take the credit for it." Sharon listened happily to the chatter and excitement building around her.

"If you think this is exciting," she told her husband, "just you wait."

"Oh, no," James faked an expression of dread. "I don't think I even want to know about it. By the way, where's that little spotted mule this morning?"

"She's upstairs playing with the paper dolls Ken gave her," Sharon said.

"I brought her something special," Sarah said. "Made them just for her." Uncovering a plate, Sarah revealed dark raspberry gelatin frozen and molded in an ice cube tray.

"Oh, brother," Ken said. "I thought we were going to get by with only two grandparents spoiling them rotten. Now I see they have four we'll have to retrain."

"Five," Sharon corrected. "Don't forget my mother."

"Oh, no," Mac said almost under his breath. "Your mother. I almost forgot her."

"How could you?" Ken said. "Your own cousin."

"It's not easy," Mac replied. "You haven't met her yet, have you, Ken?"

"Can't say that I have," Ken said.

"You'd remember if you'd ever met my cousin. Believe me, it's an experience you won't soon forget."

"Well, when's the day?" Sarah asked. "We've got work to do, Meg. Weddings don't just happen you know."

"We haven't got that far just yet, Sarah," Ken said. "But if I have anything to say about it—"

"You won't," James laughed. "You popped the question, Ken. It's in the hands of powers greater than you now. All you need to do now is show up at the right time in the right suit, and the rest is history."

"In all seriousness," Ken explained, "we really can't make any plans until the Marine Corps makes up its mind about the date of my discharge."

"And when might that be, dear?" Meg asked, trying to regain some composure.

"That is also in the hands of powers greater than mine. If I had my choice, I wouldn't even go back this evening. But as we all know, my choices aren't top priority for the Marines right now."

At dinner time, it was obvious that everyone had heard the big news except Frannie, who had lived most of the day in an imaginary world full of paper fashion models and pretend weddings.

Suddenly the child stopped eating and stared at her mother with wide eyes filled with amazement. "Mommy," she cooed, "are we going to marry him?"

"Would that be all right with you?" Sharon asked. The family held their breath until the five-year-old finally spoke.

Frannie stared openly first at her mother, then at Kenneth. "Oh, Mommy," she said, clasping both hands tightly under her chin. "Don't we love him so?"

"Oh, gee," Richie said, moaning.

Sharon closed her eyes and tried without success to control the blush she felt burning at the base of her neck and spreading rapidly toward her face.

"Oh, Mommy," Mac's cracked imitation of Frannie's comment caught the entire family off guard. "Don't we love him so?"

A moment of total silence at Mac's attempt to be funny was suddenly split by James's inability to keep his composure. "Yes, dearie," he croaked, trying to match Mac's ridiculous tone, "we certainly do."

Burning with sudden embarrassment, Sharon jumped to her feet and grabbed a damp kitchen towel. She flung it as hard as she could at her tormentor, but James caught it before it could land in his plate. Mac wasn't so quick, and a sopping wet dishrag caught him squarely across the face just as the door slammed behind her.

The two older men tried to contain their laughter while Meg and Sarah stared at their plates, motionless. Ken stifled a chuckle, then slowly stood. "I'd better go to her," he managed to say with all seriousness to the two stunned children who stared with unbelief at the scene they had just witnessed.

"Yes, sweetheart," James squeaked unexpectedly, "you do that."

"James," Sarah scolded, but then the minute the door shut behind Kenneth, she too could no longer hold her laughter. Before long, Meg was also heaving deep, uncontrollable gales of laughter. Richie and Frannie stared at the adults still seated around the table, then at each other. Richie shrugged his shoulders and smiled at his little sister, who was already reaching for her pudding dish.

"They didn't mean any harm," Kenneth said, pulling a pouting Sharon within his arms.

"I know," she said shyly. "I'm just embarrassed, that's all."

"You do, don't you?"

"Do what?"

"Love me?" he asked gently as his lips brushed across her soft long hair.

"Ken." She tightened in his arms.

"Sharon, I love you," he said freely. "I love you so much."

Pulling away from her, just enough to look her in the eyes he said, "I'd rather hear it from you than from Frannie, although I enjoyed hearing it from her too."

"Ken, I'm still afraid," she said.

"So am I, but I love you anyway."

"I know. I feel the same way."

"Are you afraid of me, Sharon?"

"I don't think so, I'm just so used to being afraid that it's hard to stop."

"Sharon, I need to hear you say it. I know it's hard for you. But I want to know from your lips, not just your eyes, how you feel about me."

"I . . ." she hesitated, dropped her eyes to the buttons on his shirt.

"Sharon, look at me," he said, raising her chin gently with the tip of his fingers. "Don't ever be afraid to look at me."

"I'll try."

"Try to what, love me or not be afraid of me?"

"I don't have to try to love you, Ken, you know that. I manage to do that without any effort at all."

Ken looked deeply within her eyes, drinking in the miraculous realization of what they had between them. Slowly he pulled her into a warm, tender embrace. Sharon relaxed against him and let all the fear drain from her body. With him here, his arms tightly around her, she knew she'd never have anything to fear from him—not ever. The impact of finding that longed for place of security within his arms brought unexpected tears to her eyes.

"Are you crying?" he asked.

"No," she said, trying to back out of his arms.

"Yes, you are," he said.

"Yes, I am," she admitted.

"And, it's okay," he said. "Go ahead and cry if you want to." Just then a tear from his own eyes traveled the length of his strong featured face and fell, mingling with hers. "Let's both have a good cry and get it over with."

CHAPTER TWENTY-SEVEN

*H*ey, Matthews!" Ken waved to the corpsman calling from across the bay from his work station. "How's it going?"

"Better than I deserve!" Ken shouted back.

Ken couldn't remember ever being so happy or full of anticipation. The only hang-up was the Marines. Paperwork always seemed to slow down within the wheels of the great military machine. However, things were settled at home, Sharon was happy and feeling more secure every day, so once again Ken quickly adapted to his routine.

"Matthews?" a uniformed enlisted man stood at his elbow. "Lieutenant Ken Matthews?"

"That's me," Ken said, dropping a wrench into a near by toolbox.

"Lieutenant?" the young man repeated. "The CO wants to see you, sir."

"Be right there," Ken said excitedly. "Just as soon as I clean my hands."

"Matthews," the commanding officer said, "I have some news about your discharge," he said, slapping a stack of papers against his palm. "You're sure about this, now? It's not too late to change your mind, you know."

"Please, sir—" Ken changed his tone and posture to military precision. "No, sir—I mean yes, sir. I've decided, sir."

"Then, Lieutenant Kenneth Matthews—Ken," the man said soberly, "on behalf of the United States Marines, I want to thank you for ten years of outstanding duty and an enviable record. At two thirty, on Friday, fifteen October, nineteen sixty-five, you become a civilian."

"No kidding?" Ken dropped all military formality and stared with wide-eyed unbelief at the officer facing him across the desk.

"It's right here," the man said, handing the orders for discharge to him. "In black and white."

"That's only a couple days away," Ken said. "I can't believe it."

"I wish you were as sorry to leave us as we are to see you go," the officer laughed.

"I'm sorry, sir. But I . . ."

"No need to explain, Lieutenant," the older man said with an uncustomary smile tugging at his mouth. "No need at all."

"Thank you, sir," Ken said. "Thank you."

"Ken," the man said, "before you go, I'd like you to know that I personally owe you a debt of gratitude."

"You, sir?" Ken listened with interest.

"I heard that you kept a generator going in Nam. The report I read said you worked around the clock to keep that thing functioning."

"Well, sir, it was . . ." He couldn't find words to finish the sentence before the officer interrupted.

"It saved my boy's life."

"Excuse me, sir?" Could Ken have heard correctly?

"My son," the man said soberly. "He was out that day and was hit by sniper fire. Unfortunately, he was hit again while being rescued. War is an ungodly way to settle this thing."

"Sir?"

"Forget you heard me say that, will you?"

"Of course, sir." Kenneth didn't quite believe he had heard the remark in the first place.

"They operated on my son in that tent that night. It's because of you he has a life at all."

"How is he, sir?" Ken hoped for good news to come out of that awful situation. Somehow it would help balance the horrible memories.

"He'll never walk again, I'm afraid."

Ken's joy sagged momentarily. "I'm sorry to hear that, sir."

"If it hadn't been for you, he would have died out there. I'll be forever grateful to you for that. Lost both his legs when they finally got him shipped to a better facility. It's hard on the whole family. Especially his mother."

Ken snapped his eyes from the papers in his hand to the eyes of the man standing before him. "Sir," he said apologetically, remembering the last conversation they had, "I had no idea. I'm sorry about the other day. I shouldn't have spoken out like that."

"Don't give it another thought," the man said. "Although, I must admit, I have."

Ken shifted his weight from one foot to the other.

"Well, Matthews, I suppose you'll be wanting to call home. Go on then, son. That'll be all." The officer stood and saluted Ken sharply. Ken returned it with as much military precision as he could manage.

"What are you going to do out there?" The officer's voice stopped him before he could go through the doorway.

"I'm buying into a small machine repair shop. And," Ken said, turning and flashing a wide grin, "I'm getting married just as soon as possible."

"Good luck, son," the man said.

"Thank you, sir."

"Go on, call your girl." The officer waved Ken away.

"No, sir," Ken said smiling ear to ear. "I don't think I will. I think I'll just go home and surprise her."

Sharon sat near the phone Friday afternoon, waiting for Ken's usual call. *He's going on duty at three,* she thought as she checked her watch. *Maybe something came up.* At two-forty-five, she decided she could wait no longer; she had to meet Richie's bus. Of course, he could walk the three hundred yards or so to the house by himself, or even James could meet him. But she knew that he needed to see her the minute he got off the bus, and their walks from the stop to the house were special times for them both.

Nearing the end of the driveway, she saw the large yellow bus round the corner and heard the brakes squeak as it came to a halt. Usually she was on the other side of the street by now; however, today she waited until the driver pulled the doors closed once again, turned off the flashing red lights, and pulled away. Expecting to see Richie standing there waiting, she felt her heart drop to her stomach when only Bobby Roberts stood in plain sight when the bus pulled away.

"Bobby! Where is Richie?" she screamed.

"He wasn't on the bus, Mrs. Potter," Bobby said. "I don't know where he is. Somebody called him out of class just before the bell rang."

"No!" Sharon screamed. "No!"

Running back toward the house, she met James in the driveway. Meg soon joined them.

"Sharon!" James yelled from short distance away. "What in the world!"

"Richie wasn't on the bus!" she shrieked.

James didn't stop to find out anything further but jumped into Mac's pickup. "Call the school, Meg," he ordered as he shoved it into reverse. "Then call the police and Jeff."

Meg hurried Sharon inside the house and dashed for the phone. Sarah quickly came to Sharon's side and began praying quietly. Within minutes, Meg returned from the phone. Her face told Sharon what she dreaded to hear.

"Someone presented himself as Richie's father and said he was there to pick Richie up for the weekend."

"No." Sharon grabbed her ribs and moaned. "Please, God, no!"

Within minutes Meg's kitchen was filled with police officers, concerned neighbors, and friends.

"Mrs. Potter," the officer in charge said, "we need you to get a hold of yourself and give us some pertinent information. Can you do that?"

"I'll try," she managed between sobs. She sat, her arms wrapped tightly around her middle, and rocked gently back and forth.

"I need to know what Richie was wearing," the man said.

"Blue jeans, plaid cotton shirt—blue and tan. And his sweater. But he was probably carrying that."

"Good. Now do you have a recent picture of him?"

"Meg?" Sharon said, turning to the woman she had come to look to for strength.

"I'll get one," Meg said. "I have the school pictures right here. They're a year old. But he looks pretty much the same. Only taller, and his teeth have come back in."

Sharon felt her insides twist, and her heart painfully throbbed in sync with her head. "Oh, Meg, he's taken Richie. Oh, God, please, don't let anything happen to my son."

"Now, Mrs. Potter." The officer squatted beside her. "I know this is hard, but it's very important. He's got dark hair, right?" the man asked, looking at the school picture. "And dark eyes?"

Sharon nodded.

"And he's got a dimple on his cheek?"

"Yes," she moaned sorrowfully.

"Any scars or birthmarks?"

"Small pox vaccination on his arm," she said quietly. "And a small scar on his lower lip where his father . . ." Her voice gave way to pain, and she didn't try to hold back the spasms that sent her running to the kitchen sink to throw up.

"What's the situation, officer?" Jeff's voice broke through the confusion and penetrated Sharon's pain-filled mind.

"Jeff, oh, Jeff," she cried. "He came right to the school and picked him up. We told them this might happen. They said it wouldn't. How could they let him go with someone they never saw before?"

"Any answers, officer?"

"As far as we can tell, he walked right in, asked someone where Richie's classroom was and spoke directly to the teacher, who obviously didn't have a clue that anything was wrong."

"Didn't the principal tell the teacher?" Sharon's voice rang with agony.

"I haven't any idea," he said. "There's a team up there talking to school officials right now."

"Anybody call Kenneth?" Jeff asked.

"I tried," Meg said, then motioned Jeff aside.

"What's up?" he said when they were in the dining room out of Sharon's hearing.

"I called and told them it was an emergency. They told me Ken was already on his way home."

"That's strange," Jeff mused. "I wonder how he knew to come home."

"I can't tell you that," Meg said. "It's not like him. He didn't call Sharon at the usual time and now this."

"Did they say what time he left?"

"That's the strange thing," she said. "They seemed to know he left at precisely two-thirty-five."

"We should be seeing him roll in within the hour then."

"I'll sure be glad to see him, but I dread telling him this news."

The phone rang and Jeff and Meg heard Sharon run for it. "Hello?" she said, then paused. "It's for you." She handed the receiver to the officer standing nearby.

The wheels on Mac's delivery truck scrunched the gravel in the driveway. Meg waited for him to come up the steps to the back porch.

"What is going on here?"

"Mac," Meg began. "Come here, sit down." Then as clearly and calmly as possible, she told him of Richie's disappearance and that Richard Potter was suspected.

"Of all the nerve," Mac said, defeated. "We thought we had it covered."

"Ken's on his way," Meg said, not knowing what else to tell him.

"Where's Frannie?"

"Oh, my goodness, the poor child. She didn't even cross my mind." Meg went through the kitchen and into the living room discovering Sarah holding a very quiet and solemn Frannie.

"Honey?" Meg asked, coming close and leaning toward the tousled blond head. "Are you all right?"

"I want my brother back," she whimpered.

"And we're going to pray for God to make that happen, aren't we?" Sarah's voice soothed not only Frannie but Meg as well. "I can handle this," she winked at Meg. "You're probably needed in there," she said, nodding toward the kitchen door.

"Just when did this happen?" Meg heard Ken's voice as she opened the door. "Sharon, listen to me. Honey, please, listen. It's going to be all right. Please, Sharon," he pleaded. But to everyone in the room, it was obvious that Ken was as upset as she was.

Amid the confusion, plans were made as to how to proceed with the search for the little boy and his abductor.

"The center will be at the station house in Redlands," the officer in charge told them all. "You're welcome to come down there if you want. But I really advise someone sticking close here at home. Who knows, the abductor may change his mind and return the child home. And no matter where we find him, if he looks to be unharmed, we'll bring him here first."

Jeff and Ken consulted with Dan and Jen Miller, who had arrived shortly after Ken. Together they decided that Jeff and Ken would go to the police station and that the Millers would stay here with the rest of the family. Ken persuaded Sharon to accept their plan.

"Honest, sweetheart," he said, "if anything at all happens, I'll call you right away. But you need to be here, just in case he decides to bring him back."

"He won't," she said tearfully. "I just know it. Not on his own. Ken, you don't know him the way I do. I should have known he'd find a way. I should have kept Richie home from school today. It was Friday. I could've let him stay home! Why, Ken, why?"

"Honey," Ken said, "don't blame yourself for this. It won't do you any good and it won't do Frannie any good either. Where is she, by the way?"

"I don't know," Sharon said, looking around the room. "I guess she's with Sarah."

"She's safe though," Ken said, relieved.

"She's been home all day. She was napping when I went out to the bus stop." Sharon's stomach tightened as she recalled the moment she discovered Richie was missing. "Ken it was awful. I waited and the bus pulled away and there stood Bobby all by himself. He didn't know there was anything wrong."

"What was his name?" the officer asked overhearing the conversation.

"Bobby Roberts," Sharon said. "He and Richie always sat together on the bus. I'll never forget the look on his face when he told me Richie wasn't there." Sharon watched without seeing as the policeman scribbled on his notepad.

"Jeff and I are going downtown, honey. I promise I'll call you just as soon as I can. Cari and Jen will be here with you, Mom and Sarah are too."

"Uncle Mac," Sharon said looking around the room for his familiar face. "Where's Uncle Mac?"

"He's outside," Jen offered. "He's taking care of Sam."

"There will be a couple of men staying here on the place, ma'am," the officer said. "Just in case there's . . . well, in case there are any changes we need to know about."

"Ken," Sharon cried as he held her close again, "I'm so afraid. I'm so scared."

"Don't give up hope, baby," Ken said, burying his face into her face and soft hair. "Just don't you dare give up hope."

Sharon felt as if her heart would rip open when he left her arms. "Ken," she cried, "I'm so scared."

Jeff slid behind the wheel of Ken's car, and Ken walked mechanically to the other side and spoke briefly to a policemen before getting in the car.

"You okay, buddy?" Jeff asked.

"No." Ken choked on the word. "No, Jeff, I'm not. I've never been so scared in my whole life."

The police station was bustling with activity when the two men walked in.

"Is it always like this?" Ken asked the officer who had been at the house.

"Not every day, but this is more or less our usual Friday night crowd," he said. Ken thought he detected a note of cynicism in his voice. "A few young toughs," he said, nodding toward the other side of the large reception room. "And, then, a hooker or two."

"In Redlands?" Jeff asked, almost surprised by the thought.

"You're a lawyer, aren't you, Bennett?" the man asked.

"Corporate mostly," Jeff answered.

"That explains it. We don't get too many corporate crooks in here," he laughed. "And what about you?" he asked, turning to Ken.

"Marines," he said.

"No kidding? How long you been in?"

"Ten years," Ken said, patting the pocket on his windbreaker just to make sure his discharge papers were still there.

"Career man."

"Not any more," Ken said. "Hey, what are you doing to find Richie?"

"They're putting out an APB right now on Potter. He's probably the most talked about person in the area right now. The *Sun* is sending a reporter over right now. You up to talking to them?"

"Will it help?"

"Maybe," the officer said. "You never know about these things. As long as we can keep it in front of people's noses, we keep the pressure on." He accepted a paper from another officer. "They're working up a description to put on the radio now. Care to come in?"

"Thanks," Ken said and followed with Jeff close behind.

"By the way," the man said, turning and extending his hand, "William Barnes. Barney, at your service."

"Ken Matthews," Ken said, accepting the introduction.

"You're the boy's stepfather, right?"

"Almost," Ken said.

"Good enough for me," Barney said. "Here's the description: medium build, black curly hair, little longer than collar length."

"Where'd you get the description?"

"From the teacher on the playground who showed him the way to Richie's classroom." Ken purposely kept his mind on the description and not what Richie must have felt when he faced his father and then was led away by him with trusted adults looking on.

"Clean cut, snappy dresser, somewhat slender," Barney continued.

"Does this sound like Potter to you?" Ken asked Jeff.

"Not the Potter I know." Jeff snatched the paper from the officer's extended hand. "Look here," Jeff said.

Ken took the report from Jeff's hand and read where Jeff pointed. *Well manicured, long fingers.* Ken stared at Jeff. "It's not him," Ken said with disbelief. "This is not the Richard Potter we know."

"So we start at the beginning," Barney said, shrugging the inconsistency off as an everyday occurrence. "Tell me what you know about Potter."

Jeff and Ken gave a fairly complete and accurate description of Richard Potter from their firsthand experiences. Muscular, stocky build, unkempt, long wavy hair, wide, dirt-encrusted hands.

"He could have had a bath," Barney quipped.

"Except for one thing," Ken noted. "He wasn't the type to go in for a manicure, believe me. It would threaten his manhood. And besides, the Richard Potter I saw had a nail biting problem. I doubt if he could have licked that *and* the drugs in the short time since I saw him last."

"You might have a point there," Barney said, making notes on another form. "The teacher said the man at the school appeared well dressed and professional. What you're telling me here," he said, pointing to the form, "is that the Potter you know would be considered more of a street criminal."

"That's what I'd say," Ken affirmed.

"Then if Potter didn't take the boy..." Barney shook his head at this latest turn of events.

"And why would Potter want the boy in the first place?" Jeff asked. "He doesn't want any responsibility. That much we know for sure. Based on past experience, it certainly isn't because he loves Richie."

"Love is seldom the motive in cases like this. Usually it's revenge." Barney slapped the clipboard on the gray desk he was sitting on.

Ken ran his hand through his hair. "I can't tell Sharon this. I think she'd be more fearful than ever if she knew strangers had him."

"No use setting her imagination on fire, eh?" Barney asked.

"We could tell her there's been some progress—not much—but some and we don't know what it all means yet. You know," Jeff said, "something to give her hope."

"I'll call her," Ken said.

Sharon took Frannie upstairs and asked to be left alone for a while. "I want to be with her."

Sitting in the rocker Meg kept in the corner of the room, Sharon clung to the child on her lap. Loneliness and loss were overwhelming, and her tears fell unchecked down her face and onto Frannie's head.

"Mommy," Frannie said, "don't cry. Jesus will help us," she said with complete faith. "Auntie Sarah said we just have to believe that Jesus knows where Richie is and that he'll be all right."

The phone rang and Sharon lunged forward, almost knocking Frannie from her lap. Inwardly she prayed for good news, then sank back weeping when she heard Meg return the receiver to its cradle.

"Jesus knows everything," Frannie said, snuggling close to her mother again. The two clung to each other and rocked back and forth, finding comfort in the nearness. "It's like David and the giant, isn't it, Mommy?"

"Uh-uhh," Sharon muttered without really listening. Mother and child fell silent again.

Before long, Frannie went limp in Sharon's arms, and her deep even breathing made Sharon grateful that at least her daughter was here, safe and sound in her arms. At the same time she felt deep inner fear that her son might be in danger with his father. Richie was very young when he knew his father, but she prayed that somehow he could remember Richard's temper and know not to push him too far. She prayed that he would do whatever Richard asked him to do rather than risk making him mad. Sharon realized how much she had done what she was mentally commanding Richie to do now. Without much thought Sharon placed kiss after kiss on the top of Frannie's head, thinking and weeping all the while for her son.

"That was Ken, dear," Meg whispered, shaking Sharon slightly.

"What?" Sharon said, sitting upright and nearly knocking Frannie to the floor. "Is he still on the phone? I didn't hear it ring."

"He said he'd be home in a little bit. There's no news, Sharon. He wants to come home and check on you."

"I want him to stay there," she protested. "Let me talk to him."

"He's on his way, honey," Meg said as she unwrapped Frannie's arms from around Sharon's neck. "She's out like a light. Let's put her to bed, at least."

Sharon moved to the side of the small cot where Frannie had been sleeping since the threat of Richard's presence became real. Pulling the coverlet up under her daughter's chin, she started to sob.

"Not once," she said tearfully to Meg, "since I brought her home from the hospital have they been separated. Not once."

"You go on down, dear," Meg said quietly. "I'll sit with her for a while longer. Cari and Jen are planning to stay through the night. I think Cari's dozing on the sofa. Jen's in the kitchen with Dan."

"Where are Sarah and James?" Sharon asked as she came in the kitchen to join Dan and Jen.

"In the guest house," Dan said.

"They're up, though," Jen said, nodding toward the window. "The lights are on."

"My guess is they're praying," Dan added.

"They'll keep it up, too," Jen said. "Just as long as necessary."

Sharon lunged for the phone the moment it rang.

"Sharon?" Her legs nearly went out from under her. It was impossible to mistake his voice.

"Richard?"

"I don't have him, Sharon." Richard's voice sounded pitiful. If Sharon hadn't been so stunned she would have noticed it immediately. "I really don't," he said.

"Richard—where are you?" she cried. "Where's Richie?" Click.

"Richard!" she screamed. "Don't you hang up on me, Richard!" Sharon sank to the floor and pulled the dead phone receiver to her breast. "Please, don't hang up on me."

Ken came in the door and found her crumpled on the floor. "It was him," she cried into Ken's shoulder as he gently lifted her to her feet. "He called."

"What'd he say?" Ken asked.

"Sharon," Jeff said, coming back with his wife. "Did I hear you say Richard called?"

"It was him," she moaned. Clutching her breast, she tried to keep her heart from breaking in little pieces. "He said he didn't have Richie. Oh, Ken," she sobbed, "what did he do to him?"

Just then she saw Ken and Jeff exchange glances.

"What?" she screamed. "What's wrong?"

"We think he's telling you the truth" Jeff said softly. "He doesn't have him."

"I didn't want you to find out like this," Ken said.

"You know something?" she begged. "Please, tell me."

"We know the man who showed up at school doesn't even come close to matching the description of Richard Potter," Ken said, trying to be gentle and direct at the same time.

"I don't understand." The strain of the endless waiting ripped savagely at her beautiful features.

"We don't either, just yet. But we know the man who came to school certainly wasn't Richard Potter. The police are questioning the teacher now. She's looking at mug shots. Hopefully she'll be able to give us more information."

"Oh, Ken." Sharon's sorrow overwhelmed her and she dissolved once again into tears.

"Take her into the other room," Ken said to Cari and Jen. "I want to talk to Jeff and Dan. Please, honey," he said, "I want you to go in and lie down. Just lie on the sofa. You need to rest a bit. I'll be right here. I'm not going anywhere without telling you first. You have to trust me, Sharon. Please."

Sharon finally let numbness overtake her heart and mind and allowed her two friends to lead her into the living room.

The man who just hours before had been overjoyed with the prospect of surprising Sharon with his discharge nearly buckled under the weight of her pain. "This horrendous affair was the last thing I expected to face when I got home today," he told Jeff and Dan. "Believe me, this is not at all how I planned to spend my first evening as a civilian."

CHAPTER TWENTY-EIGHT

*A*n hour later, Ken yanked the phone from its cradle the second it rang. "Potter!" he said in a coarse, low tone so not to disturb Sharon. "Potter, you had better—"

"I want to talk to Jeff Bennett," the man's strained voice said. "I'll call back in an hour and I want to talk to Bennett."

"Wait," Ken said urgently, afraid the man might hang up. He softened his tone. "He's right here." Ken handed the phone to Jeff. He walked to the other side of the kitchen, unable to make any sense of Jeff's side of the conversation.

Finally, Jeff hung up the phone and turned to face Ken. "He wants me to be his lawyer," Jeff said. "Isn't that incredible?"

"Unbelievable," Ken said with disgust. His anger boiled within his chest. "At a time like this he thinks of only himself?"

"Not unbelievable at all," Jeff said, slowly sinking into a chair at Meg's kitchen table. Jen came in and joined the three men.

"How's she doing?" Ken asked.

"I think she's sleeping," she said. "Cari and I took turns praying with her. Finally she drifted off."

"You better make us some coffee, sweetheart," Dan Miller said. "It may be a long, long night."

"Okay," Ken said, swinging a chair around and straddling it. "Let's have it, what's the scoop?"

"He says he has a pretty good idea who's responsible for taking Richie and why. He says they're really trying to get to him. He said if the police get to him first, he's sure we'll never see Richie again." Ken doubled his fist and slammed it on the table. "I think he may have a point, Ken." Jeff tried to be as convincing as Richard was on the phone. "Listen, will you? Just hear me out."

"Okay," Ken said between clenched teeth. Anger flashed in his eyes as Jeff began.

"Seems he's gotten involved in some pretty rough and dirty dealings in L.A. Richard Potter has finally met up with someone lower than himself. That's my personal opinion. He's scared spitless."

"He's scared? What about Richie, or Sharon?" Ken snapped.

"He said that he'd gotten a notice that if he didn't show up in L.A. and face the music, his family would be involved—one by one."

"He's wanted by more than just the police then?" Dan asked.

"Seems so," Jeff continued. "Seems as if our lowlife rapist and wife beater moved on to bigger and better forms of crime and was a bit under qualified, shall we say. He can't cut it as a hardened criminal."

"Cowards never do." Ken fairly spat out the words. "He's under qualified to be a human being. What made him think he could make in the underworld?"

"Well, all that aside for the moment," Jeff said, gathering a center of calm and objective professionalism, "Richard isn't our priority, Richie is."

"So what are we gonna do?" Ken asked.

"I'm going to the police," Jeff said.

"You're what?" Ken could hardly believe his ears. "Didn't he say that—"

"He did," Jeff explained. "That's why I'm going. To negotiate."

"Won't they make you tell them what you know?" Ken asked.

"Not now," Jeff said. "Now I'm covered by client-lawyer confidentiality."

"I'll go with you," Ken said.

"No you won't," Jeff answered. "You're not a lawyer. The rules change where you're concerned. Stay here with him," Jeff told Dan. "I want to talk to Barney myself, and I don't want him answering the phone. Don't take any chances on blowing this with your own anger, all right Ken?"

Jeff turned to Jen. "Get Cari."

"Okay."

"I'll be back as soon as I can," he said to the two men facing him at the table. "I want to talk to Cari first. I want to make sure she doesn't misunderstand what I'm doing."

"Dan Miller here," Dan said into the phone. "No, I'm a friend of the family. I'm staying here while Jeff Bennett is down at the police station."

Ken watched, helplessly wishing he could reach through the phone and strangle the caller.

"She's sleeping, just now. This is really difficult for her." Pause. "I understand that, but she needs all the strength she can get to make it through this in one piece." Pause. "I assure you, there's no tap on this phone and won't be, you have our word." Short pause. "Jeff's and mine." Dan glanced in Ken's direction, and Ken picked up the warning in his eyes. "No, I don't think so," he said to the caller. "We do too." He turned his back to Ken once again and faced the wall. "Okay, give it an hour or two. We'll keep the line open. Right," Dan said calmly. "Potter? Are you in a safe location? Good. Keep it that way, okay?"

Within an hour, Jeff returned. The noise of his car in the gravel driveway awakened Sharon, and she ran to the kitchen just as he was coming in.

"Well, folks, we have a really sticky mess on our hands," Jeff said. Cari came to his side and slipped her hand in his as the others gathered around the kitchen table. Ken took Sharon protectively upon his lap and held her tight while Jeff explained the situation.

"Seems that the police want to question Richard in connection with a gangland-style murder in L.A. We knew that already. What we didn't know is that the murdered man was a member of some underworld group, perhaps even an organized crime family."

"The Mafia?" Ken asked in utter disbelief.

"I'm not sure I'd go that far," Jeff said. "But whatever it is, he's really in over his head. Either he killed the man, or he knows who did. He's been on the run ever since. Living in the lap of luxury, fast cars, women, booze, and drugs one minute, and—"

"Wandering down lonely desert highways headed for Mexico the next," Ken said.

"You picked him up just after it happened. He was already on the run," Jeff said.

"So that's why the FBI was involved?" Dan asked.

"It's an interstate deal," Jeff explained. "Not much for criminal law myself. I don't fully understand it."

"And Richie's right in the middle of it all," Sharon said. "My innocent son is about to pay for the sins of his father."

"We hope not," Jeff said, trying to reassure her. "We certainly hope not."

"What's next?" Dan asked.

"Well, I think that's up to Richard. The police will only go so far on this. Believe me, they don't look too kindly on kidnaping, and they think even less of vigilante justice."

"What does that mean?" Sharon asked.

"It means they frown on people who take law enforcement into their own hands," he answered.

"Is that what they think we're doing?" Ken asked.

"Not yet. I think I've convinced them to let me work with my client," Jeff said. "On the one condition that he agree to turn himself in."

"But if he turns himself in," Ken said, "doesn't that put Richie in jeopardy?"

"They've agreed to hold off, but I have to have Richard in my possession, so to speak."

"What?" Cari cried aloud. "You're going to go to him?"

"Well, sort of," Jeff said. "As soon as I can, I'll have to talk him into some arrangement."

The group fell thoughtfully silent. Jeff pulled Cari close and kissed the top of her head.

"You need to meet with him face to face," Ken said as the realization finally took hold. "Some place neutral and safe, where neither the police nor the mob can get him, am I right?"

"Right," Jeff said.

"How about a motel?" Dan suggested.

"Might work," Jeff said. "There's a new motel out on the other side of Redlands. You know the one, next to Bob's."

"The Sands," Jen said.

"Would it help to bring him here?" The group barely heard Sharon's voice.

"What?" Ken nearly shouted. "Honey, you can't mean that! Here, near you and Frannie?"

"And Cari?" Jen joined in.

"Now wait a minute," Jeff said. "Calm down everybody. Let's not throw out any idea until we've thought it through, shall we? Dan," Jeff said to the calmest of the group, "I think we need Mac in on this. Anybody know where he is?"

"Walking," Jen said. "He said he'd be out walking. I think he's with Sammy."

"Sammy?" Cari asked.

"That's what he calls Richie's pup," Sharon said with tears filling her eyes again.

"I won't have him in my house," Mac growled. "I won't."

"Mac," Jeff said calmly, "I understand how you feel. I was there too, remember?" he added, referring to the day several years ago when Richard attacked Cari. "We have to put it all behind us, somehow, as difficult as that is. It's for Richie," Jeff said. "Mac, he's your grandson, for heaven's sake." As complicated as the blood relationship was, it was true. Richie was as close to having a grandson as Mac would ever get.

"I'll let you have the feed room," Mac finally gave in. "There's even an old phone out there. But I'm warning you, one step, Bennett, and that scum will not survive the walk between there and this house. I swear."

"Thanks, Mac," Jeff said with relief. "Now I'd like to have another cup of coffee. All we can do is wait for him to call again."

"Dan?" Jeff said, turning from the phone after speaking briefly with Richard, "would you mind going along?"

"Oh, my gosh," Jen said, alarmed. "Why Dan?"

"Because Ken has to stay here," Dan said, comforting his new bride. "Come on, honey, there's nothing to worry about."

"Just the mob—that's all," she said, clinging to his neck.

"Think about it, Jennifer," Jeff said. "The police don't know where he is or they would have had him in custody by now. The mob doesn't know where he is or they wouldn't need Richie."

"But they might be following you!" she exclaimed, her voice filled with panic. "What then?"

"I doubt that very much," Jeff said. "Why go to all that work when they can wait it out at a safe distance?"

"I can't believe this is happening," Sharon said quietly. "It's all a bad dream, right?"

"If it is," Ken said with his face hidden in her hair, "we're all having the same one."

"Well," Jen said just as the door shut behind Jeff and her husband, "it's a good thing James and Sarah are here. Looks like they're still on duty out there."

"God is too," Cari said, coming to stand beside the attractive redhead. "This isn't a bad dream to Him," she said, turning to Sharon. "Somehow I have confidence that this is going to turn out all right."

"Does it bother you," Jen said to Cari, "the thought of Richard coming here?"

"I'd be lying if I said it didn't," Cari answered. "But I'm not the one who's in danger—not anymore."

"What about you, Sharon?" Jen asked.

"Yes," she whispered. "Yes, it does. I never wanted to see him again."

"You don't have to," Ken reassured. "He won't be here long. Just until this is over. You don't have to see him at all."

"I wonder about that," she said. "I just wonder about that."

CHAPTER TWENTY-NINE

*H*e's here," Dan said to Jen when he came in Meg's kitchen and closed the door behind him. "He's a mess. They could use something to eat out there—coffee too."

"We're supposed to feed him?" Jen asked. "He endangers the whole family and gets his son kidnaped and we're supposed to take care of him?"

"Yes, sweetheart," Dan said, "we are. Where is everyone?"

"Sharon went upstairs about an hour ago. Cari's sleeping on the sofa in the living room."

"Meg's upstairs, too?" Dan asked.

Jen nodded. "And Mac is out walking again."

"James and Sarah still at it?" Dan inquired.

"I think so," she said. "Where's Jeff?"

"With his smelly client."

"Bad, huh?" Jen asked, wrinkling her nose.

"Worse than bad," he said. "I'm beat."

"Look at that, will you?" Jen said, peering out the kitchen window. "It's barely light out and Sarah's going out to the feed room carrying a tray."

"I'm not surprised," Dan said through a gaping yawn. "I'm going to get some shut-eye. Jeff asked me to spell him in an hour or so."

"Spell him? You can't be serious."

"We can't very well leave the man alone, now can we?" Dan asked.

An hour and a half later, Sarah came into the main house asking for clean towels and a razor. Meg hurried to fill her request before plying her with questions.

"Is he sleeping at all?" Meg asked curiously, looking in the direction of the building where Richard Potter still waited with Jeff.

"Now and then," she said. "Jeff's really beat. He's asking for Dan to come and replace him."

"Have you seen him?"

"Pitiful, Meg, just pitiful," Sarah remarked, shaking her head sympathetically. "Sin devastates a man so."

"I'll get Dan. I think he's stretched out in our bedroom. Any more news about Richie?" she asked before she left the room.

"Only in here," Sarah pointed to her chest. "I know what I know in here, that's all."

"And?" Meg asked, pausing in the doorway.

"We're just to hold on to hope, Meg." Sarah dabbed at the corners of her eyes. "And when we can't, we're to let hope hold on to us."

Dan left the house to relieve Jeff, and Sarah made arrangements for Richard to have a bath and a shave. When he emerged from the guest house bathroom, he was wearing a pair of James's clean work pants, which were several sizes too big, and a blue cotton work shirt. Sarah had already deposited his old filthy and torn clothes in Meg's automatic washing machine. Meg decided to let Sarah take care of the strange visitor in the barn while she stayed as close to Sharon and Ken as she could without interfering. Mac kept his distance, puttering around the ranch and performing the routine chores, relieving his wife for more needed activity in the house.

At ten, Jeff emerged from the room where he too had caught a couple of hours sleep. He spoke briefly to Sharon and Ken before going back out to the feed room. Dan returned to the house and instructed Jen to call his mother and tell her to be prepared to stay with the children for another day or two.

In the middle of the traumatic situation, an eerie routine surfaced. Each person seemed to slip into a definite yet unspoken role. Household chores were performed, meals were cooked, and inquisitive callers were handled with diplomacy. Sharon and Ken stayed mostly on the couch, needing to be near each other.

Jeff emerged once again, spoke briefly to Cari, and nodded for Ken to join him in the kitchen. Jen automatically moved beside Sharon in his absence.

"Well?" Ken inquired when he joined Jeff and Cari in the kitchen. "What's up?"

"I've got a name and number," Jeff said, patting his shirt pocket. "I'm going to my office to make the call now."

"Then what?" Ken asked.

"We start negotiating," he said. "I just hope I can carry it off."

"What about Barney?" Ken asked. "Will he get in the way?"

"He says he won't," Jeff said. "I hope he keeps his word."

"Can't you call from here?" Ken said. "Then we'd know right away what's happening."

"By now our phones have been tapped," Jeff said. "The FBI hasn't cut me any slack on this. Once they get wind of the fact that we have Potter up here, I'm not sure what they'll do."

"Can we move him if necessary?"

"To where? Got any ideas?"

"Sorry, I'm new in town," Ken said.

"Sharon know about you yet?"

"About my discharge? Nope." Ken ran his hand through his hair. "I hadn't wanted to tell her like this."

"She'll need to know you're not going back. Don't you think it would help if she knew this wasn't just a weekend visit?"

"You're right," Ken said. "It's just—"

"Give her something to be happy about, will you?" Jeff said as he prepared to leave. "She could use some good news right about now."

"What's this?" Sharon said when Ken handed her the large manila envelope containing his papers.

"Look for yourself," he said softly. Sitting beside her, he waited while her shaking fingers unwound the red string from the metal clasp. He watched her fine, long eyelashes sweep her swollen cheeks as she realized for the first time that Ken was home—*permanently*.

"I can't believe it," she whispered. Her eyes filled with tears, and she clutched the cherished papers to her chest. "I can't believe it—when did this happen?"

"Friday, the fifteenth, at two-thirty in the afternoon," he said quietly.

"Why didn't you tell me before?" she asked searching his eyes for an answer.

"I didn't have a chance, honey," Ken said. "We've been a little preoccupied since then."

"But—"

"It was only yesterday, Sharon," he said. "I looked at my watch and knew that Richie was getting out of school at that same moment and that I'd be home by supper if I hurried . . ." His voice trailed off, broken by emotion. "I wanted to surprise you—all of you." Ken couldn't maintain his composure any longer. "I thought it would be such a happy evening for all of us. I can't believe this is happening to us—not now. Not ever!"

This time, Sharon moved to slide her arms around this amazing and miraculous answer to her prayers and hopes—Kenneth Matthews.

"It came right in time," she whispered. "I needed you here, Ken. I would've died without you here," she said.

"I'm sorry," he said, pulling his handkerchief from his pocket. He blew his nose and took a deep breath.

"Ken," she said with sudden and surprising calm and strength, "I want to see Richard. I want you to take me to see him."

"Not on your life," he responded impulsively.

"Then I'll go without you," she said, standing suddenly.

"No you won't!" he countered. "Have you lost your mind? You don't have to ever see him—ever, ever see him again."

"I have to," she said. "I've lived with fear far too long because of that man. I want to face him once and for all."

"Mom!" Ken called to the kitchen. "Tell her she's crazy," he pleaded when Meg came into the room. "She wants to see him," he said, almost whining like a helpless little boy.

"Oh?" Meg said thoughtfully. "Sharon?"

"I have to, Meg," she said to her future mother-in-law. "It's something I have to do."

"You sure about this?" Meg said.

"Mom!" Ken protested.

"I'm positive," Sharon said.

"Do you need me to go with you?" Meg offered.

"I want Ken to go," she said.

"Kenneth?" Meg turned to her grown son, whose face registered disbelief and pain.

"I don't want her near him!" he insisted.

"I don't think this is about what you want," his mother retorted, gently but firmly. "This isn't even about what Sharon wants, is it, dear?"

Sharon shook her head.

"This is something she has to do, isn't that right?" Meg asked, turning to Sharon again.

"Yes," Sharon said. "It is."

"Then, Kenny," Meg said with a quiet urgency to her voice, "if this is the woman you are about to pledge your unfailing love and devotion to, for better or worse, for the rest of your life, I don't think this is something you can let her face alone, is it?"

"Sharon!" Richard said. His ragged face registered the shock of seeing her and the shame of the crisis he had caused. Sharon knew immediately that for the very first time she had the upper hand with him.

"Richard," she said with an unexpected calm.

"Sharon, I'm sorry about all this," he said, almost beggarly. "I can't tell you how sorry I am about the boy. After all, he is my son too."

Sharon fought the inner panic she felt just hearing her ex-husband refer to Richie. "You've caused that child nothing but pain from the day he was conceived," she said. "I think to call him your son right now is inappropriate. Please don't do it again."

"Sorry," he said.

"Richard, I want you to know something. You have caused untold damage in the lives of three, no four, people. I'm here to say something to you, something you probably don't want to hear. But I don't care, I'm going to say it anyway." She walked to where he sat at a makeshift table. Looking down at him, she saw his smallness, both in stature and in character. "I can't believe I was ever terrified of you. I don't know why I allowed myself to be." She turned her back on him, aware that he had beaten her for doing just that on two separate occasions in the past.

"Sharon," he pleaded. "I've said I'm sorry. What else can I say?"

"Plenty," she said. "I'm getting to that. But first, I want you to know that I have two beautiful children. And when Richie gets home—" She paused a minute and took a deep breath before continuing. "When Richie gets home, I want to know you will never again have anything further to do with him, with Frannie, or with me."

"I can promise you that. I can certainly promise you that."

"I don't believe you, Richard. Your word means absolutely nothing to me. I want you to formally give up all rights to the children. I'm sure Jeff would be willing to arrange the necessary papers."

"Sharon, I promise, I'll do anything—anything."

"And," she said, "I want to know why . . ."

"Why?"

"Why did you think it necessary to smash up my workshop?"

"But I—"

"And," she said, raising her voice slightly to interrupt him, "why in the world did you do what you did to that poor old dog?"

"Sharon," he said, surprising her with what she thought was remorse, "I don't know what you're talking about."

"Liar!" she spat.

"Honest, Sharon. As God is my witness—"

"Don't!" she warned. "Don't you dare do or say anything that in any way might tempt God to do what I've wanted to do for years. Not until I get Richie home safe and sound. How did you get mixed up with these people anyway? Never mind," she said before he could explain. "I wouldn't believe you anyway. Look at you. You're a real picture of success, aren't you?"

"I've made so many mistakes," he said meekly.

"Countless, I'm sure," she said. "But I'm warning you, you'll not make one false step or incorrect move that will in any way endanger my son, do you hear me?"

"You have my word on it," he said.

"No, Richard, I have God's word on it," she said calmly. "Your word is nothing to me."

"Sharon, listen to me," he begged. "It wasn't me, I swear. It was them, trying to send a message to me. I bragged that I had this son, see? That he and I were real tight. I said I came to see him every weekend."

"I can't believe this," she said with disgust.

"Believe it!" he said. "It's true, every word."

"When they found out where you lived, I tried to come to warn you, but I couldn't get near you."

"You are still the biggest liar I ever knew," she sneered. "In the situation you're in, I'd watch that if I were you. You don't have much of a limb to sit on, in case you haven't noticed."

"What can I say except I'm sorry?" he pleaded.

"Say you'll sign the parental rights thing, when Jeff can get it ready."

"Okay."

Turning toward the door, she walked quickly away from him.

"Sharon?" His voice was barely more than a whimper. "Do you hate me so much?"

"No," she said turning to face him and look him directly in the eye. "I don't. I hate what you've done to the children and me. I despise the fact that you ever touched me in any way. I'm sick to my stomach to think that I allowed my children to be fathered by you. But, no Richard, I don't hate you—I pity you." She turned and placed her hand on the doorknob. Then she faced him again. "And more than any of that, I want you to know this—"

He was riveted by her directness.

"Not for your sake, but for my own and for the children. When I leave this room, I want you to know that I'm stepping into a new life free of you, your intimidation, and your threats. You can't hurt me anymore, Richard. No more. And," she said, dropping her voice to a barely perceptible level, "I forgive you. God help me, I do."

"Sharon, I—" He tried to stand. She stopped him with a swift movement of her hand.

"Don't," she said. "This has taken all the forgiveness I have in me. Don't ask me for anything more." Without another word she turned and opened the door. Glancing at Ken, she smiled and purposely took a step out into the bright midday sun.

"Honey," Ken said, pulling her into his arms as soon as they were on the back porch, "you were wonderful out there. I can't believe how strong and direct you were with him."

"I meant it, Ken," she said. He explored the features on her lovely, tired face with his fingertips. "I really do. I can't live in bitterness and fear any longer. He's more than paid for what he's done to me and the kids, I have a feeling. Now if Richie . . ." She glanced toward the quiet driveway alongside the house.

"We'll just have to keep on hoping, right?"

"Right," she said, smiling weakly. "Hope."

hey want to make a deal," Jeff told the small family gathered at the kitchen table for the announcement. "I've talked to Richie, Sharon," he said to the worried, haggard mother.

"You did?" she cried. "Where is he? Can't I talk to him?"

"He's a little confused. Sounds perfectly fine to me other than he wants to come home."

"What's the deal?" Ken asked suspiciously while Sharon gave way to sobs of relief and confusion.

"They want us to exchange Richard for Richie. I've spoken to Barney, he's asked not to be involved in any way. Could lose his badge for this, is my guess. He hasn't asked where Potter is and I haven't said. So we wrote up a report that says we're arranging a voluntary surrender tomorrow morning at nine."

"I don't understand," Dan Miller interjected. "You're going to surrender him to the police?"

"No, we've just made an appointment to do so. If something happens to my client in the meantime, I can't help that, can I?"

"You'd actually turn him over to the mob?" Jen asked. "I can't believe you'd do that."

"Well, it's really Richard's decision. Either the mob tonight, or the police tomorrow. He's really not going anywhere in the meantime. After all, there's a police watch on

the house, front and back. Protection for Sharon and
Frannie, you understand."

"Oh, of course," Dan said. "And we're watching him
round the clock besides."

"Right," Jeff said. "Anyway, I've talked to Richard. He's
agreeable. He thinks maybe he can reason with the mob.
After all, he says, he didn't kill the guy. He only just knows
who did."

"I see," Dan said. "And they may keep him alive as a
reward for being a snitch."

"He's hoping."

"So what do we do now?" Ken asked.

Sharon listened to Jeff's plan with interest.

"We'll leave here at midnight," Jeff said. "And the cops
will look the other way, at least they said they will. And I'm
to drive him to the edge of the Seventh Street Park. You
know, over by the swimming pool."

"What about Richie?" Sharon asked. "Where's he all this
time?"

"Ken," Jeff said, "you'll be going to the laundromat up
on Yucaipa Boulevard. Know where that is?"

"I'll go too," Sharon said. "I can show you."

"No, young lady, you won't. You'll stay here. I promised
Ken would be alone." Jeff returned his attention to Ken.
"You're to take a load of laundry and put it in to wash just
before twelve. The place is supposed to close at midnight,
but they'll stay open if someone's washing. That way there'll
be someone else on the premises." Jeff was afraid to tell
Sharon the laundry's night manager was being replaced
momentarily by someone who could defend both Richie
and Ken if necessary. "Then, when it's precisely eight
minutes past midnight, a car will pull up and let Richie out
on the sidewalk in front of the laundromat. He'll be told
to go inside and of course, Ken will be there."

"I can't stand this," Sharon said hysterically. "He's in the hands of criminals and you sit there like you're planning a church picnic."

"Sharon." Cari came quickly and stood behind her friend. "Shh, honey. It's almost over. Richie will be home and in his own bed within a few hours. Hang on, don't give in to this now. Okay?"

"Then," Jeff continued, "when Mac, who will be sitting across the street in his pickup, sees Ken safely put Richie in his car and leave, he will drive to the park and flash his lights at me. Richard will get out of the car and I'll drive away."

"What happens to him then?" Meg asked.

"I have no idea," Jeff said soberly. "I really have no idea. I do know that we have an appointment tomorrow morning at nine to surrender voluntarily. Until then, he's on his own."

"What happens if he gets away?" Sharon asked quietly. "Will they come for Richie or me or Frannie again?"

"I don't think so," Jeff said. "After all, I said I couldn't do more than just put him out at the curb. I haven't made any guarantees beyond that."

Sharon glanced at the clock above Meg's refrigerator. "Ten-thirty," she said aloud.

"Less than two hours," Ken said. Sharon heard a more confident tone of hope in his voice. "Then our son will be home with us at last."

"Well," Sarah said, "James predicted we'd be pulling night duty again. If you'll all excuse me." She shoved back her chair and Dan followed her to the door.

"I'm going to send James back to the house now," he called over his shoulder. "If he hasn't gotten that sinner saved by now . . ."

Sharon paced the floor for the next hour and a half. Meg finally persuaded her to eat some toast and sip some hot tea. Ken watched anxiously as the hands of the clock moved unbearably slow past the half hour mark and creep toward midnight. Finally, he picked up the laundry basket Meg had prepared with rags and old clothes he planned to leave behind once he was reunited with Richie.

Sharon clung to him as he walked out the door.

"I'll be home within the hour," he promised. "Have milk and cookies ready, okay?"

"Okay," she promised, waving and smiling bravely. Once Ken was out of sight, all of her bravado left her and she sunk to the floor.

Meg was instantly beside her, and with Dan's help she managed to make it to the table.

"I think I heard the barn door," Dan said.

Sharon leaped from the table and before anyone could stop her, she managed to confront Richard once more before he got into Jeff's car.

"I signed the papers," he said. His tone was that of an absolutely beaten man. "I'm sorry, Sharon."

"We have to go," Jeff said, checking his watch.

Sharon stood perfectly still under the stars of the October night sky until the sound of Jeff's car could no longer be heard in the distance. *Dear God,* she prayed. Not knowing what else to say, she repeated, *Dear God!*

Ken stuffed the few rags and old clothes into a washing machine and stuck a dime and a quarter into the change receiver. He looked around for soap, then realized how foolish that was. He spotted some worn metal folding chairs on the opposite wall and silently cursed the fact that the inside lighting prevented him from seeing clearly out into the street. Picking up a tattered copy of *Ladies Home Journal,* he began to leaf through the pages, oblivious to the pictures, torn out coupons, and missing recipe pages. The washing machine whined in the background while a disgruntled night maintenance man banged pails in the back room.

"I'll be out of here just as soon as I can," he called toward the back room.

"Yeah, okay," the man barked in return.

He glanced at his watch. "Five after," he said under his breath. "Three more minutes."

Ken shifted uncomfortably in his chair. The man from the back room shoved his mop bucket toward the place where Ken was sitting. Taking out a sponge, the man began wiping around the tops of the machines nearest the door.

At exactly eight minutes past, a sleek dark car slid silently to the curb. The back door opened and Richie stepped onto the curb, turned, and waved to someone inside.

"Bye," Richie called over his shoulder, then bolted toward the door. Without hesitation, Ken scooped him in his arms, glanced around to see that they weren't being followed, and waved to Mac's truck parked across the street. Once they were in the car, Ken started the engine and headed for home. Only when he was sure they weren't being followed did he turn to Richie.

"Hey, pal, how ya doin'? Your mama's waiting up for you. She's gonna be awful glad to see you." Thankfully the darkness hid the man's tears of relief and joy.

Jeff and Richard sat in silence as they waited for Mac's truck to round the corner and flash the lights. Richard glanced nervously out the rear window a few times, then brought his attention to the dark street ahead once again.

"Scared?" Jeff asked.

"Wouldn't you be?" Richard answered. "Of course I'm scared. Who knows what they'll do to me. Maybe they won't even give me a chance to tell my side of the story."

"And is there a side to your story?"

"You bet there is. Oh, sure, I stole some money. But Bennett, it's drug money. Stolen from kids in neighborhood parks just like this one anyways."

"Well, I get your point," Jeff said sarcastically.

"Was that James fella back there on the level with me?"

"What do you mean?" Jeff asked.

"About God, forgiveness, clean slate and all?"

Before Jeff could answer, Mac's truck pulled near and the signal was unmistakable. "He's got Richie," Jeff said. Turning to Richard, he reached across in front of him and opened the door. "You're on you own, Potter. If I were you, I'd pay attention to whatever James told you."

"Can I shake your hand?" Richard asked apologetically.

"If you don't mind," Jeff said. "I'd rather not. James may have, but I'm still not there yet."

"I understand," Richard said. Slowly he turned and put his feet onto the moist grass. "I'm glad Richie's safe now anyway. It's the least I could do."

"The very least," Jeff said in a tone so low Richard couldn't hear.

"Thanks for everything," Richard said, stepping out of the car.

"Glad to help," Jeff said. He shoved the car in gear and stepped on the accelerator, leaving Richard to face his destiny in the dark park. "Glad to help Richie, anyway. I'm not so sure I helped you all that much," Jeff muttered into the dark interior of his car.

"Hi, Mommy," Richie yelled as he ran up the back steps to Meg and Mac's back porch. "I'm home."

"Richie!" she cried, wrapping her arms as tightly around her son as she could. "Richie!" Clinging to him, she felt her emotions explode into tears and sobs into his neck. "Thank God you're home."

"I'm hungry," Richie said, trying to wriggle free from his mother's smothering hold.

"I promised him cookies, Mama," Ken said, grinning from ear to ear. Just then the kitchen door burst open and Cari, Jen, and Meg surrounded the small boy, planting kisses on every exposed inch of his face and neck. "I think you were missed, son," Ken said, laughing over the hubbub.

James and Sarah joined them next and finally Mac.

"Wait a minute," Cari exclaimed. "Weren't you with Jeff?"

"No," Mac said. "I was down in the feed room, trying to get rid of every speck of—" He glanced at Richie and changed his mind about the comment. "I was righting things," he said instead. "Hey, young man, have a good old handshake for your old Papa Mac?"

"But where's Jeff?" Cari was obviously worried.

"He'll be along rightly," Mac said. Ken noticed his features were crossed by a worried expression. Sharon noticed nothing but her son, who was gulping cookies and milk.

Within minutes, both Mac and Cari relaxed when they heard tires crunching on the gravel driveway. Jeff bounded up the back stairs and came to examine the boy himself.

"You all right, Richie?" he asked. "Did anyone hurt you?"

Richie shook his head. "I'm all right, I was scared, Mommy. He said you were sick and I had to come with him so he could take me to see you. I didn't know he wasn't going to take me home."

"It's not your fault," Jeff reassured the little boy. "It's not your fault."

"I'm tired, Mommy," he said finally. "Can I go to bed now?"

Sharon and Ritchie were followed out of the kitchen by Cari, Jen, and Meg—all in an effort to help put the child to bed. Finally Sharon was able to convince them that she could manage on her own. She needed the time alone with her son. Frannie was already sleeping, but Richie would be allowed to wake her—just this once.

"Is it over?" Ken asked Jeff, who looked exhausted.

"I certainly hope so," Jeff said.

"Say," Ken said suspiciously, "if Mac was here the whole time, who was that in his truck?"

"I'm sure I can't tell you." Jeff grinned.

"And the man at the laundromat? I suppose you can't tell me about him either?"

"Sorry," Jeff said. "Don't know anything about him at all."

"Personally or professionally?" Ken pushed.

"Think they have him?" Dan Miller asked from the far corner of the room where he stood with his arm draped around his wife.

"I couldn't say," Jeff said. "I heard a rumor about the park being checked for vagrants tonight. Something about a sweep through around twelve-fifteen or so. Who knows?"

"At our park?" Jen asked. "You must be kidding."

The men in the room laughed—all except for Jeff.

"Either way, he's a dead man," Jeff said soberly. "Even if the cops catch him and put him in jail, they'll get him."

"The mob? Are you sure about that?" Cari asked fearfully.

"Positive," Jeff said. "What's more, so was he."

Ken left the room without a word. He walked slowly upstairs, trying to hear if it was appropriate to intrude on the little family that was safely together once more—*his* little family.

"Hi," he said as he approached the threesome sitting in the middle of the floor tightly entwined in a three-way hug.

"Kenny," Frannie said, making a place within the circle, "come and hug with us."

"Okay," he said. "I think I will."

*T*he next day, Kenneth came in the kitchen just as Sarah and Meg were about to serve lunch. Hugs and laughter filled the warm kitchen as much as the smells of homemade beef stew and fresh baked bread did.

"I still can't believe you're here!" Sharon said, flinging herself into his arms.

"Oh, Mommy," Frannie said, hugging Ken tightly while Richie clung to his leg, "can't we marry him now?" The whole family laughed in chorus.

"And you," Kenneth said, holding Frannie at arm's length, "are getting bigger and taller everyday. Look at you. I think they've been giving you growing pills while I've been looking the other way."

"No they haven't," Frannie said bashfully.

"And you, young man, have they been giving you growing pills too?" Kenneth scooped Richie up in his other arm and both children clung to him until Meg insisted they all sit down and eat.

"It'll be stone cold in another five minutes. Here, Sarah, hand me that plate. Mac, get that other chair from the dining room. My goodness, Kenny," Meg scolded, "if I had known you were coming home I would have made your favorite meat loaf."

"Mom," he shot back, "stop all this fussing. Remember, I've been eating military style. I'm starved."

All through lunch while Kenneth stuffed Meg and Sarah's homemade fare into his mouth, Sharon watched from her place on the opposite side at the table between the children.

"You're not eating," Ken said between mouthfulls.

"I'm not very hungry," she said quietly.

"Something steal away your appetite, young lady?" James teased.

"Someone, James," Mac joined in. "Can't you see that?"

"Look," Meg said, "the both of you—keep to your own business, will you?"

"I'm glad to see you," she said, boldly ignoring the two men.

"Not half as glad as I am to see you," he winked.

"Oh, gee," Richie groaned.

Frannie stared openly first at her mother, then at Kenneth. "Oh, Mommy," she said, clasping both hands under her chin.

"Don't we love him so?" creaked James from across the table.

Sharon closed her eyes, trying without success to control the blush she once again felt burning at the base of her neck and spreading rapidly toward her face.

"Not again," she protested. She bolted for the back porch.

"Ken, I'm not afraid anymore," she said as soon as he came to stand beside her.

"I know. I feel the same way."

"Can we get married now?" Frannie said, coming to squeeze between them. "Please?"

"Want to?" Ken said to the little girl.

"Yes!" she moaned.

"Sharon?" he asked gently. "How would you like to elope?"

"'Lope?" Frannie asked, peering up to the faces above her.

"Do you think they'd ever forgive us?" Sharon wondered aloud.

"I think they would," he said quietly. "All except for Mom and Mac. We'd have to take them along, I guess."

"What's 'lope mean, Mommy?" Frannie said, tugging at her mother's blouse.

"What about your mother?" Ken asked.

"You've never met her, have you?" she asked.

"Mommy, are we going to 'lope today?"

"Hush, Frannie," Sharon said. "I can't believe we've been through this whole thing and she's not been around since . . ." Sharon laughed.

"Since when?"

"Since Meg and Sarah tried to get her to join their Bible study."

"So what do you say?" he persisted. "Shall we get Mom and Mac and take a trip to Vegas?"

"Can we keep it a secret?"

"Sure," he said. "Okay by me. Just the kids and the folks."

"Me too?" Frannie pouted.

"Yes," Ken said, picking her up and tickling her tummy. "You and Richie and Mommy and me—shall we run off and get married?"

"Oh, yes!" she squealed. Squirming free, she hugged him around the knees before running into the house. "Papa James," they heard her squeal, "we're going to run off and 'lope!"

"Not a good idea," Sharon said.

"Getting married?"

"No—telling her. Once Sarah finds out, there'll be a wedding, pure and proper," Sharon laughed. "There's no getting out of that now—unless, of course, we hurry!"

"How long will that take?" Ken asked, almost painfully.

"How long does it take to get a license?" she replied.

"I'll race you," he said. "I bet I can get ready before you can!"

"Can't," she yelled gleefully, running in the back door and bolting for the stairs.

"Can!" he yelled back, jumping over the back steps and heading for the guest house.

"Children!" Meg scolded. "What in the world?"

"Get your clean apron on, Grandma McKenzie," Sharon yelled over her shoulder. "We're getting married!"

"Well, Sarah," James said, tipping slowly back in his kitchen chair, "guess we might as well go home."

"Just in time, too," she said. "Looks like we need to start planning a wedding—or maybe we'll be lucky this time and just have a reception."

"Well, Mac?" James said. "It's been something, I can say that at least."

"I'd better see if you've got a clean shirt," Meg said to her husband as she wiped her eyes with the corner of her apron and left the kitchen.

The four froze at the sound of Sharon's voice yelling from upstairs.

"Kenneth!"

"What?" he hollered back from the guest house patio.

"I love you!" she screamed.

"I knew it all along!" he yelled.

"Life has changed," Mac said matter-of-factly to James and Sarah. "Kids."

About the Author

*N*eva Coyle is a full-time freelance writer who is very active in the ministry of her local church. She is also the coauthor of the best-selling book, *Free to Be Thin. Sharon's Hope* is the fourth book in a series of Christian romance novels set in her hometown of Redlands, California. The first book in the series, *Cari's Secret*, was released in spring of 1994.

Neva is happily married and the mother of three grown children. Many of the story lines in this series grew out of family discussions in her own household.

Neva is also a proud grandmother.